CHINKU AND THE WOLFBOY

OTHER INDIAINK TITLES

Anjana Basu	*Black Tongue*
Anjum Hasan	*Neti Neti*
A.N.D. Haksar	*Madhav & Kama: A Love Story from Ancient India*
Boman Desai	*Servant, Master, Mistress*
C.P. Surendran	*An Iron Harvest*
Chitra Banerjee Divakaruni	*The Mirror of Fire and Dreaming*
Chitra Banerjee Divakaruni	*The Conch Bearer*
I. Allan Sealy	*The Everest Hotel*
I. Allan Sealy	*Trotternama*
Indrajit Hazra	*The Garden of Earthly Delights*
Jaspreet Singh	*17 Tomatoes: Tales from Kashmir*
Jawahara Saidullah	*The Burden of Foreknowledge*
Kalpana Swaminathan	*The Page 3 Murders*
Kalpana Swaminathan	*The Gardener's Song*
Kamalini Sengupta	*The Top of the Raintree*
Kota Neelima	*Death of a Moneylender*
Madhavan Kutty	*The Village Before Time*
Pankaj Mishra	*The Romantics*
Paro Anand	*I'm Not Butter Chicken*
Paro Anand	*Wingless*
Paro Anand	*No Guns at My Son's Funeral*
Paro Anand	*Weed*
Ramchandra Gandhi	*Muniya's Light: A Narrative of Truth and Myth*
Ranjit Lal	*The Life & Times of Altu-Faltu*
Ranjit Lal	*The Small Tigers of Shergarh*
Rashme Sehgal	*Hacks and Headlines*
Raza Mir & Ali Husain Mir	*Anthems of Resistance: A Celebration of Progressive Urdu Poetry*
Sanjay Bahadur	*The Sound of Water*
Shandana Minhas	*Tunnel Vision*
Selina Sen	*A Mirror Greens in Spring*
Sharmistha Mohanty	*New Life*
Shree Ghatage	*Brahma's Dream*
Susan Visvanathan	*Something Barely Remembered*
Susan Visvanathan	*The Visiting Moon*
Susan Visvanathan	*The Seine at Noon*
Tom Alter	*The Longest Race*

FORTHCOMING TITLES

John MacLithon	*Hindutva, Sex and Adventure: A Novel*
Tushar Raheja	*Run Romi Run: A Tale of Cricket at Mauji*

CHINKU AND THE WOLFBOY

ANJANA BASU

All characters and events in this book are fictitious and any resemblance to real characters, living or dead is purely coincidental.

First published in India in 2010
IndiaInk
An imprint of
Roli Books Pvt. Ltd.
M-75, G.K. II Market, New Delhi 110 048
Phone: +91 (011) 40682000
Fax: +91 (011) 2921 7185
E-mail: info@rolibooks.com
Website: www.rolibooks.com
Also at Bangalore, Chennai, Jaipur, Kolkata,
Mumbai & Varanasi

Cover Design: Supriya Saran

ISBN: 978-81-86939-53-6

Printed at Anubha Printers, Noida

For the 3 R's: Rahul, Rudra and Rohan,
in the order in which they came into my life

INTRODUCTION

Chinku and the Wolfboy began because the oldest of my three R's told me, 'You're an author, so why can't I have a book of my own for my birthday?' He wanted it then and there which wasn't quite possible.

The other thing that happened was that his mother told me it was my duty to help my nephews with their English. So, I suggested story writing and threw open the subject. Rahul wanted it to be about werewolves, which I thought was fair enough and I gave the subject to Rudra in Mumbai. They both stopped writing after a while, but I continued.

However, here are their stories, the best introduction I can think of to *Chinku and the Wolfboy* – even though it isn't as scary.

RAHUL'S DIVERSION

Once upon a time there was a man who was walking through the forest when he met a ferocious wolf. The wolf attacked him but the man managed to escape. Then, one full moon night the man looked at his hands and saw that he was growing long nails like me. Then he grew fur.

(He stopped and started again ...)

Once upon a time there was a man named John who was walking through the forest when he met a ferocious wolf. The wolf attacked him but John managed to escape. Then one full moon night the man looked at his hands and saw that he was growing long nails. John did not know what was going to happen to him. Then he realized that he was growing long hair all over his body. John was very scared. John did not know what to do. So he ran out from his house and went out on the road. Then John saw he was sort of a wolf standing on two feet. He went into a deep jungle until the hot sun came out. After a while John looked at his own reflection in the lake of the jungle. His face was fine.

RUDRA'S VERSION
It Came From The Forest

It was a November night, the icy cold wind drifted through the forest. The full moon lit up the dark sky. When suddenly the leaves of a bush began to rustle! A wolf jumped out. The wolf had blood trickling down its mouth. It managed to sniff its way out of the forest, but it came to the city called Jurislom. Suddenly, it heard footsteps nearby. The city constable Aamad passed. SUDDENLY, the wolf jumped up and sank his teeth into Aamad's shoulder. The wolf sank back into the darkness. It was then that it realized that it was a werewolf.

Aamad snapped his eyes open. He was lying on his bed in his vacant apartment. He looked around, it was fine. So he heaved a sigh of relief. What he didn't realize was that there was a splitting scar from his left shoulder to his elbow and blood on the bed sheets!

The next moonlit night, Aamad Norr was having a bath. When suddenly he began to grow hair all over his body, his teeth grew up to his chin, his nails grew suddenly into claws and his eyesight changed into a wolf's. He now had the insane desire to drink blood!

He jumped out of the window and landed unbalanced on the ground. Then he began to hunt. He came to Mr Bunce's turkey farm. He ate over forty turkeys. So he hid in the bushes and waited for the old man to come out. Several hours passed by, and then suddenly the sun came out. His werewolf ability shrank inside his body and he fainted.

He woke up in hospital. His best friends entered the room. His friends' names were – Rudra, Qasim and Vineet. Aamad explained his building. So they decided to surround the building with reinforcements.

The next moonlit night, Rudra and Qasim were at the entrance, Vineet and Parsn on the left, two other men on the right and back. The werewolf, not knowing that they were guarding the entrance, ran down the stairs. When it passed the entrance, Rudra and Qasim ran to kill the werewolf. It tried to bite Qasim but Rudra managed to pull out a dagger and stab it.

It was the end but as they left, two glowering eyes peeped out of the gutter.

1

The sun rose in a streak of red over the hills. It looked as though the land beyond was totally red, especially when the colour spread to the Lake of the Moon and the waters rippled red. The few women who were there early looked at the red water and backed away from it, knowing it was the sun playing tricks, but still not wanting to touch it. As they stood there hesitating, the first of the raiders came over the hills. He stood drawn in black against the red sky. Then came the others behind him swarming over the hills.

Chinku always remembered that day, first the red sky, then the dismay of the women and the way they pointed their fingers at the hills. Why had they turned to look – that was what she couldn't remember – had a hawk wheeled overhead with a shrill scream of warning? In the days when life itself was as young as the rising sun some of them knew how to comprehend the language of the birds and talked to the great mountain lords, the eagle and the lammergeier.

Her father said, 'There are some things that one should not remember. They are dangerous.'

But she did not agree with him. Nothing proved it better than that morning. First the black man then the others behind him, one after the other, slipping over the hills, holding the Mind Stealing Rays in their hands.

The first Chinku knew was when her father scooped her up from the verandah outside where she was watching the chaos by the lake. The warning flag had been run up and she turned to say something to her father about it, but he scooped her up under his arm. Hanging head down, she saw his feet crunch on gravel and then felt him roll her up and thrust her into the smallest of small holes, a hole that would cramp a rabbit, not to mention a skinny ten year old. 'Stay there. Don't make a sound. When they're gone, I'll come for you.'

The words had floated on the air outside but she could not see him, as she was crushed into the hole with frightened tears rolling down her cheeks. Then the shadows flitted past the mouth of the hole and the feet crunched. A huge black boot with teeth ran past her field of vision hunting its prey. She closed her eyes tight and clenched her fists into her stomach. The feet and the shadows moved past the mouth of the hole for what seemed like hours. She crouched there cold and cramped, but her father did not come. Finally, when the shadows grew long, she crept out of the hole.

The flag on the pole was gone. That was where her eyes first went. But the smoke was rising in blue puffs from the evening fires against the darkening sky. Someone was herding the cattle in from the fields; she could see the dust rising from their hoofs in a misty white cloud. She skimmed past the houses to her own home. The fire was lit in the courtyard there too and her heart took wings and flew free for a moment. She saw her mother and ran up to her and into her arms, crying, 'Ma, ma, I was so scared ... ' The arms were tight for a minute and then slackened, 'Chinku, you naughty girl, where were you? We've been looking for you for hours. Your father has gone to the fields to look for you! Go and wash your face and hands immediately!' For a moment she stared at her mother wide eyed. Then realized what they were always scared of had happened – the Shadow Men had stolen their memories. Tears welled up in her eyes and she jerked away from her mother, running towards the lake.

Her mother would think it was anger and not be alarmed, but before she reached the lake and while she was still out of sight of the hut, Chinku turned towards the Records Chamber. The door swung open at her touch. There was no one inside, the wooden floor-level desks gleaming clean, the Guardian's desk squarely in its place, moved not an inch out of alignment. She stood in the doorway, her head turning from side to side, wondering what it might mean. Something on the floor caught her eye, almost under one of the desks. She scuttled forward and scrabbled for it, pulling it out and up into the palm of her hand. She did not look at it until she was clear of the place, though it tickled her palm. It was a grey pigeon's feather, just an ordinary feather, except for a notch as if the bird had broken some of its plumes. Just one notch. One for sorrow.

She thought there would be other signs of warning left for her and for any other Memory Keeper who remembered, but she would have to look later.

Her father came out of the darkness at her, almost before she had time to sweep the feather into her pocket. The words he used were exactly the same as those of her mother: 'Chinku, you naughty girl, where were you?' He caught her by her wrist. For a heartbeat she waited for him to say something more, but the moment passed and she was being dragged back to her home through the dying light.

That night with her sleeping family around her she took out the pigeon feather and studied the notch by the light of the dying fire. Sorrow. That was the easy message – the harder ones were the bent flights of the plume. The Old Ones had told her that the colours too had a message but in the firelight they were hard to read. She had to be careful not to notch the feather further or clutch it too hard.

Her days had suddenly become like those of any ordinary girl in the village. She walked with her friends to the lake and filled the pots, listening to the chatter of new ribbons. She slept in the afternoon and at night, while her family slept, she would take out the feather and study it, trying to read beyond the obvious.

It was difficult because the lessons had stopped. The Old Ones had been regenerated too, or killed. She knew because she had found blood at the base of one of the caves, a smear spreading out with spider fingers still fresh and red. Her mother had looked at it and shuddered, 'Sticky gum from one of those trees. It looks like blood, doesn't it?' There was a saying that the blood of the Old Ones would always run fresh, even though it ran outside the body and beyond the veins. One of the Old Ones was there too standing a hair's-breadth away. Chinku looked at him, holding her breath.

Was it possible that he … but the Old One shook his head, 'So sad, so very sad …,' and walked away slowly.

One day when she thought she could not bear the loneliness of it any more, a boy came from over the lake. He was an easy moving figure among the cattle, all arms and legs. His walk first caught her eye because it flowed so easily. No one in the village walked that way, flowing between the people and the cattle. A boy like butter, her mother would have said. Just for a moment she forgot the feather and the things she had to write. He was carrying a bundled-up cloth over his shoulder and strode through the women to the water's edge squatting down next to her.

'You're a Memory Keeper, aren't you,' he whispered softly, so softly that she thought she had heard nothing at all.

The dish slippery with soap-nut foam almost slipped out of her fingers as she struggled to turn a blank eye on him. Look at anything blank, look at the still water in the shadows, the patches of flat white cloud in the sky, let your eyes reflect their stillness – those were lessons the Old Ones had taught her. Look blank and your secrets are safe, was what it meant.

The boy's eyes were as clear as the water, as the sky without the clouds. He held out his hand carefully with a quick glance around.

'I found these matrix stones there under the pine trees. Perhaps you should keep them.'

She looked at the stones. It was difficult to look blank now. They were of course matrix stones lying in the palm of his hand. The sunlight crossed them as it glinted.

'How do you know what they are?' she asked, wary as a young wolf. 'They look like ordinary pebbles.'

Looking at the lake water in front of them he put out his finger and made one of the secret signs in the water, a sign that the men from over the hills would never have known. Her heart leapt in a moment of happiness, even as she struggled to keep the blankness in her eyes.

'How do you know?' she said again, coldly.

'I sat in your class twice.'

She sat back on her heels. 'You? You're not one of us. How could you have got into our class? You're a liar.'

'If I were a liar, how would I know that?'

He was older by a few years, taller and looked more confident. And his smile rippled across his face like the water in front of her.

'Keep the stones,' he said, getting to his feet. 'I have to go.' And then he was moving away through the cows and the people, crossing Chinku's mother who was coming over to find out the boy's name, with an angry, 'Haven't I told you not to talk to strangers?'

It was too late to hide the matrix stones, so she played with them in the mud, throwing them like a dice or marbles and watching them spin across the water. 'Oh, he gave me these pebbles. Aren't they pretty?'

'Where did he say he came from?'

'From across the lake.'

'Strange people come from across the lake, like those who live in the village of Baghen,' her mother said. 'You should be careful. And do not go too deep into the woods.' Saying this she went away again, balancing the butter churn that she was carrying on her hip.

Everyone in the village and across the mountains had heard of the wolf people of Baghen. They ran at full moon with the wolves in the forest. Some said they turned into wolves themselves when the moon grew full and went looking for babies to turn into wolves. All it took to become a wolf man or woman was one scratch from a claw, or even a fleck of foam from their mouth when they were running with the pack at midnight. But was the boy really a wolf boy? Wolf boys had ruffled hair streaked with silver and yellow or ice-blue eyes, or so the stories went. What colour had the boy's eyes been? She thought hard but could not remember. What she did remember was the way his smile had spread from his mouth to his eyes in a slow stream of joy like rippling water. She wanted to know him better, to play the games of the matrix stones with him.

2

The next morning, after she had finished fetching water, Chinku slipped away around the lake to the forest, reminding herself that it was a long time till the next full moon and as a result the wolf people, if there really were any, were likely to be in their human form.

The pine trees shook their needles around her and the squirrels scuttled up the bark and scolded from the safety of their branches. And if they did that, she was certain there was no one around except herself.

There was a story her grandmother had told her once by the evening fire, stirring her soup pots while Chinku sat nearby. The story of a starving man in a long hard winter. He had a wife and child to feed and there had been no food for days – the lake was frozen hard with no chance of breaking the ice to spear the fish. The man had wandered through the deserted forest for days, until he was almost an ice statue himself. Then, in a mess of broken branches and ice spears in a hole, he discovered a trapped wolf. The icy-blue eyes had looked up at him through the darkness below. It was food, the man thought and warm furs for his wife and child. In his trembling hands, he lifted the spear, but try as he might he was helpless in front of that blue stare. It just looked at him and throwing the spear down and scrabbling among the branches he was able to help the wolf out of the hole, thinking the whole time,

'I am a fool, the wolf will attack me and I will never see my family again.' But the wolf did not attack him – instead, it gave him a gift.

How it gave him the gift, Chinku's grandmother did not know – there were a thousand and one ways the gift could have been given, through the wolf's breath, warm on the man's face, through a growl, or a scratch, or perhaps for a moment the wolf had taken on human speech. From then on the man had been able to transform himself into a wolf when the moon rose full and golden over the mountains and hunt with the wolf packs so that he could always scent and find food. He could walk unseen at night if required and hide his tracks the way some wolves were able to. It was a gift that the man had handed down in his blood to his sons. And the tribes lived on their own keeping to their own strange ways and even t he Shadow Slayers from across the hills did not dare to tangle with them.

'Do you remember that story?' Chinku asked her mother. 'Of how they became wolves?' But her mother shrugged and said, 'Who remembers these things?' and dragged her home to help with the washing. But there was hope, Chinku thought, because if her mother remembered the wolf people, then perhaps she remembered other things too. Chinku sat down on a grassy bank in the shade of one of the trees and wondered what to do next. The Shadow Slayers had their city somewhere to the West. She had heard of the white stone houses of Kalabash with their iron gates that closed every sunset.

At Kalabash, it was said, they ate memories and the more memories they devoured, the stronger they grew. Kalabash had no poets or storytellers, no musicians or artists. It was these things that the King of Kalabash was determined to steal from the others whenever he could.

'Why?' Chinku had asked in one of her classes, in a piercing, childishly clear voice that made the other young Memory Keepers nudge each other and giggle.

'Who knows,' the Guardian had shrugged. 'Perhaps he had a son who wouldn't sleep until he was told a story and his nurses had no stories to tell.' Perhaps the child died of crying for sleep and the King in his grief had determined to steal all the stories and legends in the world, to tell his child and make the baby go to sleep.

Chinku had not really understood it then and did not understand it now, but the tales of tribes left memoryless, storyless, began to seep in from the surrounding lands. It was the weaker tribes at first and the simpler tales of the birth of the sun from a fleck of fire stolen from the Creator's oven, or the moon dropping from Inaki Sky Queen's tear to take its place in the night and light a lamp for the weary traveller. She had loved those stories even though they were not the tales of her own tribe, but stories that a wandering storyteller had stopped to tell them at night by a fire under the stars.

Sitting in the soft sunlight, Chinku wondered whether the wolf people had stories of their own or whether the magic of running under the moon with the wing-footed wolf packs was enough enchantment for them.

'Hello, Memory Keeper,' said a voice almost in her ear and startled her. The boy was standing there, smiling, his teeth flashing white in the sun.

She tried to pull herself together and not act like the silly girl her mother often said she was.

'What's your name?' she asked. If someone gave you their name, you had their essence, the Old Ones had said.

'Nick,' he answered.

Did he look like a Nick? The name could sometimes be a lie. 'That can't be your real name,' she challenged.

'It's much shorter than my real name. A baby like you wouldn't be able to pronounce it anyway.'

'Try me,' she said, getting to her feet. Standing on the hillock gave her added height so that she felt taller than he was.

'Nekrasol Baghilov Timbre Lupineska,' he answered with a bow as springy as the tree branches. 'But you can call me Nekrasol. Now isn't it time I knew your name?'

'Chinku,' she answered simply, thinking what a horrible name he has. It doesn't make any sense, though it sounded like bits and pieces of words she knew – like the word for 'wolf'.

'Chinku. That's all,' she repeated.

'Well, Chinku That's All, what are you doing alone in the woods like this? Don't you know it's not safe?'

'I was looking for you. I wondered whether you were a Memory Keeper too.' In the dappled sun shadows she could not tell what colour his eyes were – they could have been any colour at all.

'That's not why you came,' he said. 'You were wondering if I were a wolf.' His eyes were yellow, she decided, a colour she hated and she stamped her foot. Wolf or otherwise, he was an annoying boy.

'I'm not such a curious prying creature.'

'But I am a wolf. And you are a Memory Keeper.' Too late to deny it – the word 'too' had slipped out of her mouth and she could not pull it back.

'How do you know that?'

'We can smell Memory Keepers, don't you know?' Now he was jeering at her. All the disappointment and loneliness of the past few days gathered together in Chinku's eyes and rolled down her cheeks as tears.

Wolf though he was, he faltered, then walked around her in a circle. As she fought her tears, Chinku could feel his shadow passing over her tightly closed eyelids.

'Don't cry,' he said finally, uselessly, as helpless as most boys are in front of tears. 'I know what happened to your village. We smelt the men coming.'

'Then why didn't you warn us?' she demanded, with tears in her eyes again. An arm came round her shoulders. It felt like an ordinary arm and she leant against it.

'We didn't know where they were going. And would you have listened to a warning from a pack of wolves?'

'My father would have. And at least our memories would have been saved.' Tears were memories gone sour, the Old Ones had said, except for the tears of the gods, the Sky Queen's tears that had trickled down to form the world's seas, or her son's honeyed tears that ran through the veins of trees and flowers to be gathered by the bees.

The boy was standing there firmly on his two feet. He was too reasonable, but she could not stamp her foot at him again. She knew what he was saying was true. Their tribe did not talk to a tribe of wolves. Well, she knew Nick was a wolf and now she could go back to her everyday chores because there was nothing more to be discovered that could help her.

'I have to go back,' she said lamely. 'My mother will be anxious.'

She could sit there, of course, under the trees looking at the patterns of the leaves and counting the dots on the butterflies' wings while the sun gently kissed her toes.

'Yes,' Nick answered, his smile growing longer and more wolfish. 'Run along, Memory Keeper. Go carefully, there are real wolves in the forest.'

'Where is Kalabash?' she asked him suddenly. 'Do you know?'

'Over the hills and far away,' he answered. 'Why do you want to go there?'

'If they have stolen our tribe's memories, they must have them there,' she answered.

Nick cocked his head and thought for a moment.

'It might be,' he answered. 'But I have never heard of anyone who has gone to Kalabash to steal memories back from those thieves. I don't even know how they store the memories.'

'The Old Ones say they eat them.' It was a silly thought, where had it come from suddenly, to make a fool of her in front of this wolfboy. If she looked down she would know that it came from her own sense of futility, at having to meet her parents everyday knowing that the memory of one day and a whole way of life had been taken out of their minds. No one remembered the Old Ones or left flowers at that ugly stain. And in Kalabash there was a king singing his children to sleep with their stories.

Nick smiled, that same smile she had seen by the lake. 'I can't tell you,' he answered. 'But stories aren't always the truth, you know.'

No, she knew that stories weren't always true, but she also knew that stories could shorten a road or put the blue into a grey sky. Stories could do more than that, but at ten that was all she knew.

'I had better go,' she said, half turning away from him.

'Goodbye, Memory Keeper.' There was a rustle and something moved behind her. She turned back again quickly and found no boy, just the shadows of the sun chasing each other, the squirrels scolding, and the bushes stirring softly. All at once the goose flesh prickled on her arms and she quickly ran for the path that would take her back to the lake and to safety.

3

Her mother scolded her, but no more than usual because she was back in time for the afternoon meal. When the rest of them slept, she sat under the entry gate to their courtyard with the matrix stones, trying to master the patterns of memory. When she could, she would steal some threads from her mother's weaving and knot the memory of the boy in the woods into them. Though what could she say? That the boy had told her he was a wolf and vanished? He might have been making fun of her the way boys did, for all she knew.

The black stones fell idly from her hand while she was thinking. She saw them when the lengthening sunbeams made them gleam and flash crisscross. The stone lights crissed and crossed and crossed and crissed as if they were trying to tell her something. They did it twice, once directly against the way the light fell, so that she could not be mistaken. She looked around quickly, her heart suddenly jumping into her mouth. Even in the sleeping village someone might see her. There was a sound, a scuffle of gravel nearby.

'Who is it?' She clutched the stones in her hand and leapt up, almost running.

'Are you being naughty again?' asked an amused voice. It was her father. 'Why didn't you sleep?' he asked. 'You'll be tired in the evening.'

'I'm too old to nap,' she answered, trying to put a pout into her voice.

'You were playing marbles. You're too old for that too. Let me see them.' He put out a hand.

'Why?' she asked.

'Because your mother said the wolfboy gave them to you. You should never take things from strangers, especially from a wolf.'

'But I don't know he's a wolf. And he was nice.' She clutched the stones hard in her fist and felt the edges cutting into her soft palm. Be more childish than you are, she told herself, pout more, and sulk like a baby who doesn't want to lose her toys. In the old days it would not have worked, but her father was not her father any more, just a kind stranger.

Her heart was beating hard again because this was more important than being caught doing something naughty. As she stood there looking at him, a cheel wheeled through the sky with a shrill scream and swooped startlingly close. Her father put out his hand and dragged her away in case the bird made a snatch at her hand.

'Strange bird,' he said, because the hawk wheeled up and away again, flying like a black speck through the darkening sky.

'Thank you,' she said in her mind to the cheel because her father had forgotten the stones and was pushing her inside the courtyard.

'Some danger must be coming,' he muttered. 'Go inside Chinku. Go inside now.'

He stood outside for a long time while Chinku quickly hid the stones in the hole in her pillow and came back to watch. But all that happened was the sun singing the story of night and sending the birds home to their nests. Her mother bustled past her with the soup pot and this time Chinku's father said nothing. The stones were like hard lumps under her head at night, shifting with every turn she took as if they were still trying to tell her what she hadn't understood in the evening.

After the girls had gathered at the lake and the boys had left for the fields or their fathers' workshops, Chinku slipped away with the stones back across the forest path. As usual, the squirrels scolded when they saw her and a bird came and sat quite close to her, head cocked like that boy's had been. She ignored them, scrabbling in her pocket for the stones. The sun was not yet strong enough to let her read the beams, so she sat warming them in the palm of her hand while the yellow ray crept up the bark. The next time when she took out the stones they caught the light and she spun them in her palm and let them fall. She had been taught that the stones would choose their own pattern and they did, the beams crossing against each other, once, twice, thrice. Perhaps in the hidden library there would be a book which would tell her how to interpret the lights, but who even knew where the hidden library was? She picked the stones up and dropped them again, and again they made their star patterns.

'K ... A ...' said a voice almost in her ear again, and again she was startled, though not as much as yesterday, not disturbing the matrix stones.

'You can read them!' she said accusingly.

'Not too well,' Nick answered, 'but a little. You must be a very bad Memory Keeper if you can't read the stones.'

'We don't learn that till we're ten,' she answered defensively. The boy looked alert and fresh, the wind ruffling his hair. She must stop calling him the boy.

'Nick,' she said, 'please read them for me.'

'Wolves can't read the stones too well,' he told her, for once not laughing. 'But it's almost like the way we read the forest signs.'

'What do they say?' the stones were flashing again without her having to turn them.

'I think it says Kalabash,' he said and looked at the stones again. 'Yes, that's what it says.'

'What does it mean?'

He just shrugged and answered that that was as much as he knew. Chinku thought this was even worse than knowing nothing. Now she had half a piece of knowledge that she could not even interpret. Was that why the bird had wheeled over her father, startling him away from the memory of the stones? The Old Ones had insisted that nothing in life happened by chance, that everything fell into a clear pattern if you knew how to read it. She had been thinking about Kalabash only the other day, had been talking about it and now, if the boy was right, the stones had spelt out the name. She sat there looking at the glinting pebbles thinking of nothing.

'The interpretations are in the hidden library,' the boy said.

'If it exists.'

'Oh, it's still there all right,' Nick answered. 'The Shadow Men could not find the entrance.'

'How do you know where it is?' she asked indignantly all at once. 'It's supposed to be a secret even to us! Were you spying on the Old Ones?'

'Wolves don't spy,' he answered with his voice almost dropping to a growl. It was so wolf-like that she could imagine a grey beast standing next to her.

'Then what were you doing?'

He shook his head angrily, 'What is it to you, anyway? I thought you wanted to find the hidden library. I know where it is. Isn't that enough for you?'

It actually was. She looked into his angry yellow eyes and apologized as politely as her mother had taught her how.

'You were trying to help me,' she said, 'and I was rude. I am very very sorry, Nick.' His eyes were calm again and the hair on his head flat instead of standing on end.

'You want me to take you there?' he asked.

'Where is it?' she asked. 'Will people see us going there?'

'If it were that easy for people to see,' he answered, 'it would not have been so hard to find. Come this way.'

She jumped to her feet and followed him without a second thought.

The path there took her through the fields where the cattle were wandering.

'Here,' said Nick when they had tramped through the grass and between the sheds where the cattle were kept at night.

'Where?' she looked around. She knew the place – her mother had sent her there to collect milk sometimes. The only animal in the shed at that time was the big black bull chained to one corner. He saw them and lowered his horns.

'There,' Nick answered, 'behind him.'

'How do ...' Chinku muttered. She was used to cattle, but the whole village was terrified of this bull. Once he had got loose and run through the streets trailing his chain behind him. All the children had quickly climbed the trees or run inside their homes while he roamed the village. Finally, the village men had got their pitchforks out and backed him against a wall till he could be caught by his chain and led back again. But today, the bull was ignoring her. His whole attention was concentrated on the boy, tossing his horns and pawing the straw under his feet. His red eyes looked uncertain.

'While he's looking at me,' Nick said, 'you will duck behind him. There's a trapdoor under the straw.' He stood in front of her looking at the bull and a musky kind of animal odour began to fill Chinku's nostrils. The smell of an unwashed dog, or perhaps the smell of a wolf.

The bull rattled his chain.

'Hurry!' Nick said. 'He's going to charge.'

And the next minute the black thunderbolt had rushed forward, and Chinku without any fear was scrabbling frantically in the straw. A hoof almost scraped her. Her fingers found an iron ring and pulled. The straw fell away and a trapdoor rose. She slipped through without pausing to think.

And the smell of straw, wolf, and bull fell away. She was in a room lit by the dull red glow of a lamp. It was like a lump of coal set in a silver claw, but gave no heat to her tentative fingers. The dark walls were lined with shelves and there was a rolled-up parchment lying on a desk nearby. She wished Nick would come down and join her, but the trapdoor above her head stayed shut. Still at a loss, she picked up the parchment. It had a list of names. Her finger skimmed down titles that she recognized from some of her classes. A stamp overhead panicked her, but she realized that Nick must still be teasing the bull. If he bellowed the whole village would come to see what was wrong. Her finger ran up and down the list twice fruitlessly and her heart beat so hard that it almost choked her. Looking around frantically, she saw a lizard on the wall by a niche. The lizard flickered away. Remembering the bird, she went to the niche and found another parchment stored there. Unrolling it, she read, *Interpreting the Matrix*, and without waiting to read more, rushed to the ladder that led up to the trapdoor.

Her head pushed up the wooden trapdoor. She climbed up in a rush and ran over the straw. The bull, which had his back to her, must have realized someone was behind because he turned and charged back, but just a fraction too late. She was clear. Nick was standing there smiling his pointed grin, the teeth flashing white in the sunlight. He was breathing lightly.

'Got it,' she said. 'Let's go and read it.'

'You took it away?' he asked.

'I didn't know what else to do. And there wasn't enough light ...'

Nick looked surprised and a little worried. He cocked his head thoughtfully for a while then said, 'I suppose it couldn't be helped. All right, let's go and see what it says.'

They slunk out through the cattle sheds skirting the lake until they were back in the safety of the woods. Nick took the parchment from Chinku and spread it out on a grassy hillock. He ran his fingers down it while Chinku jumped up and down in exasperation beside him.

'Will you stop doing that,' he said. 'Yes, I was right about the crisscross beams. If they flash right twice and left like that, they do spell out words.'

'Kalabash.'

'Let's toss the stones again,' he suggested. So they did, and this time he held the parchment as he read the stones. Chinku stood by with a pout while he watched the beams dance – the parchment was too hard for her to read.

'It says Kalabash,' he said finally, when the sun's light was dropping lower, too low.

'But that doesn't mean anything,' she said.

'Perhaps it means you have to go to Kalabash.'

'And then do what?'

'I don't know, perhaps recover the lost memories. How do I know? I'm only a wolfboy, not a Memory Keeper.' If she had been listening to him, she would have realized he sounded helpless, but she was too lost in her own worries. She picked up the stones while he held the parchment.

'I'll have to go,' she said. 'Or they'll start looking for me.' If she was gone too long, they missed her now, not like that other day when the men had come over the hills. Kalabash was over the hills.

'We'll have to hide this,' he said. 'Unless you want to go and put it back. Which is what you should be doing.'

She thought of the bull and shuddered. 'Can't you think of a wolf hiding place?' Suddenly, another thought struck her. 'Nick,' she said, 'aren't there any records in the Hidden Chamber?' Hope shone in her eyes for an instant.

'You silly girl,' Nick said. 'If there were any records in the Hidden Chamber, do you think it would have been spared?'

'What do you mean?'

'They would have found out and killed the bull to get at them. Until this goes back,' he said, holding up the parchment, 'it will not be safe, but for the meantime I will find a hiding place. Now go back home before they come here looking for you!'

There was a fountain in which all the colours of the world swam – reds and blues and pinks leaping up like small fish and vanishing under the swirling waters again. The water had seven streams that somehow stayed separate in the white marble basin – they flowed from a curling shell held up high by a god man she could not recognize. She put her hand in the water and a pink fish touched it lightly and then swam through her hand. At first Chinku did not understand what had happened – she thought the fish had slipped between her fingers. Then she realized the fish had swum through the flesh and bones of her hand, and startled, she took her hand out of the water and awoke to see that she was lying next to her mother in a huddle of covers with her hand out.

She lay there listening to her parents' breathing, still half asleep, when she heard somebody whisper, 'Chinku! Chinku!' It came from the window. Splinters of ice suddenly crawled on her neck. She looked up at the window and saw something move behind the glass. It was fogged as if someone had breathed on it. 'Chinku, Chinku,' she heard again. The wonder of the dream fell away from her and she carefully made her way out of the covers.

Through the glass she could see a wolf's yellow eyes. 'Come on, quickly! There's danger! Come out!'

Tiptoeing between her sleeping parents, she made her way out of the room. Fumbling at the latch she opened the door. 'How long you took! There's no time, they're coming over the hills!'

'Who?'

'The Dream Stealers ...'

'But my parents, I need to warn them ...'

'They're looking for you,' the wolf said. 'At least not you, but they think one of the Memory Keepers escaped. Now stop talking and come along.' The wolf spoke in Nick's voice. Otherwise, it was a large timber wolf. Chinku stood hesitating at the threshold.

'It will be dawn soon,' the wolf said, 'and they will be here.'

'Where do I go?'

'Get on my back,' he said. And Chinku awkwardly climbed on. There was no bridle to hold on to so she clutched the folds of fur near the neck and hoped she would not fall off. The wolf loped through the night faster than any horse, seeming to grow bigger with every stride. Chinku had not ridden too many horses so she dared not look around. Instead, she buried her face in the wolf's neck and clung as hard as she could.

'Relax,' the wolf muttered. 'It feels as if you're trying to strangle me.' The ride through the night was a strange one, with the wolf talking to her every so often in Nick's voice. Every so often frightening thoughts swirled through her head – whether the wolf could be trusted or whether she would ever return to her village – and when those thoughts troubled her, she clung harder to the furry neck.

The ride seemed to go on and on and she lost count of time. For a while she even drowsed. Then, all at once she realized the rhythmic movement had stopped and that the light creeping through her closed eyelids was red. Abruptly she sat up and found herself looking through the trunks of the pine trees at another village. It was very different from their own with its strange turreted gateways leading to pointed beehive wooden homes. Each roof had horns on top and there were crossed spears guarding every entrance.

'Get off!' said the wolf impatiently, and Chinku slid off the furry back and stood trying to wriggle life back into her feet. A man in red and black came out of one of the houses and stood in front of her.

'Is this the girl?' he asked.

'Yes Father,' said Nick. Chinku looked around and found Nick standing next to her with no trace of the wolf anywhere. Deep inside she wished she had seen the transformation – that would have been something to put down in knotted threads. But the moment required politeness so she smiled at the man standing in front of her.

'Did they see you?' the man asked.

'No Father,' Nick answered. 'I was just in time.'

'I hope so. Take the girl inside, while I go and see that there is no one following you.'

Nick put his arm around Chinku's shoulders and hustled her inside.

All the light inside the house seemed to come from a silver basin that stood on a table in one corner. She stood inside, gaping. Nick shoved her towards a chair with silver-embroidered cushions and she sat down.

'Won't they have followed?' Chinku asked, her voice thin and shrill.

'I don't think so – they will be too busy searching through your village.' She hated the way he said it. She had listened to him and come running out of her sleep, and left her parents and her village behind.

'Don't think we could have done anything,' Nick told her, as if he had read her thoughts. 'I'm only a wolfboy, not a magician.'

'We could have warned them before we left,' she muttered.

Nick shrugged, 'I don't know any of them. I only know you. So I chose to save my friend. Anyway, don't worry, everyone knows that the Dream Stealers only steal memories.'

'But they killed the Guardian,' she said, worried. 'I saw the blood ...'

It was bad in the village living with those people who did not remember, but perhaps this was worse. After all, she could have lived with her parents and friends even though they didn't have any more stories to tell her, perhaps as long as she could have cuddled safe in her mother's lap. She sat there hanging onto her tears – she could not cry in a strange place in front of the wolfboy.

A woman said, 'Your parents will be fine, child.'

Chinku looked up with blurred eyes and saw a woman towering over her – in her dazed state all she could think was that the woman was tall, and didn't have yellow eyes.

'Come and see,' said the woman. She took Chinku by the hand and led her to the silver basin. 'Look in.' Her voice was strange, like an animal purr, harsh and gentle at the same time.

Nick said, 'Ma ....'

The woman shushed him.

Chinku looked. The basin was filled with silver liquid, its soft glimmering light fading a little but still bright enough to throw light on Chinku's hand. Something floated in the middle. She blinked and looked hard and saw it was her own home, so real and solid that she could almost touch it. There were people around it, black shadows that moved in a kind of dance. One of the shadows pointed something at the walls and a thin red ray stabbed through. Chinku was about to cry out but the woman put her hand on her head.

'Wait,' she said in that rasping purr.

The red ray abruptly went out. Then the shadows faded away and her home stood there as silent as when she had left it. 'Are they safe?' she asked wonderingly.

'Quite safe,' the woman said. 'They were looking for you.'

'But how ...'

'We don't really know how they found out, but there may have been others who, like my son, knew that you were in the Memory Classes. For now you are safe. The Dream Stealers do not trouble us too often.'

Chinku looked at the silver basin and saw that nothing floated there except the silver liquid, which was gradually losing its light.

'The light goes out when the sun rises,' the woman said. 'And it waxes and wanes with the moon.'

'When there is no moon, the basin does not reflect any light,' Nick added. 'That's the most dangerous time because we cannot see danger then.'

'But you ... you hunt ....'

'The gift was given to us to use in times of great need. Except for a few, very few of us who can change shape at will,' Nick's mother told her.

The room around her was weird and wonderful in its wood and metal and silver and there were the horns of a buffalo on one of the walls. Looking at it she yawned loudly.

'The child needs to go to bed,' Nick's mother said. 'Come with me.' Chinku's eyes were almost shut as she blundered through the rooms clutching Nick's mother's hand. Then, all she knew was that she was falling on furs and deep into sleep.

There was a washroom where clothes had been laid out for her, black leggings with red embroidery and a red shirt.

'These were Nick's clothes when he was smaller,' the woman said apologetically. 'We have no little girls here. However, if you give me your night dress I can stitch you something by tomorrow.'

Chinku washed and climbed into the wolfboy's clothes wondering whether they would change her into a wolf girl. Looking into the mirror she thought she looked exactly like a boy, especially when she put the red cap on her head. That would confuse anyone who was looking for her. She pulled the cap tightly over her curls and then, clean and tidy, found her way to the outer room where Nick and his father were waiting. The windows were open and she saw that it was day time. A huge silver dish was put in front of her and just for a moment she wondered what wolves ate, whether it would be raw meat, red with blood, then, half-disappointedly saw that it was just bread and cheese and dates.

Nick asked her, 'Do you have the matrix stones with you?'

His father interrupted, 'Let the child eat. There is plenty of time.'

'I have the stones,' Chinku mumbled, through a mouthful of bread and cheese. She had put them into the pocket of her leggings and she fumbled at her side. The stones rolled on to the table in a mess of breadcrumbs. In the sunlight they flashed, first criss and then cross. Three times. Then three times again, and in the middle, a red flash – a different message from the one by the lake. Her mouth open, she gaped at the stones, then looked helplessly at Nick.

Nick's mother bustled in with a tray and said, 'Stop bothering the child and let her eat.' The flashing stones caught her eye and she looked at them for a moment, her head cocked. Then she put the tray down and started serving the meal to her husband and son.

'What did the stones say?' Nick asked.

'Eat your breakfast,' Nick's mother told him firmly.

'But they did say something about Kalabash,' Nick said.

'Yes they did, but nothing that can't wait till you've finished eating.'

Chinku wondered how Nick and his mother could read the stones. This was something the Old Ones had never discussed in all their talk about the wolf people. Nick's father obviously couldn't read them, because while he had looked at them with interest, his eyes had stayed curious. Chinku finished her breakfast and sat at the table waiting for the others. Their bowls were filled with something reddish that could have been meat, but she was not sure. What did the wolf people eat? Did they keep cattle and if they did, what would happen when the moon changed? Or when one of them decided to turn into a wolf? Nick's mother glanced at her and said, 'The stones are telling you to go to Kalabash.'

'Me?' Chinku said.

'Yes, you.' Nick's mother's eyes were suddenly cold. Like plunging into the depths of the lake in winter and looking up gasping to see the waters close overhead.

'That is absurd. The child cannot go alone.' Nick's father's voice was very close to a growl.

'I can only tell you what the stones have said.'

'Are you sure?' Nick's father asked insistently. His spoon turned over and over in his bowl and the spoon flashed almost like the stones. Chinku thought that from being the last of the Memory Keepers she had become a child being fought over by adults. She wondered whether wolves went to school. Meanwhile Nick finished eating and got to his feet.

'Take her round the village,' Nick's mother said. 'But don't go into the woods today.'

'Why shouldn't we go into the woods?' Chinku asked, the moment they were out of doors.

'In case those men are still in the forest looking for you. They might well be – my mother can smell trouble a long way off.'

'Is she a wolf too?' Chinku asked. A chicken clucked past them and she stopped to watch it go by. The wolf village looked just like her own except for the spears and the horns on the roofs and the colours daubed on the walls. The chicken was followed by a bleating kid.

'Aren't they scared? Living in the middle of wolves?'

'We don't smell like wolves to them. In fact, we don't smell like wolves at all, unless we need to, like when I frightened that bull. And my mother comes from another village, from your village in fact. She met my father in the woods and he made her a wolf after they got married.'

Chinku's mother had told her often enough not to ask too many questions. The Old Ones on the other hand said that out of questions grew knowledge. Sometimes that confused her.

'Can you make me a wolf?' she asked.

'Yes,' Nick said, 'if you want. But then you would have to live with us.' Looking around he caught her by the hand and pulled her round a boundary wall saying, 'Come on, I have to retrieve that document of yours.'

'Where have you put it?' she asked, almost dragged off her feet.

'In the woods, in a secret place.'

'But your mother said ....'

'You can wait here, if you like,' he told her. 'There's no danger for me.' Ah yes, if he saw the men he would turn himself into a wolf and they would never catch him. For a fleeting second she thought of asking him to make her a wolf too. Then, remembering the night ride, she said, 'I can always ride on your back if there's danger.'

The fact that she was disobeying Nick's mother troubled her, but she thought that if they came back with the document she would not be so angry.

Nick ran with her across a little patch of grass towards the trees.

'The woods start here. The moment we're in those trees we will be out of sight of the village, unless one of them is out hunting.'

'You hunt in the morning?' Chinku had so many things to put down once she found a thread or a feather. The silver moon liquid, for example, that lit up the big room at night and Nick's mother's eyes. Lost in thought she half stumbled then checked herself, putting out her hand and hitting a rock blindly.

'Clumsy!' said the boy. 'If that's the way you run ...'

She was too busy looking up to listen to him. The trees had opened into a clearing with big moss-covered boulders arranged around as if men had put them there. 'What's this?' she asked. 'It looks like a dance of giants.' Her hand had hit one of the boulders.

'It is the Sacred Circle,' he answered. 'The village elders gather here when the moon is full.' She thought of a pack of wolves gathered together, turned silver by the moonbeams that also painted the boulders and the valley.

'Come on,' Nick said impatiently, 'we can't stop here. Outsiders aren't allowed anyway, even Memory Keepers.' The circle would have been the obvious place to hide the document. She was half disappointed that it wasn't there.

Following Nick through the forest shadows was difficult – there were moments when he seemed to merge with the bushes so that all she could see was moving leaves. Chinku's strange new clothes did give her a kind of freedom different from her usual trailing skirts. They jumped over small streams and gnarled roots. They ducked around boulders – some of them carved into the strangest of shapes. One, she could have sworn looked like the muzzle of a wolf. At night they would be terrifying, monstrous dragon shapes and weird gaping lizards. She wondered who made them, man or wolf. Nick went up to one of the most frightening and with ease thrust his hand into the gaping mouth. Chinku waited to see the hard stone jaws close on his arm and hear the crack of breaking bone. But Nick pulled his arm out unharmed, holding a leaf packet. 'Got it!'

'Who made these stones?' she asked.

'The wind gods,' he answered, 'the day the first sun rose on this world.' Said like that with the rocks around them it sounded so impressive that Chinku shivered.

'Now come on, we have to go back before someone misses us.' He held out the leaf envelope to her and she put it carefully into the pocket of her leggings. The good thing about old parchments was that they were written on special skins that could be folded as small as small, small enough to slip through a ring if required, without breaking.

Nick put his head back and sniffed the wind that blew through the rocks.

'It's clean,' he said. 'I can only smell the forest. Let's go.'

They ran together light and easy through the sunlight and the green leaves, and when they passed the streams Chinku caught glimpses of a red and black boy-girl running behind Nick.

'No one will recognize me!' she exclaimed on a high happy laugh. 'They won't know!'

'Don't make so much noise!' Nick was suddenly alert, sniffing the air again. Chinku stopped so sharply that she almost stumbled on one of the rocks. He put out his hand, caught Chinku and dragged her out of the clearing into the shadows. Her feet scuffled through the leaves, rustling, and the birds in the trees sent out their harsh, 'Someone's coming!' call.

Most of the birds in this wolf forest were ravens and one or two fishing eagles that had wheeled overhead. Without realizing it, they had left the friendly squirrels behind. 'Quiet!' he hissed. 'Pick your feet up!' Still holding her in a pincer grip he looked around. There were no rocks, but the bushes grew thick together between some of the older trees. He dragged her by the arm and bundled her under the bushes, almost in the same way that her father had and all at once she was terrified.

'Come and hide with me,' she whispered, 'or they'll take your memory away.'

'I'll lead them off,' he answered. She caught sight of a flicker of grey. Crouching there, her heart began its dull thudding again. She was doubly terrified now and beneath the sick thread of her fear she could hear scuffling sounds, first nearby then a little further off. Above her head a raven gave a harsh croak, spread its wings and rose into the air.

There was a shout, 'A wolf, there, look!' Then the sound of a horn being blown. Then there was nothing but silence and a world washed by waves of fear.

She crouched there wondering whether Nick would ever come back and if he did not whether she could find her way back to his home, or even to her home where her parents waited. Even though they did not remember the stories of their past, they were still her parents. And what good were stories after all? Just things to entertain children with. She could live without stories if she could be rid of this terror. As she was telling herself this, the bushes rustled around her and the birds in the other trees began their shrill warning cries.

'They're gone,' Nick's voice said. She looked up and saw him standing there. There were small yellow leaves on his shoulders and a twig in his hair, but otherwise he looked exactly as she had last seen him, an eternity before the fear. 'They were hunting,' he said, 'so I flushed out a stag and gave them something to do. Now come on before they come back this way. Ma is really going to be furious now!'

She was. She was sitting in the drawing room looking into the silver basin. As they opened the door, she said quietly, 'I thought I told you not to go into the woods,' exactly like an ordinary mother, except that there was a growl at the back of her throat.

'Ma, you know why we went into the woods. You must have seen,'

'Not all of it. I started looking when I realized you were missing. How on earth could you take the child into such danger?'

Chinku quickly put her hand into her pocket and pulled out the parchment. 'We went to get this,' she said simply. 'We couldn't leave it in the forest for people to find.'

Nick's mother stretched out her hand and Chinku put the parchment into it. She looked at it carefully and then let out a long slow breath. 'No wonder the men are still here. If the king were to find this .... Get the matrix stones and let us see what they say.'

Chinku quickly took out the matrix stones and threw them on the table. As they flashed, Nick's mother looked quickly at the parchment trying to decipher their message. 'It is the same message. You must go to Kalabash. And, no ... you must go to the Lady of Kalabash. Because the stolen memories can be found there,' she said.

'Lady? What lady?' This was the first time Chinku had heard of any lady. The Old Ones had certainly never mentioned anyone except the King.

'Do you people know nothing in Qlwri?' Nick asked crooking his eyebrows. 'The King's wife is famous across the three realms. In fact, she is the one who demands the dancers and artists to come to her court to entertain her.'

'I thought it was the King who stole memories,' Chinku said indignantly. 'That's what all the old stories say.'

'Yes, it began with the old king, when his first-born died, but the Dream Stealers never raided the villages like this before. That began with the King's wedding to the Lady.' He cocked his head again, 'Of course, I really wouldn't know, but that is what my mother says.'

When she awoke it was still dark. A chink of light came through the door frame. She sat up among her furs and looked around. She was still wearing the night-clothes in which she had left home and her stomach ached with hunger. It was the hunger that had awakened her along with the pressure of the stones in her pocket. Quickly she took them out, though she could hardly see them. The stones picked up the light from the door and showed a soft running gleam. Quiet footsteps startled her and she swept the stones back into her pocket. The door was opened and the woman stood there silhouetted against the silver light behind her.

'You're awake and you must be starving. Come, wash up and eat something.' She held out her hand and Chinku took it again as she had done the night ... or was it the day before?

Nick and Chinku were sitting together in the grass outside the compound after dinner. 'It's all very well telling me to go to Kalabash,' Chinku said. 'But I'm so small. How do I get there?'

'That's the problem,' Nick said gloomily. 'Magic things always tell you what to do, but not how and what happens afterwards.'

Chinku thought it was a very strange thing for a magical beast to say. Didn't Nick realize he was magical himself? But she agreed, 'Yes, you're right. What will I do in Kalabash? I'm not old enough to do anything much.'

'Except get your memory stolen,' Nick said.

She put out her hand and plucked a blade of grass and looked at it helplessly. 'Why do the stones want me to go to Kalabash?' she said again for the three-thousandth time. 'And why me?'

The stalk was brown. A small red bug was clinging to the tip. She quickly put the blade down again and watched the bug scuttle into a forest of stalks.

'I'll go with you,' Nick offered suddenly. She started and looked at him. 'Yes, I'll go with you,' he said again, since her eyes seemed totally blank.

'Your mother won't let you. She won't say anything about me.' Chinku felt that Nick's mother, kind as she was, would only be too glad for Chinku to go back home and take her troubles with her. Not that she had said anything. Instead, she had taken charge of the parchment and said she would guard it until it was time for Chinku to go back home. As for going to Kalabash, she said she would discuss it with Nick's father and find out whether it would be possible to send Chinku with someone safe. Her eyes had frosted over when she had said the word 'safe' and Chinku had, for a moment, experienced a strange sense of hostility. Not that she had said anything about that to Nick. That was two days ago, but the subject of Kalabash had not been brought up again. Instead, she had been called twice and shown her village in the magic basin. Once, she saw her parents standing at the door of their hut and wondered whether by now they had even forgotten they had a daughter. Perhaps the Shadow Slayers had taken away whatever little memory they had left so that they would graze in the village as contentedly as the cattle in the valley.

'The only creature that doesn't have a memory is a snake,' Nick's mother said suddenly. 'Some people have longer memories and some shorter.'

'Is a story just a memory? Are they real life?'

'The Older Ones once were. That is why it is so important to remember them.'

'Good things as well as bad? Can't we remember only the good things?'

'I'm not an Old One,' Nick's mother answered, 'so I can't tell you that. But I know we learn from all our memories.' And then she bustled Chinku away from the silver basin and the shadows of her parents.

However, thinking of Nick's suggestion, Chinku said, 'You'd have to tell your parents you are coming with me.'

'No. We'd just steal away. If Ma missed me, all she'd have to do is look in the bowl.' Nick jumped to his feet excitedly. 'Let's go, now at once!'

'But we don't know the way!'

'If we find the highway, there'll be lots of wagons going to Kalabash. We can take a ride with one or the other of them.'

Chinku still sat on the grass looking for reasons not to go. Now that it was up to her, she was afraid. 'What about food and clothes and money ... we don't have any money.' What she didn't add was that adults were suspicious of children carrying money. They would be accused of stealing it.

Nick had no doubts; his yellow eyes were blazing with a happy light.

'I know where my parents keep the gold. I'll just take some.'

He made it sound so easy. Chinku looked at him wondering what would happen if he met one of his parents. How old was he anyway? He looked ten, or maybe twelve. Perhaps no one would notice the two of them, but children of her age on their own attracted attention. She felt in her pocket for the stones and clutched them for comfort. They nestled comfortingly in her palm.

The wolf village was a strange place. She had seen very few people in the days she had spent there. Sometimes she thought she caught flashes of movement behind her while running with Nick, but whenever she turned there was nothing except the wind blowing the leaves. But people obviously lived in those threatening-looking houses with their paint and polish. Cows grazed in the fields and looked well-fed and cared for. Once she had tried to ask Nick, but he had shrugged it off. She was certain now that someone was watching her from beyond the boundary wall right now, so she looked at it, but as usual there was nothing.

'You are perfectly safe here,' Nick's mother had told her. 'The Dream Stealers do not often come to tangle with wolves.' So she sat staring defiantly towards the wall till Nick came back panting. 'I found the gold,' he said and jingled his pockets happily.

'I think someone's watching,' Chinku whispered.

'Watching? Oh ...' Nick's voice changed momentarily and then he laughed. 'It's the eyes we have in the walls.'

'Eyes?'

'Yes, come, look here.' Reluctantly she went to see what it was. He pointed at one of the silver bosses that studded the red and black paint decorations.

'That's just a big old nail,' she said.

'It's an eye, actually,' he answered. 'It looks after the place for us during the day. When strangers walk through the village it sets out an alarm. All the houses have them.'

She peered into the nail trying to see the eye. 'What would happen if I stuck my finger into it?'

'Nothing. It would feel like a nail, that's all.' She stuck her finger into the boss nonetheless. It felt hard and cold like the metal it was supposed to be. 'See,' he said. 'What did I tell you? Now let's go. Stop wasting time.'

They scampered through the empty streets again. This time Nick took a totally different direction heading towards the plains on the other side. Chinku kept looking behind her, expecting Nick's mother to spring out at any moment.

'Don't worry,' Nick said impatiently. 'The stones told you to go to Kalabash. That's what you're doing.'

'But if the nails are watching us ....'

'We're not strangers. They only signal an alarm if strangers are around.'

'I think my village is much friendlier than yours,' Chinku said.

'Of course, you're not wolves. Everyone here sleeps during the day, except for outsiders like my mother. That's one of the problems with the wolf gift.'

'But *you* don't,' she pointed.

'Oh, that's because I have my mother's blood in me. I'm not a wolf wolf, you know.' She didn't know because he looked exactly like anyone else to her. 'Anyway, no one can stop you from doing what the stones say you should do. You will get to Kalabash.'

And that was that.

7

Nick might have been certain that she would get to Kalabash, but Chinku was not sure. This was the first time she was going anywhere outside her own village. Very few people travelled anywhere simply because travelling was difficult and dangerous and who knew what lurked outside the boundaries of one's own home? They knew about the Wolf People of Baghen, of course, because they were neighbours, but the rest of what they knew was gleaned from records kept by the Old Ones, records of Memory Keepers who had been beyond the mountains and who had even met the old king in Kalabash, in the days before the Dream Stealers and the Memory Stealing rays. At almost every step she kept looking around to see if the landscape would change into something strange and wonderful, which meant that she kept stumbling and slowing down. Nick was getting impatient with her.

'At this rate,' he said, 'my mother really will come looking for us.'

Chinku was gaping at a bush of flaming flowers. Each scarlet blossom looked like a dragon with a ruff and a forked yellow tongue. She was about to put out her hand to touch one when he said that.

'I thought you said nothing can stop me getting to Kalabash,' she told him pertly.

'Yes, and then I suppose you would like to travel with my father by night,' he answered. 'But I want to see Kalabash too. So don't be such a selfish little girl.'

She was about to snap at him when they heard a rumbling on the road. Nick swiftly threw himself flat and put his ear to the ground.

'Wagons,' he said. 'Let's see if we can get a ride.'

Two oxen-drawn carts came up a few minutes later, barely moving faster than foot speed. They were laden with fat-bellied barrels and driven by men who looked like barrels themselves. Nick waved at the men and one of them pulled rein.

'What are you children doing on this road?' he asked.

'Trying to get to my uncle in Kalabash,' Nick answered. 'We would be grateful if you could give us a ride.'

The other cart drew up alongside and the two drivers exchanged glances. Then the fatter one said, 'All right, hop on. We aren't going to Kalabash, but we'll take you part of the way.'

They had to squeeze themselves in behind the barrels.

'It might be better if you each got onto a wagon,' the fat driver said. 'It'll be more comfortable.'

Chinku was about to climb down again because it was uncomfortable being pressed against the wood, when Nick gripped her shoulder hard.

'We are too young to travel alone,' he said. 'Never been away from home before.'

Chinku glared at him, but Nick ignored her. The two drivers looked at each other and shrugged.

'All right. It's your funeral.' The whips cracked and the oxen started moving. The wood under Chinku creaked and the floor lurched and bucked as if she were riding some wild animal.

'The wolf was easier to ride,' she muttered.

'That's because I was careful,' Nick retorted. 'Now shut up and go to sleep.'

Instead, she peered over the edge of the wagon and watched the country creep past them. There were more bushes of the dragon flowers in shades of scarlet and pink and orange. The road rolled up and down in waves like an endless sea towards a dim blue horizon. However, except for the flowers she could see nothing very different. 'I would like to pick some of those flowers,' she whispered.

'Well don't. They scream when they're picked and their screams are supposed to bring the dragons down from out of the hills.' Nails with eyes and screaming flowers – this was a strange place indeed.

The slow roll of hills gradually began to give way to huts, small ones at first with sheep and cattle around them, then gradually bigger ones with strange decorations on the roof that glinted when they caught the sunlight – leaves cut out of metal, winged birds.

'Do those have eyes too?' she asked Nick. He was the one who seemed to be sleeping. She prodded him with a finger and he whipped awake with what sounded like a growl. The yellow eyes stabbed through her, then softened into warmer amber.

'What is it?'

'Do those have eyes too?' she asked again. He followed the direction of her pointing finger.

'Those are weather vanes. They turn with the wind. Sometimes they indicate when enemies are coming to attack.'

'What sort of country is this!' she exclaimed. 'Enemies everywhere?'

'Well if you had been as suspicious as we are, perhaps your memories wouldn't have been stolen,' he replied. 'Now if you haven't anything else to say, I'm going back to sleep.'

'But where are we?' she asked impatiently.

'I don't know,' he answered. 'But wherever we are, it looks like the wagons might stop for the night.'

Nick was right because soon they began to drive through the streets of a village. Some of the houses had bunches of grapes hanging in front of them. The wagons stopped under one of the bunches and boys came running out of the building to lead the oxen round the back. The fat driver walked round the tail of the wagon.

'Well, young 'uns,' he said, 'we're stopping here for the night. I don't know what your plans are, but I can promise that the place is comfortable and decent.'

'And do you plan to move on towards Kalabash tomorrow?' Nick asked sleepy eyed.

'We do plan to halt at Uus tomorrow evening. But that depends on the road. Do you want to come with us?'

'Well, it is on our way.' Nick said thoughtfully, but did not commit himself.

The other wagoner came to join them and listened intently in a manner Chinku did not like. She sidled closer to Nick.

'That young brother of yours is very handsome. I bet the Lady of Kalabash would like him.' His companion nudged him sharply in the ribs.

'Like him for what?' Nick asked, keeping his arm around Chinku's shoulders.

'To carry her shawls and run after her. She has a whole bunch of those young 'uns. They live like princes eating off the fat of the land.' The second wagoner was smiling in a way Chinku did not like.

'She pays good money for her young 'uns too.'

'And why would I want to sell my brother to the Queen?' Nick asked tersely.

'Why, for the opportunities, of course. A likely young lad could go a long way in a royal palace.'

Nick answered firmly, 'I don't think my family would like that. I'll take my brother inside. He's tired, it's been a long way.'

Inside the tavern was a press of people. In one corner a girl was dancing, holding out her skirt and stamping her feet. The crowds stood back for her and some of the men were clapping their hands to the beat of her movements. What Chinku found strange was that apart from the girl, there were no other women there. The girl saw them in the middle of her dance and laughed out loud.

'Look who's come,' she said. 'Two children! Sweet children! Come here my darlings, come and dance with me.'

It was good Chinku thought, to know that she was leaning against a wolf. Otherwise she would have been terrified. Some of the men looked very strange indeed, one of them seemed to have eyes like a snail's. Something was moving against her side and she realized the stones in her pocket were jumping around, but she could not say anything to Nick because he was talking to the woman.

'I'm looking for lodging for the night for my brother and myself.'

It seemed that the woman owned the tavern because she stopped her dance and said, 'That's enough. I've got to talk to these customers of mine.' There was a laugh in the way she said 'customers', but Nick did not seem to mind. The men around her melted away to sit at the tables or hang near a counter where purple and yellow bottles glowed – perhaps it was the liquid that was all these strange colours and not the glass. Perhaps the bottles shrieked when they were tilted out, the way the dragon flowers screamed when you tried to pick them. She would like to pick a dragon flower and see the dragons fly down from the hills, Chinku thought. That would be a story worth remembering. The stones in her pocket jumped again and she quickly clapped a hand over her side so that no one would notice.

The girl took them into a little room off a corridor. The room must have faced West because the afternoon sun put its long fingers inside and stroked a pot of flowers that stood on the windowsill. There was a desk with an engraved kind of surface, the dark wood was incised with deep silver letters, or perhaps they were symbols. They seemed to dance in the light and shade of the room. It was a magic room, Chinku thought in wonder.

The girl said, 'Have you two children run away from home? You're too young to be out on your own.'

Nick answered promptly, 'We're going to our uncle in Kalabash.'

'That's a long way.' The girl was looking hard at Chinku as she spoke. 'Especially if you're taking someone who looks like your brother along.'

'Why?'

'Because the Lady of Kalabash likes having young children around to serve her.'

'The wagoners we came with said something like that.'

The stones were jumping under Chinku's palm. She wondered what it was they were trying so desperately to tell her. Most likely, it was a warning. However, there was no way she could take them out and show their message to Nick unless he managed to find them a room for the night.

'Where did the wagoners put up?' the girl asked. 'You can tell me. Demetra doesn't believe in kidnapping children.'

'They said they were putting up here,' Nick answered.

'But they didn't come in with you?'

He shook his head.

'Are you travelling with them tomorrow?'

'We are supposed to. I haven't paid them for today's trip.'

Abruptly, Demetra turned to Chinku, 'Do you have a tongue in your head?'

'Yes, I do,' Chinku answered and luckily her voice came out huskier than usual.

'Can you sing?'

'A little, not much.'

'Well, little not much, if you sing for your supper, I'll see about putting you up for the night. And throw in some food.'

'We have money,' Nick said.

'But I don't take money from children. What would people call me if I did that?'

The open window looked out onto a narrow lane. The house opposite was so close that the eaves of the roof almost touched. There was someone in the alley below looking up, but whoever it was, was deep in the lengthening shadows.

Chinku said, 'I'm tired,' putting a child's whimper into her voice. She did not need to pretend, not much. And if this Demetra liked children, perhaps she would find a room for them without making her sing first.

Demetra obviously did. She took them down the corridor again, turned in another direction from the taproom and led them up a narrow flight of steps, with a door at the head of them. She pulled it open. 'Here,' she said. 'It's a nice room for children, I think. I'll come to call you at supper time.'

The room looked like a turret room with a narrow window. Outside they could see the streaked pink and orange evening sky. There was a huge bed covered with an eiderdown and a soft cushiony chair in one corner. As they were looking around the room, they heard the door close behind them. Chinku immediately shoved her hand into her pocket and pulled out the stones.

'They're jumping!' she told Nick. The stones leapt in her palm and almost jumped off. They caught the last of the light in the sky and glinted twice. Was it a criss or was it a cross? Chinku was too confused to be sure.

'What do they say?' Chinku asked.

'Something about being careful,' Nick said. 'Let me find a light.' He looked around the space and found one. 'If this has absorbed enough sun during the day it should light up now. But that depends on whether this room has been used.'

He put his finger into the wick and a ray of sunshine shot out and grew stronger. He glanced quickly around the brightened room. There was a mirror set in one wall, an oval framed in curlicues of metal. The light fell on it. Nick walked quickly over to the mirror and put the edge of his fingernail on the glass and inspected the reflection carefully.

'There's a space,' he muttered, 'so it should be safe.'

'Safe for what?' Chinku asked, confused.

'To ensure no one is watching us through a double-sided mirror. Quick, let me now look at the stones.'

She poured them out of her palm onto a table, so hastily that one of them rolled on the floor and she had to scramble under the table, pick it up and cast them again – that was the word, not throw but cast.

'Go … alone … to Kalabash. At least, I think it's alone.'

'Go alone? I'll never be able to go alone!' Chinku exclaimed.

'And I'm not letting a silly little girl like you go by yourself in any case,' he retorted. 'But wait, is it alone or along? That's what I can't tell ….'

'We should have brought the parchment,' Chinku said sadly.

'There's no point crying over spilt milk,' Nick retorted. 'In any case, the parchment wouldn't have been safe with us. Anyone could have got their hands on it.'

'But what does this mean?'

'Oh don't start that again!' Nick said impatiently. 'Whatever it means, I'm not going to take a ride in those wagons tomorrow. I don't trust the looks of those two men.'

Chinku hadn't liked them either, especially when they had looked at her and talked about the Lady of Kalabash.

'But it's a long way, isn't it … how will we get there?'

'We can travel by night,' Nick answered. 'I can turn into a wolf again. I can run much faster like that. And I can smell the way.' He glanced around the room again. 'Let's not talk here. We can go for a walk in the streets after supper and talk again.'

'But before that I'll have to sing in front of everyone!' Chinku exclaimed.

'That's all right. Nothing very much can happen in front of a roomful of people,' Nick said. 'You'd better think of what you're going to sing, hadn't you?'

'I can tell a story,' she suggested. 'That would be better than singing. I know lots of stories.'

And when Demetra came to call them down, that was what she told her she would do. The taproom was not as crowded as she feared and there was a low stool put on a platform in front. Chinku sat down on the stool and looked at the glittering eyes in front of her – the light seemed to catch only the eyes and for a while she was very frightened, wishing she had not agreed to perform at all. Demetra seemed to realize what she was feeling because she patted her on the head before turning to the audience and saying, 'We have a little wandering boy here tonight who has agreed to tell us a story. So I'm sure you'll all listen intently and kindly, because as you can see, he's very young.'

Stories seemed to be new to them because, for a few seconds, the word echoed round the room. Then the echoes were replaced by hand claps, slow at first and then, after someone shouted, 'Come on, let's give the boy some encouragement!' louder ones.

Chinku looked at the floor in embarrassment – it was an old childish habit of hers when she suddenly found herself surrounded by strangers. She had been thinking about the stories she could tell in a half-hearted fashion, because her mind was floating backwards and forwards over the matrix stones.

There were feet in front of her shuttered vision, bare feet, elaborate leather slippers with curly toes, plain leather slippers cracking at the toes, so she hastily began to tell herself a story about all those feet that passed under her nose. Rouged red feet weren't the feet of her maids: they were the soft white feet of three pampered princesses, feet so soft and white that any kind of leather chafed them. Obviously because of this problem, the princesses couldn't walk – they had to be carried wherever they went, which meant that they never set foot on the ground except in their own Persian carpeted palace.

Exasperated by this helplessness, their father, the King, swore to give their hands in marriage to whoever could find shoes that wouldn't rub their soft pink and white soles into bleeding sores. The heralds travelled all over the kingdom singing songs one mile long to announce this competition. 'Cobbler cobbler mend my shoe, get it done by half past two' – Chinku's imagination was daunted a little by the prospect of composing songs, so she substituted the nursery rhyme the Old Ones had taught her, which seemed to fit because it had a cobbler in it.

Princes from all over the world came to compete. They rode up the long palace drive on their white Arabian horses and on their long tusked bull elephants. The Arabian horses were blanketed in gold brocade and saddled in velvet and the elephants had diamonds let into their tusks. Behind each prince came a retinue of the finest cobblers, some carrying velvet boxes, some cages of silk and in each box or cage was a perfectly crafted pair of little slippers. There were glass slippers lined in fur that shattered at a kick, there were velvet booties braided in gold, there were … here her imagination faltered again because her knowledge of shoemaking was extremely limited: she contented herself by thinking of colours instead of materials. Shoes embroidered with red and white kantha stitching, elephants leaping on the toes, tigers lurking under improbable palm trees; blue velvet appliquéd with multi-coloured butterflies. One of the princes had brought a cobbler magician with him: he clapped his hands and the butterflies rose from their blue velvet bed and hung fluttering in mid-air before the enchanted court; the stitchwork tigers leapt out from under their palm trees and stalked each other on the Persian carpets.

The whole court was filled with gasps and murmurs, except for the curtained area where the princesses sat.

'Oh King,' said the eldest of the princesses, barely stifling a yawn with pink rouged palms, 'all this is truly wonderful, but I think the true purpose of the contest has been lost.'

The words fell as heavy as lead on the entranced gathering: the butterflies softly returned to their velvet existence, while the tigers retreated into their palm shades.

'Yes,' agreed the King sadly, 'let the contest continue.'

There were shoes, shoes and more shoes: three different sizes in every conceivable shape and style. Shoes that made music when they were walked on, shoes that cooled the wearer's feet, shoes – no, she was repeating herself again and her eyes were pricking with sleep. She shook her head briskly to clear the fog. Shoes … no.

The youngest princess had just tried on a pair of gauzy sandals woven from the wings of butterflies. They were shot with all the shades of the rainbow and they bestowed the gift of flight on their wearer. With a cry of delight, the princess leapt into the air and found herself hovering close to the diamond and ruby drop chandelier.

'My daughter,' quavered the King nervously, 'that looks very dangerous. Please come down at once.'

'Nonsense, Papa. It's perfectly safe,' retorted the princess who, because she was the youngest, had been thoroughly spoilt.

'I'm going to marry whoever brought me these shoes.'

The King clapped his hands thrice and ordered the court trumpeter to announce the decision. The trumpeter cleared his throat, 'Hear ye, hear ye, hear ye, Maharajadhiraja Dhirendrachandra Naranarayan Bhupati Bahadur Shah Dev, Lord of Chandravangola, Overlord of the Forests of Surajgar and Master of his own House wishes to announce that the third princess has selected the shoes she is now wearing and wishes the ruler who brought them to stand forth.'

The princess executed a graceful wriggle and came to rest on the Persian carpet – her butterfly sandals were so light that her feet still hovered a few inches above the ground, giving her an air of breathless anticipation. Everyone craned towards the great lion doors of the throne room waiting to see which prince would appear between the hallowed portals. What the other two princesses were doing in the meantime had not yet been thought of – obviously they would also have to try on the butterfly sandals, since they had their sister's seal of approval. But no ruler stepped between the golden jaws of the two guardian lions – instead, a short, ragged gnome of a man came forward.

'You?' thundered the King frowning an awfully royal frown.

The gnome bowed so deeply that his nose almost touched the Persian carpet. 'Do you have any royal blood?' the King demanded. The gnome wriggled humbly, indicating that the answer was almost certainly 'no'. The two eldest princesses, who were yet to try on the butterfly sandals, looked at each other relieved. Their sister, the two pairs of eyes signalled to each other, had been far too hasty, and look what had come out of it, such an ignoble little man, and a fate worse than death.

'How did you participate in the contest?' the King demanded, still in the same awfully regal tone, as if by the mere weight of his voice he could command this being to crumble into dust.

'Executioner,' he growled and a heavy hand descended, not on the gnome's shoulder, but on Chinku's.

It was certainly a hand on her shoulder, a hand that belonged to hobnailed boots that were not in the least poetic, firmly pinned down to the ground. She looked up and saw it was one of the wagoners. He said slowly and solemnly, 'I claim this youngster for the Lady of Kalabash.'

Few people in the room heard what he said because most of them had been concentrating on Chinku's story. And in any case the wagoner's voice when he spoke was deliberately not too loud. Chinku squirmed under the probing fingers but knew she was caught. There was no way she could just get up from the stool and escape. Instinctively, she did the first thing that came to her, which was swivel her head around and sink her teeth hard into the part of the hand nearest to her mouth. It tasted of garlic and leather but she clamped on with her teeth till he let go of her shoulder. The moment he did so she sprang to her feet and leapt straight into Nick's arms. The rest of the room too had started boiling over as people realized that their storytelling had been interrupted. Nick's eyes were glowing eerily yellow as the wagoner lumbered down from the platform towards them. Chinku felt him begin to bristle. Demetra came forward quietly and put herself between the man and the two children.

'The Lady of Kalabash's writ does not run here,' she said. People behind them were nudging each other and beginning to ask what happened.

'What did he say?', 'Good story that?', 'What happened?' followed by increasing cries for Demetra and demands to know what was going on.

Demetra did not turn her back on the wagoner. Instead, raising her voice she said, 'This man just claimed the child in the name of the Lady of Kalabash.' The whole room heard her this time and began to rumble.

The wagoner said, 'It is my duty …'

'Child hunter are you?' someone asked.

'I have a warrant from the King which empowers me to …' He put his hand into his pocket and pulled out a parchment, which spilled like water on the floor. Demetra picked up one end of it distastefully as if it were a dirty tablecloth and ran her eyes over the print. In the light of the moon sconces the writing seemed to stand out clear in letters of fire. Chinku could see the letters leaping like tongues of flame then wondered whether she had imagined it because the next moment the page was just a page.

'It is certainly a writ of a sort,' Demetra said slowly. 'And yes, it empowers you to recruit children for the King of Kalabash. With the expressed permission of their parents.'

The room was crowding in on them from all round, a press of elbows and angry bodies. Chinku felt that Nick had stopped bristling and was secretly relieved – if he were to change into a wolf in front of a roomful of people, it might cause more chaos.

'Do you have their parents' permission?' Demetra asked.

The man stopped shaking his hand and said, 'They're runaways, both of them. I found them on the high road. They're fair game.'

'Did they say they were runaway?'

'Some stupid story about an uncle in Kalabash. Lies, all of it.'

Demetra said, 'I can think of some children from our own town who disappeared and whose parents had certainly not given them permission.'

'The King and his Lady will pay good money for a storyteller like this one. Enough gold sols to make us all rich!' The wagoner was beginning to bluster and Chinku could see the hobnails shifting backwards and forwards and wondered wildly whether they had eyes too.

'The wealth we require would be beyond their means,' Demetra said quietly. Then she turned to the other people in the room and said, 'I think this man has trespassed on our hospitality long enough. See him out for me, some of you, and our storyteller can get to work again.'

There was a low murmur like the surge of wind in the mountains or sea. The wagoner began backing away, his face suddenly pale, muttering, 'I have the right ....'

Chinku sat down again, but after the disturbance it was hard to slip back into the story. Had the slippers taken flight and born the gnome away from the executioner's hands? Yes, that was a possibility, there in front of the roomful of people; the gnome had hopped neatly into those shoes and risen up into the air. He had begged the executioner for the right to die with his own shoes on his feet and seeing those shoes, the youngest of the princesses had wept – though she was secretly relieved that she would not have to marry the gnome. After all, once her pampered feet were pleased she would still have to live with a man who was no fairy tale prince. But then seeing the gnome hovering on those magical shoes amongst the crystal chandeliers and watching her father's guards try to catch him with leaps and bounds, the youngest of the princesses thought that for a gnome he had a strange kind of courage and deserved to have an enchanter wave his wand and transform him into a person as unique as his shoes. Her sisters were standing around with the butterfly pairs on their feet thinking that their lives would now be even more comfortable than ever before because now they would be able to dance without allowing a single footfall to touch the ground, totally unfazed by either the executioner or all the excitement.

The youngest princess, despite being pampered, like all youngest princesses was tender-hearted. Seeing the confusion in the hall and the shoemaker's possible bloody end she tried to intervene.

'Father!' she shouted, loud above the chaos that filled the durbar hall. 'You gave your word! What will history write about you? What will people say?'

The King replied firmly, 'I will not allow you to marry that man!'

'I'm as guilty as you are, I said I would marry him.' The gnome was still circling overhead – there was no way he could get out of the room because the large French windows were closed, and once the executioner had entered, the elephant and lion doors too had been shut with reverberating bangs. The elephant doors were pure carved ivory and the lion doors made of the eight sacred metals. Most criminals remembered the closing of those doors as the last beautiful memory of their lives. The ones who were still to be found in dungeons beneath the palace could sometimes still be found discussing the magnificence of those doors.

The King looked up at the gnome hovering round the diamond pendants of the chandelier, 'Will you accept money for your shoes?'

'The youngest princess, or nothing,' the gnome retorted.

As soon as the story was finished, Demetra hustled the children away from the crowded room.

'I don't want any more people getting ideas like that wagoner,' she said. And she put them into her office behind the desk. 'Don't move from here. I'll bring you something to eat.'

'That was a good story,' Nick said to Chinku. 'Was it one you'd heard?'

'No,' she answered. 'That was one I was trying to make up.'

'But you're seriously good,' he told her. 'If you were a man you could make a living going from village to village telling stories like that. And on the way you could make up even more stories from what you saw.'

'But I'm not a man,' she whispered and lowered her head. They were both silent when Demetra bustled in followed by a girl with both hands full of platters. Delicious-smelling steam suddenly filled the air and both the children realized that they were very hungry.

'Eat!' Demetra said, 'And worry about nothing.'

Their hostess had been generous – there was a grilled trout with slices of lemon, so fresh that it almost still smelt of the mountain streams from which it had been caught. There were peaches and apples and cups of a creamy drink flavoured with wine. Silence followed silence but this time it was a happy contented kind of silence. After they had emptied the plates, it was too late to feel anything except sleepy and long for bed. The girl who had followed Demetra looked in and when she discovered that they had finished, hustled them back up to their little turret room. As she was leaving she said, 'Mistress said it would be best if you locked the door.'

Nick was swift to do that.

'Now take out the stones once more,' he said, 'and see if the message has changed.' Sleepily, Chinku pulled out the stones and cast them in the lamplight. They made crosses in the air this time, three of them. She glanced at Nick.

'Nothing,' he said. 'Just the same thing about going to Kalabash alone. No warnings.'

'What will your parents do when they find us gone?' 'They already know we're gone,' Nick answered. 'And my mother will look into the bowl. So they know everything that is happening.'

'But they can't help us if danger strikes, can they?' Chinku asked.

'No,' he said. 'They can't. Go to bed now. We have a long way to go tomorrow.'

The beds were soft and warm and despite the fact that she was far away from home, Chinku slept soundly, dreaming only of the gnome's flight on the butterfly slippers with the princess. Because the moment she had said, 'Rather than have him die, Father, I will marry him,' he had changed into a tall handsome young man, the hero out of a thousand-and-one dreams. He was a ruler's son, he said, and he had asked a powerful enchanter to put a spell on him so that he could find the right princess to marry. With her words, the spell was broken. Now why should that be – the thought floated even through her dream. Why could he not have stayed gnome, the short and the tall together, beauty side by side with deformity? If she had told it that way the people would have probably thrown her to the wagoner.

The wedding was celebrated with all the pomp and ceremony that the occasion demanded. And the princesses flitted between the assembled guests in dresses made of fabric that looked like butterfly wings, to match the butterflies on their exquisite slippers. The only drawback, if you considered it a drawback, was the fact that the young man could no longer make exquisite slippers. It was probably part of the spell, or perhaps it was part of the story that she had not quite been able to work out; after all, at ten, that was a lot of story to spin.

Demetra came to wake them early in the morning, so early that morning was barely a red thread against the darkness of the sky. Chinku blinked up at her. 'What time is it?'

'Almost dawn. Come, get up. I want you to be ready to leave before the sun is high.'

In the semi-darkness Chinku caught the yellow glint of Nick's eyes and knew he was awake too.

'It is best,' Demetra said, 'before any more people get ideas like that wagoner. Your little brother is a master storyteller. Your parents must be proud of him.'

'Yes,' Nick answered. 'They are.'

Shaking off the warmth and dreams Chinku splashed her face and hands with water. As a bath, it would have made her mother shudder. And she was still wearing those clothes that she had run away in. Demetra looked at her with a frown.

'Those colours are so bright, it would be better if you were less conspicuous. A lot of people saw you last night and they will be talking about you.'

'What can we do?' Nick asked. 'These are the colours of our village.'

'I shall lend you some cloaks,' she said. 'They will at least hide you from those looking for a child dressed in red and black. Now come and eat and I will send you part of the way with one of my servants.'

She went to one corner of the turret room and pushed against the stone wall. One of the stones silently swung open and Chinku could not help but exclaim out loud. Demetra took out something that looked exactly like dried leaves. They rustled in her hands and, in the half dark were almost invisible. 'Here,' she said, holding them out. 'Put them over your shoulders. When you are outside, draw the hoods over your heads.'

'Are they Invisibility Cloaks?' Nick asked, excited.

'No, but they do have special powers. The old elves made them from leaves. Like leaves they grow to cover whatever they touch and they blend into the landscape around them. Now come.' She swung the stone back into its place and hustled the children down the stairs and through a twisty corridor that led outdoors. The children found themselves standing under the fading night sky facing a grove of trees.

'Now cover your heads,' Demetra said and whistled. Through the early morning birdcalls they heard the clopping of hoofs. A cart drawn by a shaggy brown horse stopped in front of them.

'Good morning, Scrimshaw,' Demetra said. 'Here are your passengers.'

'Bright and early too,' said a cheerful voice. 'Well climb up, youngsters. We have a long way to go.'

'Be careful,' Demetra told him. 'There will be eyes on the road looking for the little one.'

'Yes,' answered Scrimshaw, 'I heard that. The palace has a shortage of new stories. And it's sad that it's a boy, just the kind of little boy the Lady likes.' And he whipped up his horse and the cart drew away from Demetra into the gathering daylight.

'What do you mean by *shortage of stories?*' Chinku asked after a while.

'Eh? Did I?' Scrimshaw sounded light-hearted and cheerful.

'You did,' Nick said.

'Well what I hear, and I do get around these parts a great deal, is that the young princes are tired of listening to the old stories. They want new ones. And drinking memory juice has not made the Memory Stealers or the Dream Stealers more inventive.'

'Storytellers walk the roads of every village,' Nick told him.

'Yes, so they do, but the storytellers are a little wary of treading the roads to Kalabash. Too many of them have never returned.

Now, if you ask me, the King should have been more generous with his gold and less generous with those armies of his. But then, I suppose that's why I drive a cart for a living instead of sitting on a gold-and-ruby throne.' He shrugged cheerfully. 'Now bury yourselves under those cloaks of yours and lie still till we get out of these trees. I don't want people to see you.'

They quickly did what he asked, even though Chinku wondered how the rusty old cloaks could possibly cover anything. She peeped out once from under hers and glanced at Nick and then pinched herself because all she could see was a pile of old dusty leaves lying there. She lay there under the warmth of her own cloak and wondered at the magic that Demetra had put into their hands. With cloaks like these a whole village could perhaps hide from the Dream Stealers. They would come with their Stealing Rays and find only drifts of leaves lying around. Except, what would happen if they kicked the leaves? She thought of kicking Nick to see, but then decided it was better to lie still as Scrimshaw had told them.

'She has given you a great gift,' Scrimshaw said when they halted in another grove of trees. 'She lost her husband to the Lady of Kalabash years ago. And now she runs the tavern and hopes that one day he will walk in through the front door as whole and handsome as when he left her. He was a storyteller, you see, and the Lady sent for him in the days before we realized how dangerous the Dream Stealers were.'

Chinku murmured, 'But I thought the little prince died because he was so unhappy and there were no stories to distract him.'

'That's what they say,' answered Scrimshaw. 'And it's a sad story too for a city like Kalabash filled with so many marvels. Do you know that in their palace the painted birds on the wall have the power to fly free? They can calculate strings of figures a mile long in their heads and double them and triple them and turn them inside out without ever getting a wrong answer.'

'You sound like you've been to Kalabash often,' Nick said. 'Aren't you scared?'

'Me? An ordinary elf like myself? I've got no stories to my name. And even if you filled me with Memory Juice, no stories would come out of my mouth, that's for sure.'

'Do you work for Demetra?' Nick asked.

'Yes, I travel all over the country buying supplies for her tavern. Wine and suchlike. Here, you must be hungry. She told me to stop and feed you when it was safe and I reckon here in the wood, it's safe enough.' He fumbled out a knapsack from under the front seat and began to spread it out on the grass. Bread and cheese and fruit – simple food, the kind that is practical to carry on picnics because it doesn't crumble and the ants don't get at.

Perched on tree stumps and rocks they listened to Scrimshaw while they ate. 'Demetra's husband was such a master storyteller that they said the beasts and birds in his stories roamed free amongst his listeners as he told his tales. If he talked about the Were Tiger of Igbashu, then you could be certain that the Were Tiger would stand upright with a fearsome roar and send the children scuttling for shelter. No one for a thousand leagues around, they said, had his gift.'

Chinku dreamily munched her apple and cheese and thought about her flying shoes again.

'When the stories ended,' she asked, 'did the creatures return to the world they came from?'

'Returned of course. What a problem that would be if they stayed in the living world. He would have had to conjure up heroes to fight the Were Tigers and the dragons. Not that he couldn't have, mind you. The way Demetra speaks, he could have done anything with his stories.'

'Did you ever hear him?' Nick asked.

Scrimshaw looked a little wistful, 'I wish I could have, but when I came to work at the tavern, he was long gone.'

'Can Demetra tell stories too?' Chinku asked.

'No, she never did, though she remembers the stories her husband told and sometimes tells them to us. Pale shadows those stories are, she never had his power of words. Come on then, it's time to get moving again. Huddle up under those cloaks of yours.' And the pony cart began its jolting again over the roads that Chinku could not see. All she was aware of was the changing shades of light above the green canopy that covered her, from pale green to the yellow of noon, to the darkening of jade. She fell asleep in a huddle, thinking drowsily that she would make a very sad adventurer indeed. She was awoken by a hand shaking her and she sat up with a jump. It was Nick.

'Come on. This is where we get off.'

The cart was standing by a stream. She could see the moonlight glinting on the water, so that it became splinters of silver.

Scrimshaw said, 'Take the bridge, go straight down the road and you'll come to a small village. If anyone stops you, say you are on your way to your uncle's house, and carry on walking. Once you are through the village you'll find a barn. You can stay the night there. Keep those cloaks over your shoulders, you should be safe.'

They waved goodbye to him and set out over the small bridge that curved over the stream. It was hardly a bridge at all, as the stream was hardly a stream. The cloaks hid them well, because as they began to walk through the village streets, none of the few people they met glanced in their direction, even when Chinku's sleepy feet scuffed over a stone. It was early of course but the moon was rising almost full disc in the eastern sky. Nick was unusually quiet as they wound their way through the moonlit streets, not even scolding her when she stumbled. She thought he was tired as she was.

The barn was like a dark hole pierced with rays of light here and there. It was filled with bales of straw and Chinku felt she was in the heart of a moon ball. She collapsed on a bale of hay with a sigh of happiness.

'You think your mother can see us?' she asked, nestling into the soft hay. It had no prickly bits so it was obviously freshly gathered, but she did not stop to wonder who might have done that. She could see Nick's shadow dancing in and out of the rays. He was not sitting down.

'Nick,' she said, 'is anything wrong?'

'Yes,' he answered and his voice was the low growl voice that signalled danger. 'I forgot that tomorrow will be a full moon.'

'So?' She looked at the toes of her boots silvered by the moon. They were almost like a map of the countryside, the ups and downs and curves of the leather that were no colour in the light.

'Where will we be tomorrow night?'

'On full moon nights,' he said, not answering her question, 'I have no choice but to turn into a wolf. And I behave like a wolf sometimes.' The shadow stopped pacing up and down and she could see his yellow eyes in the darkness staring at her.

'What do you mean?' she asked, suddenly frightened.

'On full moon nights we hunt with the wolf packs, or if there are no wolf packs, we hunt alone. That is the one night in the month when we lose contact with our human selves altogether. Haven't you heard the stories?'

Chinku remembered what her mother had told her that day by the lake. 'I've heard something. But what does that mean?'

'That means I will have to leave you somewhere safe before nightfall tomorrow and then disappear till dawn.'

'But why can't I be with you?' she still could not understand what he was saying.

'I won't remember who you are,' he growled. 'I might even attack you. Don't you understand that's why the other tribes leave us alone?

'But your mother … she's one of us ….'

'Yes, but my father made her a wolf, so she's half a wolf and in no danger.'

The shadow rustled fiercely through the straw, up and down, up and down. 'I should have remembered …'

Chinku thought hard, 'Can't we stay here? Then I could hide in the barn and you could go into the woods.'

'That will be one day wasted. You need to get to Kalabash.'

'But if I was in any danger, the stones would be jumping in my pocket,' said Chinku.

'Tomorrow, they will,' he said definitely and with a trace of hopelessness in his voice.

'I'll ask my stones tomorrow,' she told him. It was sad to see Nick suddenly so lost; she had never seen him like that before. Part of her found it hard to believe what he was saying about wolf people. The other part, the storyteller part, was curious. She wanted to see him turning into a wolf in front of her eyes. His eyes would be the same, of course, because Nick's eyes were already wolf-coloured. Whatever he was, she thought confidently, she would always know him by his eyes.

'I'll write a story about you,' she told him. 'And I'll tell the whole world how brave and kind you are. Now come and sit down and let's go to sleep. When morning comes, I'll take the stones out and you can tell me what they say.'

'Not right now. You stay under the cloak. Let me see if I can get some food from the tavern.' And then the shadow was gone, leaving her in the darkness. Almost immediately, she heard the bark of a dog followed by scared yelps and wondered whether Nick had anything to do with that. She was not scared of being alone in the night, if she had to be scared, she would have been afraid in that hole into which her father had thrust her.

She lay dreaming in the hay under her cloak and waited, telling herself the story of a wolf knight called Nick to pass the time. A perfect knight with hair as silver as the moon who went to rescue his ladylove disguised as a wolf. An enchanter hid her away in a tower, which could only be seen by the light of the full moon. Otherwise it was a dark patch of shadow in a green valley. The only problem was that at the full moon, the knight became a wolf without any memory. That would be a story she could tell one day, she thought comfortably. She could hear the dogs yapping outside the barn, but Nick had shut the door behind him so she was certain nothing could come in without her knowing it. And then a breath of wind touched her cheek and a voice said, 'It's starting.'

'How did you get in without me hearing you?' she asked.

'That's a trick wolves have,' he answered. 'Didn't you hear the dogs? They were running from me in the streets. Luckily no one noticed. Here, I managed to get some food.'

She could smell him too, she thought, a strong kind of smell; though none of them had taken a bath the whole day. But there was time enough to worry about that tomorrow. She settled down comfortably with her dreams, though wolves raced through them all night.

The problem was when the sunlight pierced the interior of the barn and woke her, Chinku found herself alone. She sat up and looked around, but except for a bundle of disturbed straw nearby, there was no sign of Nick. Even his leaf cloak was gone. When she had shaken off her sleepiness, she was angry because he had crept away like a thief in the night. It was so like a boy to slink away when the moon was hours away from rising. Uncertain of what to do, she peeped through one of the chinks outside the barn. It was broad daylight. There was no one outside except a chicken fitfully scratching at the earth, so she cautiously stepped out of the barn. What she needed was water to splash on her face and some food, but since Nick had all the gold, there was nothing she could do about the food. Why, she couldn't even read the matrix stones because the silly boy had slunk off leaving her helpless. The burst of anger brought her close to tears. Helplessly she began to look here and there. If this was a barn there must surely be a well nearby.

Her eye was caught by the curve of a stone wall and, carefully covering herself with her cloak, she ventured further out till she found the well. There was a bucket on the windlass and she sent it down into the water. At least it wasn't too rusty for her to turn. She washed her face and hands as best she could, thinking that she needed new clothes. The cloak would have to make up for it. What did people see when they looked at her, she wondered? A swaying bush?

Feeling fresh she sat by the well huddled in her cloak. Was she to move on? But how? She had no idea which way to go. The stones in her pocket were still, that was the only consolation. She took them out and looked at them as they flashed, very like normal stones in her hand. But then, their messages were only for people who could read them. She heard a noise and swivelled around. Nick was standing there, a very strange, tense Nick. His face seemed to have grown more pointed overnight and the tips of pointed teeth were visible under his lower lip.

'I thought you had gone!' she exclaimed with a relief that was stronger than the strangeness of him. His voice was harsh and so low that she had to bend to hear him.

'Stay here. Can't move today.' It was hardly human at all. 'Stay ... distance ....'

'Read the stones,' she insisted. 'They'll tell us what to do.' She held them out to him, but he did not put out a hand to take them. 'Throw ...'

The relief was beginning to ebb now and his strangeness was dawning more strongly on her. Warily, she took the stones out again and shaking them like dice threw them down on the clear stones beside the well. Nick cocked his head to look and she could see the teeth more clearly now, sharp dagger points. Then he shook his head. 'Can't ...' The stones suddenly flashed their light straight into his eyes. He blinked. 'Hurts ...'

'They're trying to tell us something,' she said.

'Wait ... help ... help will come ...'

She could hardly understand him and then, all at once, she understood why he had left her. The sun was high, but he was a mix of wolf and boy, unlike that night at her home when he had been all wolf, speaking with a human voice.

'It's always night somewhere,' he muttered when she asked him. 'My father told me that.'

Despair nagging at her, she caught him by the arm, which she discovered was bristling with hair, and half dragged him inside the barn. There in the shadows he seemed calmer and she cast the stones again, hoping that this time he would be able to read them with more clarity.

'Told you,' he said with an effort. 'Wait ... help will come.'

There was no use asking what kind of help. She sat down on a bale of hay and said, 'We'll need food and water. Give me some money, I'll go and buy some.' It was a brave offer because she had never done it before – in her own Qlwri everyone knew everyone and people ate together as friends. There was no buying or selling of food.

Nick was huddled on the floor of his barn. He looked up at her. 'I can get food … not safe for you.' And before she could stop him, he was out of the barn again, leaving her nothing to do except trust that the stones were right.

The sun rays had shifted across the floor by the time Nick returned. She saw there was a trickle of blood at his mouth and leapt up with a cry, 'You're hurt!'

He shrugged her off and threw a bundle on the floor, pointing her to it. She found a flask and shook it – its weight shifted with something liquid swirling around inside. There was more bread than fruit.

'Can't light a fire,' he told her. 'Smoke will attract people.'

It did not feel very safe to her but she sat there staring as he wiped the blood from his mouth with a wisp of straw. 'Chicken, ate …' he rasped, thinking he owed her some explanation. After he had wiped his mouth, he seemed to fall asleep so there was nothing much for her to do but nibble at the bread and watch the trail of the sun across the barn floor. Finally, she went to sleep out of sheer helplessness, half-knowing that when she awoke she would be alone again. And she was. The moon rays filtering through the barn were brighter than last night – they would be, it was a full moon, after all.

Even though it was probably not very late she could hear the dogs yapping. The barn door was shut and she knew the dogs would not come in – they had not done it the night before. But then she heard a high, long howl that could have been dog and the yaps around ceased abruptly. There was an ominous silence. Wolves, she told herself, did not hunt around villages, not unless they were man-eating wolves. Nick had not explained exactly what it was that happened to him at the full moon except that he could not control it. Did it mean that if he met her he would not recognize her and attack her? It seemed very likely that that was what he had meant. But if he changed while it was daylight perhaps he would change while it was still night because the sun had risen somewhere else at the edge of the world. This did not make any kind of sense to her.

After a while, tired of clutching them, she pulled the stones out and saw that they were glowing gently. They seemed to draw the moon's rays and glow even stronger until she could see the bones of her hand silhouetted against the silver light. The light spread up her arm and bit by bit over her whole body till she thought she must also look like some kind of moon. It spilled over the floor and grew and grew until the barn glowed with it. And even then it did not stop spreading, climbing up the walls and to the ceiling. She was swimming, she thought in the silver light. It reminded her of the moon bowl that lit up Nick's home and Chinku wondered whether Nick's mother was somewhere close at hand watching. And then she discovered that she could see through the barn walls.

It was a strange and fantastic landscape she saw, one that looked nothing like the outside of the barn. Dragon flowers, their heads proudly erect, were growing just outside. Each flower, she could now see, was a living-breathing dragon because flames flared from their mouths. They had eyes that glittered in the light and the whole tree was alive with them until she wondered why it did not take flight into the sky with so many dragons in it. The well was another kind of silver, chequered stones with ripples flowing to and fro through the stones. For a moment she got to her feet and thought of running outside to lose herself in the wonder of what she saw. She had quite forgotten the howls of the wolf and Nick's strange behaviour. And then her eyes saw other things, shadows that came rippling into her field of vision. Thrown against the stones of the well they looked like a transparent curtain of animals running, and she had to strain her eye to make out the different layers of things. Was it dog shadows? It could have been. Then came someone who was no shadow – Nick, in his human self, looking tired and lost and rumpled. She was so glad to see him human again that she actually leapt to her feet.

Nick was looking at the barn and even the silver light could not quench the yellow flame of his eyes. He came towards it in his usual swift wolfish lope. The night trembled to a deep roar, not a wolf's howl, but a belching kind of roar. She saw that it came from the tree of dragon flowers because the dragon heads were thrown back. Nick checked almost at the door of the barn. He looked afraid and she wanted to go to him. The light trembled again and he was running backwards now, still in that same fluid run of his. 'Nick!' Chinku's throat was sore with the strength of her cry but he did not seem to hear her. She ran to the barn door and threw it open.

It was night outside, plain ordinary night, still, with no dragon flowers or roars. A wolf's shadow slipped away under the trees. Then there was silence. The stones in her hand glimmered quietly with none of their extraordinary light. Something stronger than her own will made her shut the door. Quietly she sat down on the straw in the middle of the silver pool of light and began to record her first memory, knot by knot, plaiting the straw – the record of a wolfboy and the dragon flowers.

Tomorrow, when the world went back to being hers again she would look outside the barn to see whether the moon had left any rocks behind. One of those would add to her memory knots. Her plaiting complete, she curled up on the straw to wait for what the morning would bring.

The morning brought a pale, drawn-looking Nick. When she woke up, Chinku found the barn restored to its normal daylight colours. She blinked around her, finding it hard to send the silver memory away from her eyes. The plaited straws were there next to her. She was about to pick them up when her eye fell on an out-flung hand and she realized Nick was back. She sat next to him quietly for a while, studying him. The claws she had glimpsed on his hand were gone and as he breathed through his open mouth she saw that the white pointed teeth were also normal again. His eyes opened and he sat up in a gathered kind of leap.

'You don't look well,' she said, and he wasn't. He looked as though he were recovering from a fever.

'I'm all right,' he answered, in his normal Nick voice. 'I'll be better as the sun gets higher. Now we have to get out of here and onto the road.' He looked around the barn and then asked awkwardly, 'Did anyone, anything come here last night?'

She picked up the plaited strands of straw and told him briefly what had happened. He let his held-in breath out with a whoosh. 'That's all right then, at least we know that the stones will look after you.'

After they had washed, they left the barn in search of food. Chinku could not help glancing at the dragon tree outside the barn but the flowers were just flowers again with no magic in them.

Nick took her back into the village that they had left behind. There was a baker's shop that smelt of fresh bread. While Chinku was tearing into a still warm loaf, Nick asked the baker for directions. He told them there was a passenger wagon that could be boarded from the crossroads and it would take them to the nearest big town. There was a network of passenger wagons that ran on the highway to Kalabash.

'But are they safe?' Nick was concerned.

'Safe enough,' the baker answered. 'The King's Dream Stealers guard the road after all. Travel a few more miles and you will be in the King's dominions. You children must be strangers in these parts otherwise you would know about the travel wagons.'

When they came out of the shop, Nick told Chinku to pull the cloak around her shoulders but not over her head. They discovered that when she did that, it acted like an ordinary cloak. Nick sniffed the air and then took her on another path which eventually led them out of the village.

'What did you smell the air for?' she asked curiously.

'If the wind is blowing in the right direction, it tells me where people and horses have travelled. A highway smells very different from a village. The wind moves faster there.'

They took a zigzagging road and Nick stopped several times to sniff, raising his head like a dog. Once, he hustled her into a clump of trees and waited for a while. When the road stayed silent for some time, they moved on again. Finally, they came to where four broad roads met. Horses galloped down one even as they got there, sweeping past in red dust clouds.

'Pull the cloak around you,' Nick told her. 'You'll swallow less dust that way.' A man driving a donkey came by. He stopped when he saw the children.

'Are you waiting for something?'

'The passenger wagon,' Nick said.

The man squinted up at the sun. 'It should be here by noon,' he said cheerfully, 'if it isn't late, that is. There were Shadow Riders on the road this morning. That always throws the traffic out of gear.'

'Shadow Riders? What were they looking for?' Nick asked.

The man shrugged, 'Who knows? One of the Lady's errands, or the King's. It's better not to know. Anyway, I had best be about my business. Hiii Dobbin!' And he whacked the donkey with the driving stick and the two moved on.

'What is a Shadow Rider?' Chinku wanted to know.

'The Dream Stealers, but mounted. They wear black and ride black horses with red eyes. I saw one near our village once. The horse almost trampled me because I was sleeping under the bushes.'

Chinku wondered what a black man on a black horse with red eyes would look like, but she did not have time to wonder long. Soon a large carriage lurched up. It was drawn by four sturdy horses with a driver in yellow. People bulged out of the windows and there were even some sitting on top, clutching bundles and live geese. The driver pulled on the reins and the carriage doors opened.

Chinku managed to squeeze herself between a fat woman and her equally fat husband. The fat woman muttered something about the manners of children these days. Nick found himself a space between two windows and the door and was standing braced against the wall, hanging onto a strap. He swayed easily on his feet when the carriage lurched into motion. 'Graceful boy,' someone said. 'Do you work in a circus then?' someone else commented. Nick did not answer.

As it happened they did not ride very long in the carriage because after a little while, it came to a sharp halt that threw her fat neighbour almost onto Chinku's lap. As the woman lurched against Chinku she suddenly realized the woman's hands were feeling carefully down her sides, probably groping for her pocket. Pinioned between the two fat people, Chinku could not move, but the woman suddenly gave a scream. The coach had come to a complete halt by then. In the commotion Chinku had not noticed what the fat lady was up to. Suddenly, a shadow blotted out the light from the window.

'What is that noise?' asked a rasp of a voice, a cold kind of voice that made Chinku shiver even between the heat of the two bodies.

'It's this boy, your honour,' she heard the woman say. 'He has weapons in his pocket.' A fat hand thrust her off the seat into the middle of the wagon.

Chinku saw the head and shoulders of a man in black blocking the window. He wore what looked like a black mask that covered his head and left only his nose and mouth exposed. There were eye sockets that glinted red.

'Bring the boy out,' ordered the raspy voice.

Against the wall, Nick was stiff and bristling. 'He's my brother,' he said.

'Then both of you come out.' There were hands enough to shove them out of the coach. Chinku thought the fat woman would follow, but she did not. As they stood in the sunlight, the man held out a black-gloved hand.

'Empty your pockets, boy ...'

It was the end, Chinku thought, the stones would glint in the light and flash their warning and the red eyes would know instantly what they were and who she was.

Nick said, 'My brother has no weapons. The woman was probably trying to pick his pockets ...'

The black hand did not waver. Surrounded as they were, Chinku had no choice. Half of her hoped that Nick would turn into a wolf and tear the man to pieces and run off with her. The other half doubted whether the pale, tired Nick would be able to do anything at all. Helpless, she put her hands in her pocket and pulled out the stones, not daring to look as she did so.

'Marbles!' she heard the angry voice hiss. 'What kind of trickery is this? Bring that woman to me!'

Knocked from her hand, the stones fell at her feet and she quickly scampered to pick them up, while the feet around her bustled back and forth. 'The woman must be a pickpocket,' she heard Nick's voice growl. 'Trying to rob my brother.'

Clutching the marbles she glimpsed the hoofs of a black horse stamping to one side. The hoofs flashed as they rose and fell and she wondered what kind of metal they were shod with. She glanced up and saw the toe of a black boot framed by a stirrup. The boot had a cruel spur on its heel like a cock's beak. She shuddered for the horse and looked down again at the matrix stones in her hand. They did not look at all like marbles to her but she supposed it was part of their magic – to look like marbles to outsiders. Nick's grey fur boots came to stand close to her.

Huddled close to him she looked up in time to see the woman brought out of the carriage clucking like a disturbed hen. The Shadow Rider held his horse in on a tight rein and she could see its anger froth white around the bit. It did indeed have red eyes.

'False accusations,' hissed the Shadow Rider, 'bring their own punishment.'

'It isn't false,' said the woman. 'Those things in his pocket hurt my hand ...'

'And what were your hands doing in my brother's pocket?' Nick demanded, as quick as the pouncing wolf that he was.

'Good point,' said the Shadow Rider. And he flicked out his whip, caught the woman in it, then started his horse with a flick of his spur. The woman was dragged after him as he galloped away, on her feet for a while and then a helpless bundle trailing after him in the dust. The people who had been in the coach stood around frozen with horror. Chinku quickly thrust the stones deep into her pocket.

The dust behind the rider subsided as did the woman's screams. The rest of the passengers quietly climbed back into the coach, though they were careful not to sit too close to Chinku. She huddled herself in her cloak and sat next to Nick. The Black Rider had terrified her even more than the Memory Stealers and she hoped she would not encounter more of them on the road to Kalabash.

The coach passed into the King's dominions a while later. Chinku saw a pillared building flash past. Then the coach stopped. 'Check post,' the driver announced through the window. 'Everyone out. You will have to go through the turnstiles there.'

The children climbed out uncertainly.

Nearby were guards in grey and black carrying what looked like Memory Stealing rays in their hands. The passengers from the coach were forming a line in front of the building that Chinku had glimpsed. 'Are we going to go in there?' Chinku whispered to Nick.

'We shouldn't,' he said. 'If we're trapped in there then I don't know how we'll get out.' He looked around and saw that people were still filing out from their coach and that there was another coach drawing up. No one was looking at the two children.

'Cover your head with the cloak,' he said, and doing the same thing he ducked between the two coaches with Chinku at his heels. Once she thought she heard a shout, but she could not be sure. Then they had crossed the highway and were running over the undulating turf on the other side. The grass was long and tangled with her boots and she stumbled and ran out of breath.

'Trees,' Nick said. 'We'll wait there till dark.'

'And then?'

'Then you'll ride on my back and we'll cross over.'

Chinku wondered what it was that they would cross over. There was no boundary beyond the building to tell her that they had crossed the King's dominions. From what she had seen, the road continued on its journey unhindered.

'There must be something,' Nick said. 'Black Riders possibly, or some kind of guards. Perhaps the buildings have eye-nails like ours at home. I don't know! We'll just have to sit still and wait for the dark.'

And so they did. Night seemed to take hours to come, but finally it was there. The light faded from the sky and the birds came flocking home to their nests. Soon, fireflies began to flicker in the trees.

'All right,' Nick said, after standing up and sniffing the air, 'now.' And the wolf was standing next to her again.

She could see the long shape in the darkness and glimpse the yellow eyes. For a moment now she was scared. She remembered the blood trickling down his mouth.

'What's the matter?' the wolf asked and the yellow eyes turned full on her, as large and glowing as twin moons in the early evening. There was really nothing she could say. She quickly slung her leg over his back and crouched low on his neck.

'It isn't a full moon,' he said quietly, before he launched into his loping stride.

They came out of the wood onto the highway. 'I'll have to go this way because I don't know the road. Hold tight in case I have to run.' She could see the walled building because it was lighter than anything else on the surrounding plane. The wolf came almost up to then turned sharply past it, taking the road the coach would have followed. There was another gate at the back wall of the building with a stag on top. She was just able to see it as she craned her neck.

'There are people there,' the wolf said. 'And horses, I can smell them.' He could also smell something else, something that was not quite human and not quite animal, but he did not want to scare Chinku. At least not until he had figured out what it was. There were no lines or stop posts. The road wound ahead like a ribbon. She had expected sconces on either side, something to mark the fact that it was a road in the kingdom of Kalabash, but there was nothing at all to set it apart from the road they were leaving behind.

She could feel the muscles rippling under the wolf's skin. His ears flicked back. 'There's something following us,' he said. He did not pause as he spoke, just quickened his lope. After a while Chinku could hear a dull pounding behind them, heavy mallet blows.

'What is it?' she whispered.

'I don't know, but we'll have to get off the road. Among the trees we'll have a better chance.' He swerved as he spoke and ran diagonally off the road, looking behind him once. She looked back too but could see nothing in the darkness except for some red flecks that might have been fireflies.

'Did you see anything?' she asked, because she could still hear the dull pounding.

'Don't … talk …' And then they ran. He kept turning and she realised that he was trying to travel parallel to the road so that he would not lose his way, but that was all she could take in. It was so utterly dark that Chinku could see nothing except when the trees cleared in front of them briefly and star points of silver pierced the night. Then the trees closed over them again. Lying almost prone on the wolf's back she could still hear that dull pounding but fainter now. In fact the beating of the wolf's heart was almost as loud. They galloped and galloped into the night. Slowly the birds began to call in the trees and she saw it was almost morning. 'We'll stop now,' the wolf rasped and she could tell he was very tired.

She almost fell off his back and landed softly in a pile of grass. The moment she did, he tumbled down beside her and without further thought they were fast asleep, totally oblivious of the hard ground and the stones that rolled away from under them.

11

'Wolf!' Chinku's eyes flickered open. It was morning. Huddled in her cloak she had been so comfortable that she had not even registered the changing of the light against her eyelids. There was a shadow looming over her, no, not a shadow, a man with a sword. She sprang up.

'Don't move, wolf!'

'Guard the child!'

She looked around and saw the wolf was on his feet. There were other men around him with knives in their hands. Chinku realised what must have happened. Nick had been so tired last night that he had fallen asleep without changing back into his boy self. The wolf had his head low and was moving in a tight circle as the men surrounded him. One of them ran to her to scoop her out of the way. A knife flashed dangerously close. 'Stop!' Chinku screamed. 'Don't hurt him! He's my wolf!' She kicked the man and ducked through the knives to Nick's side, throwing herself over him.

'Mad child! Get him! The King …' But stopped when they saw that the wolf was not attacking her. Nick's hair was still bristling on his neck. She stroked him hard.

'He won't harm anyone,' she said, not caring whether she sounded like a boy or not. 'He's my friend!'

'A wolf makes a very dangerous friend,' one of the men said.

'But he's not attacking me,' she said. 'And he'll listen to whatever I say. Sit!' she said to the wolf, looking him hard in the eye. The yellow eyes looked a little sceptical, but the wolf sat down. 'Paw!' she said, holding out her hand. Reluctantly a paw was extended.

'By the Lady!' exclaimed one of the men. 'A tame wolf. This they must see!' She wondered who they were because they were not dressed in black. 'Well child,' one of the men, who seemed to be their leader, said. 'It seems we must take you and your wolf with us. This is dangerous territory for anyone, even for a child guarded by a wolf.'

'Where are you taking us?' Chinku asked, still clinging to Nick's paw. He shook it angrily and she quickly dropped it.

'To Kalabash,' the man said. 'We're the King's huntsmen. We can't leave you in the woods like this.' He gestured to the others and one of them came running with a leather leash towards the wolf. Nick growled threateningly. 'You can't tie him,' Chinku said.

'Then how will he travel with us?'

'We could drug him perhaps,' one of the men suggested, 'put some pills into a roll of meat.'

'He will follow wherever I go,' Chinku said. The huntsmen scratched their heads and looked at her standing with her arms round the wolf's neck. 'The horses wouldn't abide it,' one of them observed.

'A cage,' suggested one. 'He would have to travel in a cage.' Chinku glanced quickly at Nick, but he did not meet her eyes. In any case what could he do? He couldn't speak to her in front of the others.

One of the huntsmen sounded a horn, three long notes and two shorts ones that were obviously some kind of signal.

'You're lucky we found you, boy,' the Chief Huntsman said. 'Dangerous things travel these woods at night.'

'But I have my wolf for protection,' Chinku answered perfectly truthfully. 'And he's never been caged before.'

'Well, he can't ride with you on horseback, so he'll have to travel in a cage.' They were certainly not going to let them go because they were in a ring around her and Nick. In answer to the horn they heard a rumbling of wheels and a cage drawn by bullocks was brought up.

'That's for your wolf,' said the Chief Huntsman. 'Luckily we were out trying to trap deer for the Lady.' They opened their ring to let the cage back in and some of the huntsmen began to advance on Nick. The wolf gave a low threatening rumble in his throat.

'I'll have to lead him in,' Chinku said quickly. She glanced at the cage, it didn't seem too small. 'And I think I should travel with him in the cage. He'll stay quiet that way.' The Old Ones would have been proud of her, she thought, for her quick wittedness. At least this way she and Nick could stay together.

'Are you sure? He might turn vicious in that cage.'

'He won't harm me,' she said. And putting her hand on Nick's neck, she led him up to the cage. As they walked he bared his teeth at the men and their swords. He was doing his bit, she thought, to pretend that he was a real wolf. With a smile inside her she led him up into the cage. It was lined with prickly straw. Arranging her cloak around her, she sat down. The men quickly slammed the cage door shut. Nick circled the place for a bit before sitting down. 'At least we'll get to Kalabash,' she muttered. He flicked an ear at her before sinking his head on his paws.

The huntsmen mounted and arranged themselves on either side of the cage. The Chief Huntsman sounded his horn again. Chinku thought, it sounded more like a conch shell than the clear shrill of a normal gold horn. In her village conch shells were used to announce the sunrise and sunset and the call to prayer in their homes.

'This is very strange,' she muttered to the wolf. He did not raise his head but rolled a golden eye at her in warning. It was going to be very dull she thought, travelling with Nick who did not talk to her, but perhaps she could pretend that it was all a game. At least through the cage she had a clear view of the roads they travelled. They were also, as a result, the centre of attention wherever they went. Whenever the hunting party came to a village, people rushed up to look at the boy in a cage with a wolf.

'Is he a wolf too?' some of them asked, poking their fingers through the bars of the cage and snatching them away again whenever Nick raised his head. Chinku was annoyed. 'Do I look savage?' she asked angrily. A troupe of little boys ran up to mock her accent; sticking their tongues out, dancing round the cage.

'Yah yah, wolfboy …' The huntsmen reined in on their horses and grinned from ear to ear. 'You had a choice, boy,' said the Chief

Huntsman. 'You could have ridden on horseback with us.' But they showed no signs of driving the irritating boys away until Nick suddenly sprang to his feet and made a snap through the bars in the direction of the ringleader. It was such an angry leaping snap that the claws on his front paw grazed Chinku.

'Watch out, boy!' yelled the Chief Huntsman and raised his whip at the village urchins who, in any case, were running backwards terrified by the wolf's sudden rage. Nick settled down again into his peaceful wolf incarnation. Chinku rubbed her arm.

'If he does that again,' said the Chief Huntsman, 'we'll have to take you out of the cage.'

'Did you hear that?' she muttered to Nick who was remorsefully licking her arm. 'Now keep quiet no matter what those boys do.' Loudly she said, 'And if you try to take me out of the cage, my wolf will tear you all to pieces, so please don't even try.' After that the huntsmen made sure they surrounded the cage whenever their road led through a village.

Gradually Chinku realized that the road was getting broader and smoother. Traffic on the road became more frequent – carriages, carts, strange horseless things that whizzed by, seemingly propelled by magic. Nick, his head on his paws, was watching the road with her and she wished she could ask him what he knew. Curled up against his side she ignored the people who pointed whenever they passed and instead amused herself by counting the horseless wagons.

How, she thought, did the horses feel when they passed a wagon like that? Did they wonder how the strange thing was moving along on its own? There were few of them and they seemed to belong to very gaudily dressed people. A lady with a bright red mouth and crimped golden hair stuck her head out of the window of one that passed them. The lips formed a perfectly astonished O when she saw Chinku sitting next to a wolf. Then she waved her scarf at the huntsmen, stopped the wagon, and came dancing out on dainty green high-heeled shoes to look at the child and the wolf. If anything, her questions were sillier than those of the boys.

'Is that a wolf child? Can it talk? How much would you sell it for? With the wolf of course. They'd look so nice carrying the glasses into my dining room when I have guests for dinner. The wolf can have a harness with the tray strapped to his back ....'

The Chief Huntsman laughed with her, because she was obviously a very important lady but firmly refused. 'We have orders to take them both to the Lady.'

'I must speak to the Lady then,' Red Lips and Golden Hair pouted charmingly, and danced away into her wagon again leaving a trail of flowery fragrance on the air.

After a distance the countryside vanished and brick and stone houses came crowding in on them, more and more and more. They squeezed their way through a marketplace where men and women were standing by carts piled with fruit and vegetables, greens, yellows, peaches and browns jostling for attention in the sunlight. The huntsmen used their whips and elbows to get through, and then turned into a narrow cobbled road that ended at a wooden gate studded with brass knobs. The gate squeaked open at the Chief Huntsman's shout. Chinku and Nick saw a stable yard. The huntsmen dismounted as the grooms came crowding around to take the horses. The Chief Huntsman went to the cage.

'We've arrived,' he said. 'I'll take you and your wolf to the menagerie. You can see him safely housed there. And then you will be taken to the Lady.'

Nick was uncertain how to react, Chinku could feel that. She stood up, keeping her hand on Nick's head. 'Can't he be chained in my room?' she asked. 'He was brought up in our house. He's never been caged.'

'Hold onto him,' the Chief Huntsman said. 'We'll open the door of the cage.'

Cautiously, they approached and unlocked the padlock on the cage and threw the door open. The moment they did that, they backed away, expecting the wolf to spring out. However, Chinku and Nick came out quietly. The wolf was being Nick in wolf's clothing rather than a wolf, but only Chinku knew that.

Standing on the cobblestones they were instantly enveloped by the bustle of the courtyard. The horses in the stalls were laying their ears back and lashing out. One of the grooms picked up his pitchfork and pointed it threateningly in the wolf's direction.

The Chief Huntsman said, 'Put that down.'

The groom said, 'Unless you take that wolf out of here, I won't be answerable for the consequences. The King will get angry if his prize racehorses are lathered up.' Nick's ears flicked when he heard that. Chinku held on tightly to the scruff of his neck.

The Chief Huntsman said, 'We don't intend to hang around here in any case. The Lady has asked for the boy.'

Chinku turned her head to look at the Chief Huntsman, 'The Lady sent for me?' She felt a flash of instant alarm and realized Nick had too because she felt the coarse wolf hair bristle under her hand. The Chief Huntsman did not answer but hustled them inside, leaving the indignant groom and his temperamental horses behind. Chinku repeated her question.

'I have orders to bring any child I find in the countryside to the Lady. Especially one like you who is travelling with a wolf.'

'You mean there are other children with wolves?'

'No, no! The Lady loves a story. I thought you with your wolf; you would have an interesting story to tell. Now keep hold on that animal. I don't want to be responsible for what happens if any of the ladies-in-waiting scream.'

Neither child nor wolf – because of course, in his wolf's form Nick could not be called a child – had time to look around. They found their feet sinking into green carpets as soft as moss. The walls were decorated with painted tapestries and gilded bird-shaped sconces held bowls of light high above so that the corridor was as bright as day. The Chief Huntsman led them to another huge door guarded by men who looked very like the Dream Stealers, with long slim tubes in their hands.

'Where are you taking that thing?' one of the Dream Stealers asked. 'Dangerous animals are not allowed in the castle.'

'The child won't be separated from it. It's going to be chained in the boot hall. It should be safe enough there.'

The men reluctantly let them go by. The room they came into had wide windows that opened to the sky and to tall buildings with hanging gardens.

'Is this Kalabash?' Chinku asked, as she looked in wonder at the windows.

'Don't you know anything?' the Chief Huntsman asked. 'Yes, of course this is Kalabash. But then what would a child from the woods like you know?'

Her parents' memories were here then and so were the memories of the Old Ones.

12

The way to the boot hall apparently led through more winding corridors. Chinku had a feeling that the Chief Huntsman was deliberately taking them the long way round so that he could show off his discovery to as many people as possible. The rooms in themselves were marvels of beauty. Birds hung in golden cages in one where they found themselves confronting a group of ladies with trailing skirts like peacocks' tails. The ladies whisked their skirts away from Chinku and the wolf and clustered together with little shrill cries that the birds echoed.

'What a savage little boy,' one of them said aloud and the others hastily shushed her. The Chief Huntsman paused to tell them his tale about how he had discovered Chinku fast asleep with her arms around the neck of her pet wolf. Hearing the story, one of the ladies, greatly daring, darted up and brushed the top of Chinku's head. Chinku started and almost lost her grip on Nick. The wolf whirled around and leaping up, snapped. Luckily, all he caught was the trail of the lady's sleeve.

In an instant the place was swarming with the Dream Stealers who pointed their tubes at Chinku. 'It's the wolf, you sillies!' roared the Chief Huntsman.

The lady had fallen back and was inspecting her sleeve.

'That wolf should be killed,' she screamed. 'Do it, now!'

'Princess,' said the Chief Huntsman cautiously, 'that is for the Lady to decide. Until she chooses, I cannot give any orders.'

'But it attacked me,' said the princess.

'Because he thought you were attacking me,' Chinku told her. Thinking, at home we would know better than to come close to a wolf. 'The wolf protects me.'

The princess stared her straight in the eye but Chinku did not turn her gaze away. Finally, the princess had to avert her face. 'Very well, but I will tell the Lady what happened.'

The Dream Stealers were mumbling together. One of them said, 'You cannot take that animal through the palace quarters like that. He is dangerous.'

'As long as no one tries to touch me,' Chinku said, 'he is perfectly safe.' Her heart was beating as she looked at the tubes, but she said those brave words. The Dream Stealers fell back and they moved on. 'Don't do that,' Chinku said to both Nick and the wolf that Nick was pretending to be. 'If you're hurt, you won't be able to look after me.' It was all right to say that – they would expect a child to talk to his pet.

'You're a brave boy,' the Chief Huntsman observed. 'I certainly wouldn't keep a savage animal like that.'

Chinku repeated, 'He's perfectly safe.'

'And what about when you fall down and bleed?' the Chief Huntsman asked. 'Doesn't he lick the blood from your wounds? Won't that give him a taste for human blood?'

Chinku thought of Nick with the trickle of blood from his mouth, but said nothing.

'Well, the sooner a thick steel chain is round that wolf's neck, the happier I will be,' declared the Chief Huntsman. 'Come on.'

They went through more rooms, each grander than the other. Finally, they reached a hall divided by the fall of a thick, silky curtain. Two guards in leather with crossed pikes barred the way. 'That animal cannot be taken into the presence of the Lady.'

'But I have a story to tell her,' said the Chief Huntsman.

The two guards consulted briefly with each other, then one of them ducked behind the curtain. As the curtain swayed, Chinku smelt a strong overpoweringly sweet smell that could be flowers or incense. Nick sneezed at it, a wolfish sneeze. They stood there patiently for what seemed ages to Chinku before the guard came back. He was carrying what looked like a long silk ribbon in one hand. 'This goes around the wolf's neck,' he said. 'Then you go in.' The Chief Huntsman pointed at Chinku. She took the ribbon and gingerly wound it round Nick's neck.

'Tightly,' said the guard. 'If that wolf gets loose, he'll have to be killed.'

She tied the short end into a knot and held the other one. It was surprising how strong it felt, more like spun steel than silk. The moment it was done, the guard held the curtain back.

At first the smell held them prisoner, almost like a curtain in itself. Then the light dazzled them. Not the light of the sun or the moon but another kind of strong beam that bathed the room in gold so that the people looked almost like statues. There was a murmur as Chinku and the wolf entered, which was quickly hushed.

'Bow,' hissed the Chief Huntsman as he did so himself. Chinku was so busy taking it all in that for a moment she did not hear him. When she did, she bowed deeply, though she could not quite see whom she was bowing to.

'You may rise,' said a deep husky voice. 'Come closer.'

When she raised her head, she could see a golden idol sitting on a dais hung with tapestries. The idol looked like something out of one of the old legends, a goddess with four arms and different flowers in each of her hands. She clung to the end of Nick's leash but kept one hand on his neck to give her courage.

'What is the story of this child and wolf? Huntsman?' the voice asked.

The huntsman briefly explained how he had found Chinku and the wolf asleep.

'Is the wolf tame?' the Lady asked.

The huntsman hesitated.

Without waiting for permission, Chinku said, 'He is my wolf and tame to me.'

There was a murmur that echoed through the hall. She realized she was not supposed to speak without permission.

'Peace,' said the Lady, 'the child is a stranger. Does your wolf do tricks, child? And what is your name?'

'Chinku,' answered Chinku, without really thinking. The wolf flicked an irritated golden eye at her. In the strange light it looked doubly gold. She wondered why they had no windows in this hall, or whether the Lady was averse to fresh air.

'Chinku,' the Lady tried the name on her tongue. 'What does it mean?'

'It is a kind of fruit,' Chinku said. 'The tree grows near our house. My mother said my cheeks reminded her of the fruit on that tree.'

Nick turned his eye away from her with a scornful sniff. She felt like slapping him.

'Well, Chinku,' said the Lady, 'Entertain us. Does your wolf do tricks?' Chinku looked doubtfully at Nick and wondered whether she should confess to telling stories. On the other hand, if Nick did tricks there was always a chance that he would be well looked after and kept close to her.

'He's not a tame wolf,' she said slowly, 'but he does do a few things. Nick, bow.' The wolf gave her an incredulous kind of look but bobbed his head and raised a paw.

'Dogs do that,' said someone among the assembled courtiers. A woman – she wondered whether it was the same woman whose sleeve Nick had ripped. 'A wolf is far more difficult to train than a dog,' she said, glancing at the golden idol. The idol looked frozen. Sending Nick to fetch a flower would mean slipping him off the ribbon. She bit her lip wishing that the floor would open up and swallow her.

'He dances,' Chinku said finally.

The idol clapped. 'Music,' she commanded. 'Let us see this dancing wolf. What music does your wolf dance to, child?'

'Anything,' Chinku answered miserably, not knowing what else to say. She had no idea what the musicians in Kalabash played and all she knew was that Nick could play the flute. The wolf had turned his head when he heard Chinku and given her an amazed look, that is, if you believe that wolves can look amazed.

The musicians began to play in a harsh clashing clanging kind of tune. Chinku held out her arms to Nick, still holding onto one end of the leash. The wolf awkwardly reared up on its hind legs. Chinku caught the forepaws and began wheeling him around as best she could to that no-music sound. Dancing with a reluctant wolf is not easy. Certainly almost as difficult as dancing with a reluctant Nick who was dancing with paws instead of feet. Add to that the fact that he towered over her like an animated fur coat. They managed two circles before he tripped over the toe of her boot and Chinku found herself sitting down hard on the stone floor with frantic wolf paws scrabbling all over her as Nick tried desperately to regain his footing. The hall around them resounded with titters of laughter.

'Your wolf needs a dance master, child,' the golden idol said laughing. 'But still, it was entertaining. I haven't laughed so much in a long time.'

Chinku slowly scrambled to her feet. Nick was on all fours again and glaring at her.

'Chief Huntsman,' the Lady said, 'come forward.'

The Chief Huntsman walked up to the dais and dropped into a worried bow. 'You did right to bring this child and wolf to me. They shall stay in the palace.' She threw him a small sack that clinked. Then she clapped her hands again. Chinku noticed that the two extra arms strapped to her back flapped when she did that. A short bald man dressed in cinnamon and gold scuttled up and bowed deeply.

'Major Domo, find this child living quarters,' ordered the Lady. 'Make sure he is comfortable.'

'And the wolf?'

'Put him in the menagerie.'

Chinku, who could not hold her tongue said, 'Oh no!'

The golden head turned to her. Was it gold paint, Chinku wondered for half a fleeting second. The etched eyebrows drew down into an angry kind of scowl over the slit eyes.

'Why did you interrupt, child? I will forgive you this once, but know this: no one speaks when the Lady is speaking. The next time you will be punished.'

'He'll be miserable away from me. He'll howl and howl and howl.'

'If I may speak, Lady, the animal could upset the menagerie keepers and the other animals,' said the cinnamon major domo.

'Then where should it be housed? We cannot have the wild animals of the forest roaming free in the palace grounds.'

The major domo thought for a while. 'One of the turret rooms might be ideal,' he said. 'There are embrasures where the wolf could be chained or the adjoining garde robes where he can be locked.'

'Then take them there,' the Lady ordered. 'And find clothes for this boy. We cannot have him running around in these savage things that he is wearing.'

The major domo looked them both up and down before nodding and beckoning to Chinku. He led them back out through the curtain and down another hallway. Chinku held tight to the leash as they were surrounded by a wave of exclaiming courtiers. 'My wolf gets upset if he sees so many people,' she said desperately. 'Please keep them away from us.' Somewhere in this palace, she thought, as she clung to the leash, is the King's secret room where he stores all the memories.

But it would be hard to find out where that room might be, given the endless halls and corridors. The palace looked like it had been built with a thousand-and-one stories, not as if it belonged to a race of people who had no imagination. One had walls with great painted trees and actual moulded fruits, ripe glowing peaches and plums that looked so real, her mouth watered.

There were guards in unexpected places, some with the memory tubes and some with long spears that reached up almost to the ceiling. A guard running with a spear that long, she thought, would be bound to trip. In one hall they passed, she glimpsed groups of children sitting around. Some of them had musical instruments in their hands, others seemed to be writing, their heads bent over sheets of parchment. They were arranged like a garden of flowers, in rows of pinks, blues, greens and yellows. The blue clusters were the writing ones, Chinku noticed.

It was strange how silent the Hall of the Children was. Normally they would all be chattering away like parrots. These were whispering together in huddles. 'You will be joining those,' the major domo told her, but he did not take her through the hall. Instead, they turned another corner and came to the bottom of a flight of narrow spiral stairs, the kind she had come to realize meant a tower.

The steps were guarded by the men carrying tubes in their hands. When they saw Chinku and the wolf, they backed away a little. The steps turned and turned and brought them to another floor where a barred and bolted door blocked one end.

With a flourish the major domo pulled out a bunch of keys and selected a large iron one. 'Help me with the bar, child,' he said to

Chinku. And the two of them wrestled the wooden plank out of its sockets.

Chinku expected to find another room like Demetra's on the other side of the door, but except for a bed and an old table, this one was bare. The major domo walked them inside and looked around. There was another door at one end, which he opened. It was narrow dark room with shelves on the wall and a bathing alcove to one side.

'You can keep your wolf in here,' he said. 'Be sure to lock him in when anyone comes, because if he causes trouble, it's straight to the menagerie. I'll send someone with clothes. We should have something in your size.' And then he shut the door on them.

13

The moment the door was shut, Nick changed back into a boy, panting with relief. 'That's the longest,' he said, careful to keep his voice down, 'that I've had to be a wolf. And as for that dancing …' Chinku, though she was glad to see him in his normal shape, was busy looking around the bare room. It was as vast as a cow field, well almost, and the walls were hard stone. It looked as though no one had lived in that room for ages. She poked the bare mattress on the bed. It was almost as hard as the stone walls.

'You should have let them keep me in the menagerie,' Nick told her. 'I could have slipped out of there easily and explored the castle. On this floor anyone can catch me.'

'This is a prison,' she said, not paying attention to him.

'What did you expect?' he asked. 'They're bad people. Everyone knows that.' She pointed out that the palace downstairs hardly looked as though it belonged to bad people.

'In fact it doesn't look like they needed to steal people's stories.'

Nick threw himself on the hard mattress. 'They say that the palace was bare and gloomy before the King started stealing stories,' he said. 'But that isn't the point, we need a plan. And until I can get out of here, nothing can be done.'

'Well you can walk out,' she told him. 'No one here has seen you. Take one of the shadow cloaks and go down the stairs.' If it came to that, she thought, they could both hide under the cloaks and escape, or hunt for the Story Vat or do whatever it was that the matrix stones wanted them to do.

'And then what? At some point I will have to take it off and everyone will recognize me for a savage. You heard what the Lady said.'

There was at least a window, which looked down on the pepper pot and candelabra towers of Kalabash. Chinku craned down to look but a jutting shelf with a dragon's head that stuck out immediately below blocked her view. 'Pay attention,' Nick snapped.

'I'm listening,' she said, annoyed because he was distracting her. She should be putting down her thoughts of Kalabash on those strips of hide she had in her pocket. She had never ever seen a place like this before.

'We need to ask the stones what to do,' Nick said. 'And before someone comes with clothes for you, take this.' She turned and saw him holding out a nail.

'What will I do with that?' she asked, thinking, just like a boy keeping strange things in his pocket.

'This,' he said, 'is one of the nails from my home. Wherever you go, try and stick it into a wall or a door. It will record whatever happens in that room.'

'A nail?' She remembered what he had said about the spying nails in his village. 'How do you know it will work here? Have you ever been out of your village?'

'They work anywhere.'

She took it from him gingerly. 'I don't know, the doors look very hard ....'

'Well, a curtain then. Just make sure no one sees you ....' He sat up abruptly.

'I think someone's coming. Let's go and look at that other room.' Even as he spoke there was a rattle at the door.

'Wait!' Chinku called desperately. 'I have to tie up my wolf!' They scampered to the narrow garde robe and she shut the door before whisking over to the other one.

'You can come in now,' she called. The door opened a chink and the point of a spear was thrust in.

'Are you sure the wolf is safe?' a voice asked.

'Quite sure,' she said. The door opened wider and a page, who didn't look very much older than she did, was escorted in by one of the guards. The page had his arms full of clothes in those bright flower colours that she had seen the other children wear. He himself was dressed in saffron and gold, a kind of echo of the Lady's golden glitter. The guard watched as the clothes were put down on the bed.

'Is that wolf of yours all right,' he asked suspiciously. 'He seems awful quiet behind that door.'

'He's fine,' Chinku assured him. 'I just put him there. He's a very good wolf.'

The page flashed his eyes curiously at her, but did not say anything, waiting with folded arms to be let out again. 'They'll send food soon,' the guard said. 'So keep that wolf in there.'

'Food for me and my wolf?' Chinku asked.

'I suppose so. By rights that animal should be in the menagerie. He'll be better looked after there. But I suppose you know what you're doing.'

After the door closed behind the two she let Nick out. He went to the bed and riffled through the pile of clothes. He held one of the tunics up against himself. 'This seems like it might fit,' he said. 'Let me try it on.'

Chinku said, 'Shouldn't we ask the stones what to do first?'

'Yes, but quickly before someone comes again.'

However, when the stones were pulled out of her pocket they just lay there without a flash or a roll. 'You're not doing it right,' Nick said impatiently. 'Cast them again.'

She did. However, all that happened was that they rolled across the bed like the marbles she had called them.

The children looked at them in dismay. Chinku wondered whether the fact that they were now in Kalabash had taken the flash and roll out of them. Nick shook his head, 'I've never heard anything like that about the stones. Perhaps they don't have anything to tell us just now.'

'Perhaps someone is spying on us. After all if you have spying nails, they might have them here too.' She glanced at the stone walls. Nick said the stones would probably have warned them if that were the case. Hanging her head Chinku picked up the stones and was about to put them back into her pocket when Nick said,

'You'll have to change your clothes first. Don't leave them lying around in any old pocket.'

So she took the smallest set of clothes into the other room and changed into them. They were very different from the clothes Nick's mother had given her and certainly not at all like the dresses she wore at home. The cloth flowed like water between her fingers; silky blue changing from light to dark as it caught the tiny glints of light in the room. She wished there was a mirror where she could see how she looked but she supposed a boy wouldn't think like that. When she came out into the bedroom Nick had already changed into the long blue tunic. Somehow, he still looked wolfish.

'Now,' Nick said, 'all I have to do is get out of here and lose myself in the hall of children.'

She said, 'Someone will notice you.'

He shook his head. 'I don't think anyone looks at those children, just at their clothes.' Nick could always put the shadow cloak over his shoulders and go downstairs in his normal shape. He could then get into the halls and throw off the cloak and mingle with the others. But what then?

As they sat on the hard bed to think about what to do, there was another knock on the door. Nick dived for the other room while Chinku let the page in again. This time he was balancing a tray of food in one hand and what looked like raw meat on a pitchfork kind of thing in the other. He held the pitchfork gingerly at an angle so that the drips of blood did not fall on his suit.

'You can give me that,' Chinku said. 'You don't have to come in.'

He handed over the pitchfork with a sigh of relief. 'If I get drips on my clothes,' he told Chinku, 'they'll send me to stir the Story Vat for hours and hours.' Just before Chinku could ask what the Story Vat was, a harsh voice told the page to hurry up there. The page, startled, gave Chinku the plate of food and admonished, 'You be careful – that meat's fresh,' before vanishing again. Chinku heard the door being bolted on the outside.

Gingerly holding the slab of meat at arm's length, she went over to the closed garde robe and knocked. Nick opened it.

'This is what they sent for you,' she said. Nick standing there like a blue shadow in the semi-darkness made a face. 'That would be generous if I was a wolf. Now ….'

'Well you can always turn back into a wolf and eat it,' she pointed out. He came out of the room and glanced at the plate she held in her other hand. Green and red vegetables, fruits, and something in a sauce decorated with slices of lemon. He took the tray from her and put it down on the bed.

'Where do we put this?' Chinku asked.

'If we're here till the full moon, I'll probably be glad to eat it,' Nick said grimly. He picked up a slice of melon and bit into it.

'Well, we can't leave this lying around,' Chinku told him. 'Are you sure you can't turn into a wolf and eat it?' Nick was certain. Holding the pitchfork she went over to the window. 'If I had a knife I could cut it into small pieces,' she said. 'Then the birds could eat it.' There was no cutlery on the tray except for a spoon, so obviously the guards were being careful.

Nick sniffed, 'What kind of birds would eat raw meat? And horsemeat from the smell of it.'

'Eagles and hawks,' she answered.

'You don't get eagles and hawks in cities like this,' he told her, licking his fingers. 'The meat will lie there and rot.'

Nonetheless, she put the meat on the ledge just outside the window. If nothing, it would at least be hidden. As she drew her fingers back she felt a snap of air. Something had moved. She glanced down. The meat was gone. Only the blood drips were left.

'Nick,' she cried, 'the meat's gone.'

'You must have dropped it,' he answered. 'Now come over here and eat something before I finish it all.'

Reluctantly, and a little puzzled, she went back into the room. They had at least been generous with the food on the tray. Even after Nick had eaten there was enough to fill her stomach comfortably. As she ate, he lay on the hard mattress and looked at her.

'You know,' he said, 'you could probably stick that nail through one of those buttons.' He fingered one of the large wooden buttons that fastened the tunic. They were like hollow lozenges. Taking the nail from where she had left it, he carefully threaded it through the hollow. 'Will that do?' she asked. 'Doesn't the head have to be upright?'

'It might work,' he said. 'And it will be better than your sticking it into a wall and trying to bring it back again later.'

'But then it will only see whatever I see,' she pointed out. 'Nothing else.'

He left the nail in the button. 'Let's try it this way first.'

After they had finished eating they tried to figure out what to do next. Nick thought it would be a good thing if he could get out of the room. They both agreed that she would leave him in the garde robe when the page next came and he would see whether they left the door unlocked once Chinku was out of the room.

Chinku carefully took the heap of clothes and the shadow cloaks into the garde robe where she put them on a shelf, covering them carefully with the clothes. 'That,' she said, 'is in case they want to take the other clothes back. They won't dare while you're in the room.' At least, both of them hoped no one would dare. Too much of what they were doing depended on luck rather than magic and without the protection of the stones they felt quite helpless.

The page, escorted by the guards, came for Chinku a long while later. The shadows were creeping across the floor by then. 'Where's the wolf?' the page asked, peeping carefully round the edge of the door.

'In the garde robe,' Chinku answered demurely.

The guard came in too, this time, with his spear at the ready. The page took the tray and said, 'You are to follow me. I hope the wolf hasn't made too much of a mess with his meat.'

Chinku did not answer that question because she was busy hoping the page would not ask for the rest of the tunics back. She kept fiddling guiltily with the button in which Nick had stuck the nail. Once outside the door, she was happy to notice that no one bothered to lock it.

'As long as that wolf doesn't get out,' the page grumbled.

The guard replied, 'Behind a solid wooden door? Not likely. And the staircase is guarded.'

It was, but the guards carried tubes rather than spears or knives.

Led by the page, Chinku returned to the hall where she had seen other children in the morning. The only person there was a rather sad-looking man who was gazing out beyond one of the velvet curtains. When he heard them he dropped the heavy folds and turned. The page bowed to him and said, 'Sir this is the child who came this morning.'

'The one with the wolf,' said the man. 'Word of your arrival took wings through the palace.'

His eyes brightened slightly as he spoke to Chinku. 'What is your name?'

'Chinku,' she answered, slightly hesitating, but she had given her name once before and no one had said that it was a girl's name.

He repeated it, seeming to try it on his tongue.

'It is a fruit,' she said, since he was taking so long about pronouncing. His eyes met hers.

'Yes, a sweet fruit. It grows near my country. I know it well.' There was something in his eyes that worried her, a glint of knowledge that she had not seen in the eyes of the Chief Huntsman or even those of the golden idol.

The guard said, 'You will be responsible for the child. The Lady wishes to hear the story. She will send for you at twilight to find out what your assessment is. We will be outside if you should need anything.' It sounded almost as if Chinku was going to be put through an examination.

'Sit down child,' said the man. 'And tell me your story.' He indicated a cushion.

She sat down on it and looked up at him. It was a class, almost like with the Old Ones. Except that she was sitting there alone with him. Would it be good to tell her story quickly or in the elaborate storytelling manner she had been taught? While she was thinking, the man asked her where she came from. Caught unawares, she took the name of Nick's village, and then thought, if the man knew anything about Baghen he would know that the Wolf People lived there. This time the man did not repeat the name. Instead, he said, 'Tell me how you made friends with the wolf. Does he have a name, this wolf of yours?'

So she told him how, one golden morning while she had been playing in the woods, she had heard the whimpering of something from the hollow of a tree. Greatly daring, because her parents had told her never to go near baby animals, she had gone to look and found a bedraggled wolf cub. He had seemed lonely and deserted and had licked her fingers frantically. No mother wolf sprung out to tear Chinku's throat. She thought that the cub's mother must have died or fallen prey to hunters, so she had taken it home with her. Though her parents were uneasy, she had begged and pleaded with them to keep the cub. Finally, they had given in. She had called him Nick after a baby brother who had died and the wolf followed her everywhere, sleeping by her bed at night, protecting her from harm.

The man seemed to be listening to her, but sometimes she had the feeling that he was actually listening to something else. Her voice had stopped for quite a while before he said, 'Yes, yes, I understand. And where is your wolf now?' She said he was in the garde robe of her turret room, while wondering whether he had been able to slink past the guards.

'Well Chinku,' the man said, 'I think we can have you ready to present your story to the Lady in a few days.'

She was a little annoyed at the few days because after the incident in Demetra's tavern she was convinced she could tell stories with the best storytellers in the land.

The man must have noticed her annoyance, because he said, 'Don't feel too badly. There are certain rules about storytelling here, which all children have to learn. Now you are free to do what you choose for a while. I will call for the page and let him take you around the palace.' He clapped his hands and sent the guard away to fetch the page.

'Use your eyes, boy,' the man told Chinku. 'That is the best way to learn.'

'Do all the children here tell stories?' Chinku asked.

'No, some sing, some paint, some dance. The Lady gets tired of one kind of entertainment. So do the princes. If you are really good, you will be sent to the Painted Nurseries to tell your tales to the youngest prince.'

The page returned, this time with an air of self-importance about him. 'Follow me,' he said to Chinku.

'What's your name?' Chinku asked. 'I can't keep calling you Page.'

'Fowler,' the page answered. 'There are stairs here, be careful.' He led Chinku down a short flight of steps to a large room. It was empty but there were drums and stringed instruments scattered around.

'This,' he said, 'is where the musicians practise.' The room opened out into another which had shelves on the wall. Chinku's eyes picked out beads and strings, and parchments. The room looked very like her classroom back home. 'You will start classes here from tomorrow morning,' the page told her.

'What about the hall upstairs?' she asked.

'Oh, that's for the better students and the singing girls,' he answered. 'Down here if you make mistakes, no one can hear you.' That room also opened out into another one. She found it strange that there was only one entrance to each of the rooms. Then she realized that no one could go in or come out without being seen.

'Aren't there any guards on this floor?' she asked, trying to make the question innocent. Fowler seemed not to have heard. He showed her the other rooms then turned her round again and brought her back up the steps. She was certain that she had seen nothing of any importance.

'What happens if you sing badly?' she asked, since she felt she should be asking more questions.

'You're sent to stir the Story Vat,' he answered. That was the second time he had mentioned the Story Vat.

'What's that?'

'It's a huge vat with all the stories of the world dissolved in it,' he answered, without any hesitation at all. 'It's the heart of the palace.'

'Can I see it?' she asked.

He shook his head. 'It's the most secret place in the palace. You only go there if you're punished. And the corridor is guarded.' She was almost certain that that was the place where their memories were stored. Fowler turned several corners and, after a while, she realised that he was taking her back to her turret room.

It was empty when the guard opened the door. As she dashed for the inner room, she heard it closing behind her. A wolf looked up from the gloomy interior with a snarl that checked midway.

'It's you!' exclaimed the wolf.

'Of course it's me. Who else would open the door?' The grey outlines blurred in front of her eyes, the shape elongated and seemed to rear up, the air melted and then there was Nick, blue tunic and all.

'There's a Story Vat hidden somewhere in the palace,' she burst out. 'We have to find it!' And she told him all that had happened.

When she had finished he said, 'Give me that nail.' She had almost forgotten about it, she thought and twiddled it out of her button. He took and put it to his eye. She was a little disappointed as she watched him do that because she had expected some wonderful feat, the pictures from her morning shown larger than life on the stone walls.

Nick said, 'They don't work too well here, but at least we can see things,' He handed it to her and she put it to her eye. Ringed with silver, she saw a pinpoint room and the man who she had met. The man's mouth moved and the image wavered up and down with occasional flashes of blackness.

'You were moving quite a bit,' Nick told her accusingly, 'so it missed whatever happened when you moved.'

Still, she thought, it was wonderful enough. And handing back the nail and forgetting all about the Story Vat for the moment she dashed to the bed, took out her memory strips and began plaiting.

Nick followed her, 'You were supposed to tell me about the Story Vat,' he said accusingly.

'Ssh!' her fingers flashed back and forth.

Nick quietly sat down next to her, his shoulders hunched as he watched. 'What are in those other straws?' he asked when her fingers seemed to have stopped.

'Those are about you,' she told him.

'What about me?'

'The full moon night,' she answered and saw him flush.

'It's not right to put down things about other people,' he told her in a low voice.

'But that's how we learn things,' she replied. 'And no one can read it except the Memory Keepers.' Quietly he shrugged off his anger though he did put out an involuntary hand to touch the straws. 'When your people regain their memories,' he said, 'they will be able to read all about me.'

'Do you know what happens on full moon nights?' she asked him curiously.

He got to his feet and turned away from her without answering. The answer was there in the set of his shoulders.

'The Story Vat must be in the deepest heart of the palace,' she heard him say. 'I need to get out of this room.'

'You can't run wild through the palace as a wolf.'

'No, but I can change back into my original shape. As a boy among other children no one would notice me. They know what you look like after all.'

Chinku took out the matrix stones again but they did not flash or catch the light. Without their help they could rely only on Nick's shape shifting power and the eye of the nail. Together they sat looking out of the window watching the sunset fly its blood-red flags. Dusk fell quickly at Kalabash and turned the buildings into grim forbidding shapes. A strange sound made Chinku shiver, but she realized it was some kind of horn blowing. 'They must be shutting the city gates,' Nick said.

As the last of the light faded, the walls of the room began to cast a glow. It started dimly, like the embers of a fire and then gradually brightened, almost in the same way that Nick's home was lit by the light from the silver basin. Nick went to the walls and touched them gently.

'Perhaps they absorb the sun's light during the day and cast them back at night. Much in the same way that this nail absorbs images and holds them.'

No one came to provide them with sheets or pillows for the bed, so they spent an uncomfortable night. Chinku used her discarded clothes for a pillow, while Nick made do with towels and the extra tunic and the cloaks. At dawn they were woken by the horns blowing again. Nick groaned, rolled over and covered his head with a towel. Chinku scampered up and went to the window to see what she could. The streets below were flecked with pinpoints of light, where the night torches were still burning. She could see movement in the streets if she craned round the angle of the dragon's head below.

Food arrived for them early. Nick just had time to yawn himself awake and scamper into the garde robe. Chinku opened the door and found Fowler with a tray and the chunk of meat on a pitchfork. He looked as if he had just woken up himself and this time there was no guard with him.

'You're early!' Chinku exclaimed.

'You have a class,' Fowler said. 'I have to take you to the Master in a little while, so feed yourself and your wolf as fast as you can.'

Chinku took the tray back into the room. Nick came out to see what there was. 'Throw that meat out of the window again,' he told her. So, gingerly like the last time, she went over to the window. This time it was gone before she even had time to turn away.

'This is very strange!' she said and began turning her head this way and that, trying to solve the strange mystery. She could see the blood drops from the meat.

'It's the birds. They're probably looked after as badly as we are,' Nick told her, chewing his way through a crusty roll. 'Come and eat.' She wasn't listening. Looking down carefully, she saw something amazing. There was a drop of blood on the stone dragon's mouth. She looked harder, was the stone throat moving? It was. The scales flickered for a moment as the shadows danced over it.

'Nick!' she called.

'What?' he asked through a mouthful of bread. 'Come here.' He came reluctantly in a shower of breadcrumbs.

She pointed to the dragon. 'Look at it,' she whispered. 'It's alive.' The dragon seemed frozen, but not frozen enough. The throat moved again. Chinku looked at Nick, 'What does this mean?'

'That the King has the dragons imprisoned in some way so that they guard his palace. Most people think the dragons went back to the hills and lie hidden there.' His mother had told him that the soldiers of the King had driven the dragons away after his marriage with a dragon princess. Some had turned mysteriously into flowers. The rest had vanished and people said that they were waiting for the Kingdom of Kalabash to fall before they returned.

'How strange,' Chinku said. 'And all the while the dragons were here, guarding the palace.'

Nick said, 'That's why the matrix stones aren't working!' as if he had only just thought of it. 'You don't find those stones anywhere except in dragon's caves,' he explained. 'They're supposed to be frozen dragon's tears. When dragons are around, they lose their powers. It's very lucky that the Dream Stealers dropped them when they did.'

'But that must be a long time ago,' Chinku said.

'Yes, so very long ago that no one alive remembers when. Didn't your Old Ones tell you anything about dragons?'

Chinku shook her head.

'Then people began to say that the dragons were evil and that it was just as well ...' Nick suddenly leapt to his feet and ran to the garde robe. Almost immediately came a knock on the front door. Chinku went to open it and found Fowler there with one of the guards.

'There were voices coming from here,' the guard said suspiciously.

'Voices,' Chinku said innocently, her heart thumping, 'but there's no one here except me and my wolf.' She turned, 'Shall I show you my wolf?'

Both Fowler and the guard replied Yes.

Chinku went to the garde robe door and opened it. They could hear a threatening growl. The guard went forward thinking perhaps that he should look inside, but the growl grew in intensity and he jumped back.

'You must have heard wrong,' he told Fowler. 'There couldn't be anyone inside, not with a vicious wolf like that.'

'Lock the door,' Fowler told Chinku.

'I'll shut it,' Chinku replied. 'Wolves can't open doors.'

Fowler was looking around the room as he spoke, 'I need those old clothes of yours,' he said. 'They have to go to the Boiling Vat.'

Chinku put her hand out to the door again. 'They're in there,' she said.

'Don't waste time,' the guard told Fowler.

'You should have taken those clothes before. The Wise One is waiting.' She had a story to tell the Wise One now, she thought, a tale of a palace borne on the wings of dragons. Why, she wondered, had the dragons allowed themselves to be taken prisoner?

The man she had decided to call the Wise One was waiting for her in the hall. She was told she would have her classes by herself until she made her presentation to the Lady. 'Then you can join the others if the Lady is pleased,' he told her.

'And if she is not pleased?' Chinku asked. A look of sadness flitted across the man's face.

'We hope she is pleased,' he told her. 'Now pay attention to me.'

Storytelling in Kalabash, Chinku discovered did not jump straight into events with a *Once Upon a Time there was a little girl*, or even *A king with three daughters*. It seemed to open with a statement of time and place, as in *Once upon a time in the days before reason when darkness ruled the minds of men, the Wise Ones in the Heavens decreed the birth of a man who would bring a ray of light into the darkness*. What he was telling her, she realized, was the story of the Titan who had stolen fire from heaven. She sat back and listened to him, trying to understand it, though every so often the words escaped and wove such patterns that she lost the thread of the story.

'What do you mean?' she asked once and he checked his flow and, she thought, almost laughed. However, the smile lines quickly straightened almost as if they had been pressed with a hot iron. Perhaps they did not laugh very often in Kalabash. She understood why the princes were told stories at bedtime. With stories like these they would very quickly fall asleep.

She was not quite sure what to do with the *Once upon a time in the dark days*, so she improvised with a *Once upon a time when the spring days were long and April was a month kissed with unusual warmth*, and hoped that that would do.

Sometimes she lost track of what she was saying. Once the class was interrupted when a page, not Fowler, came scuttling with a bottle and glasses on a tray. The bottle was like a sapphire tear and held a greenish liquid which was poured out for her.

The Wise One told her, 'It refreshes the throat and is good for the memory.' It tasted, she thought, like liquid grass and she forced it down her throat. Once down, it was actually refreshing and her tongue stopped stumbling over the formal sentences. A drink to help her tell stories, or clear her mind! That was new. She wondered where the Kalabash people had discovered that.

The lesson continued for a few hours. Sometimes they were interrupted by other children who would run in with questions. Once Fowler came in and whispered into the Wise One's ear. But otherwise it continued in an unbroken monotony. She polished sentences and re-polished them. The Kalabash storytellers apparently memorized their tales and recited them word for word. She thought that was stupid.

'Couldn't I please,' she said, tired of wordsmithing, 'bring my wolf in with me? He would make the story so much more interesting. The Lady liked the dance we did for her.'

'Take a wolf into a formal storytelling session?' the Wise One's eyebrows shot up so high that they almost disappeared into his hair. 'I hear your wolf snapped at one of the court ladies.'

'She startled him. He doesn't like it if people rush up – he thinks he's being attacked.'

'And yet he is so gentle with you ...' He fell into silence and, thinking that was all, Chinku lowered her head and stumbled back to the next sentence. 'I think I need to see your wolf,' he told her quietly and clapped his hands. She stopped in mid-sentence gratefully. Fowler appeared with the guard at his side.

'I need the wolf brought here,' the Wise One said. 'Take this child with you.'

The guard protested, 'That might not be safe ...'

'The Lady has gone riding in the country with her court, the King is hunting ... what danger could there possibly be?'

So Chinku found herself returning to the turret room and opening the garde robe door while Fowler and the guard waited outside.

'You're to come with me,' she told Nick. 'The Wise One wants to see you.'

Nick was still in his wolf's shape. 'What am I supposed to do?' he asked. 'Is there a chance I can escape today?'

'I don't think so. I'm supposed to practise my story with you.'

'What's taking so long?' asked the guard waiting outside.

'Nice, Nick, good Nick, come on, Nick Nick Nick,' purred Chinku immediately.

'Stop that,' Nick growled. 'Find that silly leash.'

'I can't find the leash,' she said loudly and rummaged in the pile of clothes. Luckily, she found it and looped it carefully around Nick's neck and led him out.

'Careful,' said the guard pointing the memory tube at Nick. 'Not one false move.'

'He's a wolf,' said Chinku. 'What will that do?'

The guard lowered it, but he was obviously angry at his loss of control. 'I should have brought a spear,' he grumbled, 'wild animals roaming around a palace like this ...' Both he and Fowler kept a safe distance. The guards at the bottom of the turret steps also sprang apart to allow the wolf through. The few people they met in the corridors skirted around the procession. Chinku was wondering whether she would have an opportunity to slip the leash, but she soon realized that without proper planning Nick would find it difficult to get back to her.

The Wise One was pacing up and down the hall as if he were annoyed at the delay or worried about something. Chinku held the leash tight as he came towards them.

'So this is your wolf,' he said, without any sign of fear.

'Nick, give him your paw,' Chinku said, thinking that that might be a good start. Nick obeyed.

'You can take it,' Chinku told the Wise One. 'He won't attack.'

'I can see that.' The Wise One took Nick's paw in his hand even as the guard and Fowler muttered words of caution. He held the paw for a little while longer than was necessary before letting it drop.

'I see the problem now,' he said to Fowler and the guard. 'Stay outside should I need you.'

As soon they were alone, the Wise One came up to Chinku and said, 'Is he really a wolf?'

Chinku's heart started thudding and she looked down at Nick. 'Of course he's a wolf. Why should you think otherwise?'

'I don't know,' said the Wise One slowly, 'something about his paw. It felt almost like a hand ...' Chinku glanced at Nick to see if he had taken it in, but the wolf's head was turned away. He was watching a bird fly past the window.

'Paw!' she snapped. Nick started, whirled and held up his paw. She felt it but could feel nothing but the hard pads, claws and fur. She shook her head at the Wise One. 'It's a paw.'

The Wise One said, 'I have heard stories of wolves who were actually people. Men who changed into wolves during the full moon and attacked villages.'

Chinku mumbled that stories were like the Whispering Game, the more you whispered, the more the story changed until in the end it was nothing like the original at all.

The Wise One shrugged. 'Well, show me how you plan to use the wolf in your storytelling.' He seemed to have suddenly lost interest in the whole thing. Chinku pushed and prodded Nick as she told the story again and this time she told it in her own style of storytelling, using Nick to hold up his paw pathetically when she was describing the lost wolf cub that she had found. She had Nick pretend to carry things backwards and forwards across the room. Once in a while the guard peeped around the curtain, but seemed to be satisfied with what he saw, because the head soon disappeared.

The Wise One said, 'I once knew one of the wolf people, a man called Lobo.' Both Nick and Chinku started because by now they were convinced he wasn't paying attention to them. Nick was in mid-caper and almost lost his balance. 'He was the Chief of the Wolf People,' the Wise One continued. 'He lived in a village with wooden houses that had horns of steel.' It sounded very much as if he had been to Nick's village, though the name Lobo meant nothing to Chinku. She glanced at Nick. His ears flicked back and forth but he sat there quietly, his mouth slightly open as he panted.

'Did he attack you?' Chinku asked because a deadly silence seemed to threaten.

'No, but then I was never at the village during the full moon. People from other villages around told me about the attacks. Not that anyone could document them. It was all part of local legend.'

Chinku met his eyes fearlessly and answered, 'I have had my wolf for many full moons. He has never attacked me.' Nick rose and skittered across the room, his claws making a click-click sound on the marble floor.

'But the name is strange for a wolf, you must admit,' the Wise One said. 'Nick is a boy's name.'

'I named him after my brother,' Chinku answered. 'My mother said I had a little brother who went away to the Cloud Folk.' She thought of something more to say, 'And my wolf needs exercise. He gets restless in one room for so long. Can I take him for a walk?'

'That,' said the Wise One, dropping the subject of the Wolf People, 'may be difficult. However, yes, your story does seem to have more life when the wolf is with you. Let me see.' The guard was sent for. He did not seem to be terribly happy with what he was told but he agreed to take Chinku and Nick to a corner of the palace that had a long corridor where the wolf could pace up and down, 'without getting under the ladies' skirts.'

The corridor was beyond six more halls, all of which were empty and it was certainly long, running like a dim, cool arrow through the heart of the palace. 'I'm standing here,' said the guard. 'Don't try any tricks.' Chinku tugged at the leash, but surprisingly, Nick stood there. He seemed to be sniffing something, his nose close to the ground. He sniffed and moved in quite another direction, tugging Chinku behind him.

'Oi!' the guard cried, 'What's going on?'

'He smells something,' Chinku answered, though she thought it was quite obvious from the way Nick was behaving.

'That way is barred,' the guard said. 'Stop your wolf now.'

'Nick!' she said desperately because the man was beginning to look quite threatening. She clutched the leash close to his neck. Nick turned his head around and his eyes glowed an angry yellow.

'He's restless,' she babbled, 'he's been cooped up for so long.' Nick began to do his imitation of a wolf on the verge of attack, which worried the guard even more.

'Control that animal,' he said, 'or I will not be responsible for the consequences.'

She let Nick drag her a little way in the forbidden direction, murmuring to him and pretending to soothe him.

'Don't worry,' she said to the guard. 'As soon as he calms down, I'll bring him back here. We won't go far.'

They turned a corner and for a second they were out of sight of the guard. Another corridor stretched ahead, a seemingly bald, blank mass of whiteness. 'Nothing I've smelt before,' Nick whispered. 'Coming from this way.' He said it in the low voice, which most people would mistake for a growl.

'Well, we can't go any further,' Chinku mumbled. 'The guard will come to see what's happening.'

Just as she spoke the guard's voice startled them, 'That's enough. Come back here.'

'Can't he run down this corridor?' Chinku asked. 'It looks empty. I won't have to tug him back then.' She spoke in her most appealing voice, quite forgetting that the guard thought he was talking to a boy, like the rest of the people in the palace.

The corridor ahead of them stayed empty. She hoped very hard it would stay that way. If Nick's strange smells took shape then they would be hustled out of there quicker than quick. The guard seemed to be in a quandary. He paused and scratched his head. 'There's nothing here,' Chinku pointed out, making the motions of tugging at the leash. Nick's nose remained obstinately pointed in the other direction.

The guard finally shrugged. 'All right, all right. But just towards the end of the corridor. I lose sight of you and that's it!'

Nick leapt like an arrow down the corridor almost before the guard had finished, dragging Chinku after him. It was a little, she thought, like being lost in the hollows of a seashell, white and whirling, curve melting into curve. What she had not realized when she had first seen it, was the way the walls of this corridor curved overhead. Nick had dragged her forward too fast for that. Sounds echoed because of those walls, funnelling towards one end. Nick went faster and faster on his skittering paws, his ears pricked and his nose twitching. Ahead, the walls looked as if they were twirling smaller and smaller, the roof was sloping over their heads. Terrified, Chinku put her weight behind the leash, 'Nick, stop, stop!'

'Come back here, you two!' the guard called almost simultaneously. 'That's enough exercise!' Reluctantly, Nick turned. They returned to the guard and he led them back to the turret room.

Nick was out of his wolf's skin almost before they heard the lock of the door. 'It's there!' he growled.

'What is there?'

'The Story Vat.'

'How do you know? And supposing the guard had opened the door again and caught you.'

He shrugged, 'Well he didn't, did he? We have to go back to that corridor and see what lies at the end.'

'The roof closed in,' Chinku pointed out.

'I don't think so,' he told her. From my viewpoint it seemed to be perfectly straight.'

'You didn't look up,' she retorted. 'Only dwarfs can go in there.'

'But we will have to go in there. Tell me, is that nail still in your button? Did you put it back?' She fumbled it out of its hollow and handed it to Nick. He went to the window and put the tip of the nail to his eye. As he did it Chinku asked, 'Who is Lobo?'

'Eh?'

'The Wise One mentioned a Lobo. Is he someone from your village?'

Nick raised his head, 'My grandfather. The Wise One has been to my village.' He did not seem at all disturbed when he said that. She had the feeling that the knowledge might be dangerous. If the Wise One knew there were people who turned into wolves then he might suspect that the wolf with her was also a human being – in fact he already had. Nick was peering into the nail and turning it this way and that.

'We have to go back to that corridor,' he told her. 'Or at any rate, I need to go back into that corridor.'

'If you disappear,' she said, 'the Wise One will know you're not a wolf.'

'He hasn't said anything yet,' Nick pointed out. 'He might not be sure.' Of course, he could be a friend, Chinku thought. She hoped that he was. Then there might be someone on their side who would help them to where they wanted to go.

16

She was determined when she saw him the next morning to try and discover whether he was on their side. 'Don't rush at it,' Nick warned her. 'Remember, we don't have the stones to tell us what to do.'

'Can't the dragons help us?' she asked hopefully. She had just finished feeding them Nick's scraps of meat. This time she had stood at the edge of the window watching, and seen the stone mouth reach up and catch the meat. They were grey like the pigeons and their scales flashed with the same purples and greens as the pigeons' feathers when the sun caught them. The stones in her pocket were still marbles. She even took them out to play with, tired of the empty room after sunset.

'The dragons are so old that no one really knows what they will or will not do. Your Old Ones would have been able to tell you if they still had their memories. Do I come with you now or not?'

They heard the guard's rap at the door and Nick ran to the other room. When Chinku opened the door, she was told she had to bring the wolf with her. So, like the day before, she put the leash around Nick's neck and the two of them walked down to the hall where the Wise One was waiting for them. Sadly, he was not alone. There was a group of children sitting there, in red and blue tunics. Chinku realized that they came from two different classes because the red ones were carrying flutes and theorbos.

The Wise One said, 'I was wondering whether music would help you narrate your story better. That's why these children are here. The ones in the blue tunics are from your grade. They are here to watch. As to the red ones ....' He smiled and told the children to play.

The first attempts were a little uncoordinated because the children were distracted by Nick's presence, but gradually they fell into place and the music began to sound rather nice.

'If you tell them your story,' the Wise One said, 'they can figure out how to keep pace with you.'

But rather than do that, she impulsively caught Nick's paws and whirled him round to the music. Clumsily, but with enough grace to make the children clap. 'I have heard of this,' said the Wise One when she dropped Nick's paws and stood panting in front of him. 'This was how you entertained the Lady on the first occasion.' He would have said more, but they were interrupted by a rush of running feet.

Fowler burst into the hall, 'The King! His Majesty is on his way here!' He stopped so abruptly that he almost fell over, panting and sweating nervously. Nick put on his disturbed wolf act, a sudden growl and leap. Chinku almost dropped the leash because he took her by surprise, but just managed to grab it at the last minute. Only the Wise One was calm. 'Child, control that animal of yours. The rest of you stay still.' As he finished saying that, the tramping of feet filled the hall.

The curtains were flung apart and a boy, who wore the same kind of clothes as Fowler, but more ornate ones, stepped through. 'His Royal Highness King Viraz the Magnificent of Kalabash, Overlord of Helegon, Duke of Prismia,' he announced and then doubled over into a deep bow. The King stepped through the curtains. Chinku's first feeling was one of disappointment because the King, when compared to his gilt idol wife, looked so thin and worried. His mouth was a narrow slash and eyes so deep set that they vanished under his brows. His clothes were stiff gold-and-silver brocade things that looked very uncomfortable. A hand came down on her head and forced her to bow. She realized it was the Wise One before she ducked her head obediently.

'My wife has told me about this wolf,' she heard the King say, while her gaze roamed over the toes of a pair of mirror-polished brown boots.

She was a little disappointed by the boots. The King should have raised one foot and stepped into the air with chains of dragons behind him instead of Dream Stealers. She heard him speak in a deep rumbling voice, which too was unexpected.

'My wife has been telling me about this child and his wolf. I thought I would come to see for myself.'

The hand stayed on her head, so Chinku kept looking down at the shoes and listening to the voice, the voice that was very different. If you listened to it, you almost forgot that it belonged to a mean man.

'Let the child look at me,' said the voice.

The Wise One's hand moved away and Chinku raised her head. Nick had dropped into stillness next to her.

'Let the child speak,' the King said.

'With your permission, Sire,' the Wise One said, 'he is not ready.'

'Did I ask for stories?' the King enquired. 'I want him to show me what his wolf can do.' To Chinku, he said directly, 'I want to see your wolf dance.'

'How fortunate, Sire,' said the Wise One. 'The musicians are also here. Well, child, show the King your wolf dance, as you showed it to us just now.' The musicians started the rumble of their theorbos again. Nick reluctantly allowed her to raise his paws and circle him around the dance floor.

'Remarkably graceful,' the King observed. 'Almost like a girl rather than a savage from beyond the hills.'

Chinku stumbled when she heard that.

'The child still has much training ahead,' the Wise One said. 'If he appears before the Lady now it will just be a repetition of the same performance.' The King put up his hand and the music stopped. Chinku and Nick stopped two beats after.

'There is of course another alternative,' the King said. 'To let one of the trained storytellers practise with the wolf.'

'That might be dangerous for the storyteller, Sire. The wolf is not tame.'

'There are some interesting experiments being carried out,' the King observed, 'even with the memory of animals.' He stopped as if he had said too much. 'However, that may be premature. Continue with your classes.' And he abruptly turned his back on them and swept out of the room with the guards and the page in his wake. Chinku looked at Nick. The yellow eyes gazed back into her own. She could see that even he was worried. Where did a wolf's memory go then? Surely not into the Story Vat with human memories? What could you do with a wolf's memory? Give it to the Shadow Riders and let them use it to destroy people?

The Wise One said, 'There is nothing to worry. His Majesty was just thinking aloud.'

For Nick the rest of the day, as he told Chinku later, was sheer torture. He was danced up and down, in slow four steps and quick mazurkas, as the Wise One tried to see what kind of pace would suit the formal storytelling method best. In the middle of that came a summons from the Royal Nurseries – the young princes had heard of the dancing wolf and wanted to see him. The message was brought by a plump lady with silver hair dressed in silver brocade. The Wise One seemed irritated at this interruption.

'How am I to send a wolf to the nurseries?' he demanded. 'Would that be safe?'

'The princes have demanded it,' the silver woman replied. 'There is no way you may refuse.'

'Is His Majesty aware of the request? Or the Lady?'

The woman shrugged, 'It was the Lady who told the princes about the wolf. And what she said excited them so much that they were desperate to see the animal. Now they refuse to eat unless the wolf is taken up to them.'

The children sitting behind Chinku set up a buzz. She thought of the story she had heard about a prince of Kalabash who had died because he had not been able to sleep. Were the royal children so indulged then? The Wise One reluctantly allowed Chinku and Nick to be led away between two armed guards.

The nursery had model ships on the walls that bobbed up and down on strange blue waves. Another wall had what looked like rampaging horses. Every so often the horses jumped down and galloped around the room. In the middle sat the two princes. The older one hung back with a sulky look on his face but the younger one was small as an elf with a smile that broke unexpectedly on his face. Because that smile set her lips dancing, Chinku thought that he was perhaps the nice one. The younger prince pointed when he saw Nick and was about to leap forward when his nurse stopped him. Both the princes had nurses, Chinku saw, white haired very sensible-looking women dressed in black from head to foot. She wondered who the silver woman was. Perhaps a royal grandmother? Or was she a fairy godmother? In this strange place, anything was possible. Chinku observed that the younger prince was surreptitiously digging his nails into his nurse's arm, that smile still flickering on his face like a will o' the wisp. The nurse stood there unflinchingly.

'Wolves bite, Your Highness,' she told him.

'But he's not biting that boy,' the prince said, pointing at Chinku.

'He's his pet.'

'Hold on tightly to that beast,' the other nurse ordered Chinku. 'The princes want to come closer.' One of the guards muttered something about how unwise that would be. 'And do you know the consequences of refusing an order from the princes?' the nurse retorted.

Chinku saw the princes getting to their feet and she quickly grabbed Nick by the scruff of his neck. What a day it was, she thought, first the King and now these two children who she would probably have slapped if she had met them in school. Nick was squirming because her grip was too tight, but she dare not loosen it in case he decided to play wolf again. Lay one tooth on either of the princes, she thought, and it would mean being sent to the King's laboratories.

As quick as lightning, the younger prince dropped his nurse's arm and came up to Nick. He was cautious at first, keeping his distance. Then, when no one expected it, he pulled the wolf's tail and darted away again. Nick started.

Chinku said, 'Don't touch him!' The nurses squealed and fluttered and muttered many reproachful, 'Your Highnesses ...' The older prince cautiously circled Nick. 'If he can touch him, so can I,' he said. 'You, give me your wolf's leash.'

'He doesn't like strangers,' Chinku pointed out.

'Tell him to behave. If he doesn't, I'll tell Father and he'll have him turned into soup in the Story Vat!' She gripped Nick hard and did not know what to do.

'I'll hold him by his neck and you can hold the leash. Would that do?' Chinku tried to find a solution. The eldest prince thought awhile and said, 'My word on it,' and held out his hand. Chinku carefully gave him the end of the leash. Nick stood perfectly still and showed no signs of wanting to attack the prince.

'Can I touch him?' the prince asked, stretching out a hand towards Nick's nose. The wolf's nostrils flared a little, but that was all. He sniffed the hand and licked the fingers. 'Now let go of him,' the prince said.

'I ...' Chinku said hesitantly, but Nick's tongue was still flicking out at the fingers and it was obvious that he had no intentions of attacking the prince.

'No!' chorused the royal nurses anxiously, but even as they did, Nick twisted and Chinku temporarily lost her grip on his neck. They stood there then, the prince and the wolf on the leash.

'Open the door!' the prince ordered. 'I'm going to walk him through the palace. This is my new pet!'

'You can't take him from the boy, Your Royal Highness,' his nurse pleaded. 'He doesn't belong to you.'

'Everything in this palace belongs to me,' the older prince retorted. 'Open the door!' The guards did so without a murmur. 'Come on,' the prince said, flicking the leash. 'Come on, wolf. Let's go for a walk!' That was when the little prince darted up and pinched him hard. The older prince cried out, 'Ow!' and dropped the leash. Nick pounced towards the open door, scattering the two guards and disappeared like a streak of greased lightning.

At first Chinku did not believe it. She stared at the open mouth of the door. How could Nick have bolted like that without saying a word to her? Then the whole room came to life again; at least the humans in the room, since the horses and the ships on the walls had not stopped their magical movements. The elder prince slapped his younger brother who promptly dissolved into loud howls.

The guards grabbed Chinku by the shoulder. 'Come on boy, we have to get that wolf back!' They ran her towards the door and out into the corridor.

17

The corridor was empty. The nurseries were on another floor and Chinku had lost track of the twists and turns and stairs in the palace. Here the walls were painted in soft shades of sea green and pink, dotted with flowers and blades of grass that moved as if in some invisible wind. Despite her worry the beauty caught her eye. Then she was running again with the guards tugging at her. This way and that way, wherever the corridors turned, desperately seeking the flash of a grey tail. Unfortunately, they could find nothing. The guards looked at each other in dismay.

'It's your fault, boy,' one of them told Chinku. 'The King will have your head for sure.' However, his voice sounded unconvincing.

'What shall we do?' asked the other. 'The King will have our heads as well if he hears.'

'He won't be able to get out of the palace,' said the first guard. 'Someone will track him down. But until then ....'

'If word gets to the Lady ...,' the second guard looked even more horrified at this thought. In the end they decided that the best thing to do was return Chinku to her room.

'My wolf will come looking for me after a while,' she told them hopefully, even though she was not certain that Nick would do any such thing. Drat that boy for not telling her what he planned to do. Of course, she could not blame him. No one had known the princes would behave like that.

It was lonely in the turret by herself, even though she went to the window to look at the dragons. They were as still as stone because she had no meat to offer. She wished she knew their language – then she could have spoken to them and flown away from the castle. Finally she curled up on the hard bed and burst into tears. Anyone seeing her at that moment would have known she was not a boy, but Chinku did not care whether anyone saw her or not. After a while, she heard feet approaching her door. It was opened without a knock. The Wise One stood there.

'I heard about your wolf escaping,' he said, stepping inside and shutting the door carefully behind him. 'He isn't really a wolf, is he? Dry your eyes,' he added glancing at Chinku and pulling out a soft white handkerchief from his pocket.

'Whatever you think,' the Wise One told her, 'I am a prisoner like you. Now tell me – is that wolf really a wolf?'

Chinku slowly shook her head.

'I thought not,' the Wise One said. 'That means that they won't find him, will they?'

'I don't know,' Chinku answered.

'Well, there will be chaos in the palace for a while, then when they don't find the wolf, a few people will have their memories altered and no one will remember that there ever was a wolf. That, I am afraid will include you and all the other children in the hall.'

'Surely not the princes,' she said defiantly. 'It was all their fault.'

He sighed, 'Not the princes, not me because my teachings are too valuable to them. Ever since I was brought here...' he broke off. 'No point troubling you with my stories. I have to find out how to get you out of here.'

A thought suddenly occurred to her. 'Are you Demetra's husband?' she asked.

There was a sudden spark in the Wise One's eyes. 'You know Demetra?'

'We came from there ....'

'Is my wife well?' the Wise One asked with concern in his voice.

Chinku told him what had happened in the tavern, even though what she wanted to do was talk about Nick. He listened intently and for a moment Chinku thought his eyes were glistening with tears. Then running a hand over his face he said slowly, 'The guards may not notice a new boy in the palace, provided he is wearing the right clothes.'

Chinku tugged at her own tunic. 'He is wearing one of these.'

'How did you get an extra tunic?'

'They gave me three sets to try on.'

'And they haven't discovered that an extra set is missing?'

'I kept them in the garde robe where Nick was,' Chinku replied. 'They were too scared to go in there.'

'We must get to him before the guards, not that they will suspect that a wolf can be a boy.'

She said, 'He will try to find that strange corridor like a shell.'

'Where the Story Vat is kept?'

'I don't know,' Chinku answered. 'It was just a corridor. And Nick said that there was a smell he could not recognize.'

'Do you know what the Story Vat is, child?'

'Is it where everyone's stolen memories are kept?' She looked up at him, her heart beating. 'They came and stole everyone's memories early one morning. My father hid me in a rabbit's burrow so I was able to escape. Nick and I are trying to recover the memories.'

'We will have to find Nick.' The Wise One strode over the door and rapped on it hard. A guard came and opened it. 'I am taking this child with me. He may know where the wolf has gone. At any rate, the creature will respond to his master's voice wherever it is hiding.'

The guard did not seem to know what to say. He wiped his face and whispered, 'There is chaos in the nurseries. So far word has not reached the King, but if it does this boy will be blamed.'

'But it wasn't my fault!' Chinku exclaimed indignantly. 'It was ...' before she could say any more the Wise One clapped his hand across her mouth.

He told the guard, 'Then the sooner we find the wolf, the better.' Holding Chinku firmly by the shoulder, the Wise One led her down the stairs. 'We need to retrace our steps,' he told the guards. The guards were too distracted to even want to follow them.

'Those princes deserve to be beaten!' Chinku said.

'Ever since the King lost his eldest son, no one has laid a hand on the princes.'

'How long ago was that?'

'That happened three kings ago, however long ago that may be,' was the answer. A life without being told what was right and wrong, a life filled with storytelling sessions? Chinku thought it was unbelievable. She stumbled after the Wise One until she found herself outside the hall where the classes had been held. The Wise One took a turn and led her up another flight of stairs. Occasionally they met people running frantically here and there. No one glanced at Chinku, but she realized that in her blue tunic she looked like any other child.

'Your wolf has created quite a furore,' the Wise One told her loudly as they walked up the stairs. She soon realized what the loud voice was – the guards were still there at the top. 'A child for punishment?' one of them asked.

The Wise One said, 'Have you heard the news?'

'What news?'

'There is a wild animal loose in the palace.'

'It must be that wolf for sure,' one of the guards said, nodding his head wisely. 'It came up here the other day.'

'You didn't see it?'

'No animal came up these stairs.'

'Nonetheless, I need to check for myself,' said the Wise One. And taking Chinku firmly by the hand he turned the corridor away from the guards in swift footsteps. They did not challenge or run after him, even though she was expecting a shout to come after them at any minute.

'I stay here of my own free will, you see,' the Wise One told her. 'So I am allowed certain liberties.'

'Of your own will?' Chinku asked, confused. The corridor began its shell-like spins in front of them. The Wise One strode briskly forward without showing any signs of stopping. There was no sign of a cockroach, let alone a wolf in that twisting whiteness. 'He's not here,' she said sadly. 'And I can't smell anything.'

'You're not a wolf,' he answered striding on, despite the fact that the ceiling seemed to be closing in overhead. Involuntarily, she ducked.

'Don't worry,' he said. 'That is one of the defences of this corridor. Walk on and hold your head high.' And he held out a hand to her. She took it and they walked on.

Every so often, her neck deceived by her eyes cramped down for protection. 'Stand upright,' said the Wise One again. 'It is only your eyes. Few thieves dare come this way,' he added. 'The illusion is too strong for comfort.' She could see the corridor funnelling to an end, corkscrewing. 'Close your eyes,' he told her. 'This is the difficult part.' So she obeyed blindly because it was better than looking at those walls closing in. Surprisingly, the moment she did so, she relaxed. Holding on to the Wise One's hand, she moved forward. 'Now you can open your eyes,' he said. As soon as she opened her eyes she saw a door in front. It was painted a shimmering colour that was white but not quite white, rainbow, but not quite rainbow, moving and shifting like the waters of a stream. The Wise One put out his hand and touched the door. He must have touched a panel or a particular part but the shimmering image in front of her made that hard to tell.

'You will now see,' he told her, 'the greatest secret in Kalabash. Few come so far and leave the palace.'

Inside she saw a huge shadow that glimmered here and there surrounded by tall pillars. There were spiral stairs leading up its side. All the light in the room came from the ceiling above that shape. A man in a long white coat appeared out of nowhere. 'Has the child come to stir the vat?' he asked the Wise One. 'We are short of stirrers these days, all the children are behaving so well.'

'No, I have been told to show him the vat as a warning,' the Wise One replied. 'He is new and not yet disciplined.' As he spoke, he moved towards the spiral stairs, his hand firmly on Chinku's shoulder. The stairs spiralled like the corridor they had left behind, so narrow that they had to walk in single file. It would be difficult for anyone to approach the Story Vat, Chinku thought. The light grew brighter and brighter as they rose upwards and she could smell a fragrance that seemed to belong to all the flowers of the world. It was so sweet, she found tears clouding her vision.

'Now you understand why it is such a punishment,' she heard Demetra's husband telling her. His hands from behind steadied her but the sweetness became so cloying that she almost retched.

Climbing the stairs they now reached a platform. Cautiously she looked up and saw a silver edge and beyond that a sea of colour. The colours were never still. At one point the sea blushed pink, then suddenly a green ripple ran through it or a wave of purple. Then it was still and silver until blood red currents ran through.

The colours were fed by a pipe that led from the ceiling. They gushed out of its mouth creating that overpowering white light.

'All the memories of the world,' murmured the Wise One.

'How do children stir this?' Chinku whispered, her eyes and nostrils full of that scent and brightness. The Wise One pointed to the tall silver rods hanging from some kind of rack to one side of the vat. 'With those,' he said, 'one at a time, to make the colours change faster.'

'But what do the colours signify?' she asked.

'Different kinds of stories and memories,' he answered.

'Then my village's memories are somewhere in there,' she said, forgetting her distress at the smell.

'Quiet!' he hissed and almost immediately they heard footsteps below.

'Is there a problem, Nostromo?' a voice asked.

'No,' the Wise One replied. 'It was just this child asking a question.' Chinku clung to the rim trying to think. This was where she had wanted to be and here she was, but Nick was nowhere near. And the vat of colours was so huge that she could not imagine how she would be able to steal her village's memories back from it. Something cold stung her finger like a whiplash and she jerked her hand away.

'Careful,' said the Wise One, or Nostromo as he was called. 'The colours have powers that no one can ever guess at.'

'But how do the princes get told the stories from here?' she whispered, shaking her finger.

'They take a little bit at a time, a drop, on a brush. Flick it once on anyone and the person immediately begins to tell the most wonderful stories. They say all the tales ever told since the dawn of time are in this vat. Now come, we must leave this place and find your wolf.'

She found herself wishing that Nick were with her to see what she had seen. She told herself that she needed to see what the Story Vat stood on. If they were, by some magic, to overturn it so that all the colours spilled back into the world, it would have to stand on something tiltable, like a wood-cutting wedge. She kept looking hard as the stairs wound their way round the vat and down.

Going down was not so difficult because the smell and the stinging in her eyes receded. However, the colours still dazzled them and cast a rainbow over everything she looked at. Below the vat it was as dark and still as when she had left it. The Keeper in the white coat ushered them out solemnly and shut the door behind them.

'Is it kept locked?' Chinku asked.

'No,' Nostromo replied. 'No one goes into that room willingly. At least, none of the children do and the guards are kept terrified by stories of memory altering.'

They came down the stairs and went past the guards. As they did so there was a sound like a growl and Nick came scampering out of another corridor followed by shouts of, 'Catch him! There he is ...' The two guards nearby looked at each other, wondering whether to move or not, raising and lowering their Memory Tubes. Nick ran straight up to them, and leapt up at Chinku, putting his paws on her shoulders and licking her face. Her heart raced as she patted him. 'Down boy, good boy...'

'That is something achieved,' Nostromo said. 'Now if no harm has been done ....'

The people chasing Nick dashed up to where they were and came to an abrupt stop when they saw Chinku had hold of him.

'The wolf has to go to the menagerie,' one of them said panting. 'If he escapes again ....'

Chinku clutched Nick hard, almost strangling him. He uttered a muffled yelp.

One of the guards said, 'Sir, if word of this gets around, the King will not spare the wolf ....'

'It was bad enough,' Nostromo answered, 'that he was allowed to enter the royal nurseries. Yes, it certainly seems as if the menagerie would be the best place, but this child will have to practice with him everyday...'

'Surely the Lady would not wish ...'

'I have no instructions from the Lady to discontinue the performance,' Nostromo answered. 'My orders are clear and I must do whatever is required to carry them out.' He looked at Chinku and Nick for a long moment before saying, 'Perhaps it would be possible for the wolf to share my quarters. There he might not find it so easy to escape.' It seemed obvious that Nostromo would win. He faced the men with such certainty and confidence. 'In any case,' he said, 'the wolf did not escape from this child here. It escaped...'

The guards did not let him finish the sentence, 'Yes, yes, we know all that.'

'This would be the best way,' Nostromo told them. 'He can be removed quietly to my quarters without disturbing the whole palace. For those who know of the wolf's escape, we will allow them to think that he was recaptured and removed from the palace. In fact bring this child too. He can stay there as well. No one, as you know, escapes from my quarters.'

Nick's furry ear was over Chinku's mouth. 'I saw the Story Vat,' she whispered into the ear while the guards and Nostromo were talking. The ear flicked and Nick stiffened. However, she did not dare say more.

The Wise One turned to her and said, 'Follow me.'

Nostromo's quarters, as he called them, were a series of rooms that opened out one from another. There was a balcony at the very end, which looked out on the gardens below with a wall immediately underneath edged with the teeth of broken glass. Nostromo told Chinku, 'Escape is impossible. When I first came to the palace I would sit and plot so many times and so many ways. Then I thought the best way was to submit.' As they were looking down into the garden, Nick had quietly turned back into a boy. He came out onto the balcony and stood beside them. Nostromo started slightly then held out his hand, 'It is good to meet you in your true shape. You have the look of someone I once met.'

'My grandfather,' Nick told him.

'Lobo ...' Chinku asked Nick, 'Where did you go?'

'I went looking for the corridor that led to the Story Vat, but I kept running into guards everywhere. I thought I'd wait for night to fall before trying again. Anyway, you've seen it. Now what do we do?' He sounded a little annoyed that Chinku had seen it before he had, but she did not blame him for that. It was something they should have done together. Quick as thought she twiddled with the hollow of her button and pulled out the nail. Without words she held it out to Nick and, equally wordlessly, he put his eye to it.

'What is that?' Nostromo asked.

'It's a nail from his village,' Chinku said. 'It captures images of whatever it sees.' In all the passing back and forth it was a lucky thing that it had stayed in Chinku's tunic. Nick had his eye to it for a long time. Then he finally raised his head with a deep sigh.

'I wish I had been there. But now we must work out how to get all the memories out of the vat.'

'What is this?' Nostromo asked. 'That same desperate dream of yours?' So the two children told him how their trip to Kalabash had come about, though this time they told him about the message of the matrix stones. Chinku took them out of her pocket and showed him the stones as still as marbles. Nostromo took up the stones and spun them this way and that, but no light reflected from their surfaces.

'Strange,' he said, 'what has happened to these stones?'

Chinku murmured, 'Dragons,' and then glanced quickly at Nick. He did not know that Nostromo was here of his own free will and she wasn't sure how to tell him that.

'Dragons? There are no dragons in the palace except the Lady with her dragon's blood and the sculptor that came from Dragonara.'

Nick suddenly asked, 'Sir, how were you captured?'

'Not captured exactly. In the beginning the King sent for storytellers from far and wide. He wanted as many of them as he could to keep the Lady and his sons entertained. He was offering good gold. So we all flocked to the palace. It was only when we were here that we realized we were prisoners. Those who chose not to cooperate with the King had their memories stolen. I preferred to keep my memories and continue telling stories and teaching others to do the same. At least that way I could remember my dear wife as I had left her.'

'You could have escaped,' Chinku said indignantly.

'And gone where? They would have sent the Shadow Riders to my wife's tavern. I would have brought disaster on them all.'

'But the stones told me to come here,' Chinku pointed out. 'There must be a reason.'

'There is a tank on the palace roof where all the memories are gathered. They are then filtered through the tubes into the vat. The room itself has no outlet, or so it seems. When she showed it to me, the Lady said that it was built by a very special kind of magic.'

'And what do the old stories say about the dragons?' asked Nick.

'The stories say that the old king sent his Shadow Riders into the mountains seeking out dragons. When they finally returned, they brought with them the dragon flowers and the story of the

Kingdom of Dragonara, which they said was a human kingdom.'

'That can't be true,' Chinku said.

'It wasn't,' Nostromo agreed. 'At least, Dragonara was not human as we know it, though it was ruled by a king who walked on two legs. The dragons were a peace-loving race and lived side by side with the different peoples, even with the Wolf People. What was more important was that the Shadow Riders told the king that the dragon flowers chased away bad dreams because the last of the old dragons had turned into flowers. The old king, when he heard that, decided to make a treaty with Dragonara so that dragon flower seeds could be brought into the kingdom and planted.'

'Is that why the stone dragons are carved around the palace?'

'Yes. The old stories also talk about a girl who will one day come to save the dragons. But those stories seem to be inaccurate – part of the story cycles around the main matrix.' Chinku did not understand what a story cycle was, but she felt proud that it was to be a girl who would save the dragons.

'The stone dragons are alive,' she said, thinking what a day it was for the telling of truth. And she told him what she had seen.

He looked at her with sudden interest, 'Are you really a boy? Because if you are not, then …' And that spark she had seen before lit up his eyes again.

It really was almost too much happiness for one day to hold. Almost as much as being hugged by her parents would have been.

They had to have a plan – that was obvious. Despite being so much older than them, Nostromo did not seem to have any better ideas. All he could do was take the nail from Nick, with one ear to the door for approaching footsteps, and put it to his eye. Through the silver tunnel he too could see the marvel of the Story Vat.

'There is one thing,' he said slowly when he finally raised his head. 'To take the stones to a place distant from the palace and see if they have a story to tell there.'

'Can you read them?' Chinku wanted to know. 'Because I cannot.' Nostromo admitted that he could not either.

'Then Nick will have to go with us,' Chinku said. 'He is the only one who can read the stones after a fashion.'

Nostromo felt it would not be too difficult to take Nick out of the palace as a wolf and smuggle him back in human form. He said it might even be easier that way, especially if he said the wolf was behaving wildly and it would be better to release him outside the castle walls. The guards, he said, would only be too happy to see the last of the wolf, because if the story of Nick's escape spread, their memories would be in danger.

Nick said, 'Don't they already know?'

'You would be surprised to know how slowly word spreads here. No one wants the King to hear about their mistakes. Too many people have lost their memories altogether.'

The man was cautious for someone so wise, though Chinku had observed that grown-ups were usually slower to act than children. They would say, 'Hang on, wait, there might be something dangerous lurking in there.' And think and think until the children went mad with tension. It had been so easy for both of them – Nick had just run out and then the rest of the events had fallen into place. As if he understood her thoughts, Nostromo said, 'Even if you are the Chosen One, nothing is to be gained by rushing. I will have to ask the Lady for permission. And that can only be granted after you have performed for her one more time.'

'I have to tell her that story again, the way you told it to me?' Chinku asked in disbelief.

'Yes,' said Nostromo. 'It is the only way. No,' because Chinku had leapt up, 'listen to me. The wolf will be part of this storytelling. He will pretend after a while to be gloomy and put his tail between his legs. The Lady cannot bear gloom in her presence, in man or beast. That will give me an opportunity to ask.'

Without waiting to listen to their arguments, he went to his door and opened it – unlike their turret room, Nostromo's door was left unlocked. However, Chinku and Nick, hiding behind a curtain since he was taken unawares, both caught a glimpse of a guard outside.

'Tell the Lady I wish to present my pupil's first efforts to her tonight. Send me a page and I will entrust the message to him.' He shut the door again.

'You are lucky,' he told Chinku, 'that there are very few stories about the Chosen One. A girl with a pet wolf would cause no end of chaos in the palace!'

'Does the King know about the Chosen One?' Nick asked.

'No. Most people have never even heard the story, but I found it in the Story Vat once.' He shivered, 'That was a bad day.'

'In what sense?' the children asked.

'The Dream Stealers had returned with more memories. I was still new here and terrified because with each one of their raids they travelled closer and closer to my wife. The fear paralysed me that day as I was telling a story to the Lady.'

He had sat in front of her in the ceremonial storyteller's fashion and found that he could not remember a single word of the elaborate tale he had been telling. He sat there wishing the earth would swallow him up. Nothing like that had ever happened to him in all his storytelling days.

'I don't know why it happened,' he said again. 'Perhaps it was that golden woman who sat there like a statue waiting for me to make her smile. I would not have minded the princes so much, horrible as they are ...' The Lady had of course become impatient. 'At Kalabash they have always been impatient, easily bored, they are constantly on the lookout for something new. Almost like ...' Nostromo was going to say 'children' but he looked at the two who were sitting there staring at him and quickly changed the sentence. 'Almost like some women I know,' he finally said.

Chinku asked, 'But then what happened to you?'

Nostromo shook his head sadly, 'As I sat there, the Queen clapped her hands and three of the pages came running. She told them to go to the Keeper of the vat and ask him for a drop. I did not know then what it meant, of course. There followed an interminable period of waiting which was filled by one of the Queen's ladies who displayed her juggling talents. She took up fruits from a bowl, soft squishy kumquats and threw them in the air so skillfully that they circled like green shooting stars, even seeming to glint in the light of the torches. I sat huddled and miserable in the middle having given up the idea of even looking for another starting sentence. Nowadays I do my best to ensure it does not happen to any of my students, which is why they are taught singing and dancing as well.

'The pages returned escorting a man in a white coat. He held up a long splinter of what looked like a rainbow. The colours were so vibrant that it seemed he was holding the living colours between his fingers. Looking at that play of emerald and jade and peacock's tail would have been enough to set my tongue rolling again, but the man came close, so close that I could feel his breath on my cheek. And then I felt a pain as if a splinter of ice had stabbed me. He was so quick that I did not realize he had jabbed my arm with the tip of the rainbow. For a minute there was a streak of blood and then the colours started flowing under my skin, spreading up and up and up ...' before he had known it, the words had started rolling off his tongue. The story had completed itself and he had sat there in all the wonder and pain of the colours, not knowing it.

Chinku and Nick sat there for a while wondering what it would be like to have a rainbow spread up your arm. Nostromo told them his tongue had never moved so quickly, but after it was over, he could not remember a single word of the story.

'It was probably one of the most wonderful stories I ever told,' he said, 'but it is gone. In any case, we cannot sit around like this. I have to prepare the message for the Lady.'

There was of course a format for submitting proposals to the Lady. The request had to be written in the form of a poem, a fourteen-line sonnet, Nostromo told them, as he chewed the end of his pen and crossed and uncrossed lines. If the sonnet amused the Lady, she would pass the request. Nostromo changed a word and muttered that it would all have to be written out afresh. By the time he was finally satisfied Fowler had arrived and was standing in the doorway shuffling from foot to foot while Nick, who had changed back into a wolf, was tied to the balcony railings. Fowler took the poem on a golden cushion and dashed away with it. He walked as if he were on wheels Chinku thought, with tiny mincing little steps.

'Don't tell me,' she said to Nostromo, 'that is the court walk for a page delivering a message to the Lady?'

'Quite right,' said Nostromo. 'As to the Land of the Dragons, I have never heard reports of dragons in Dragonara for generations. And the Lady would be the last person to keep such a secret to herself. What I do know is that the stone dragons were sculpted by a craftsman from her kingdom. After he sculpted the dragons, his memory was taken from him so that his gift could be passed down to generations of sculptors at will.'

'And what happened to him?' Nick asked. 'He has a room in one corner of the palace. He can't sculpt a thing now, because he does not remember how to, but he is treated as an honoured guest. That is more than the Lady does for most people.'

Perhaps it was because she was a Dragon Princess that she covered herself in that gold paint, Chinku thought, and felt sorry for the poor sculptor. 'If you splashed him with fluid from the Story Vat would he regain his memory?' she asked aloud.

'Quite possibly,' Nostromo replied, 'but no one can do that without permission from the King.'

The rest of the day was dull. Fowler did not return, though trays of food came and went. Nostromo could not leave the room as long as they were there. Nor did he want to take Chinku and Nick wandering round the castle until he had the required permission. Chinku and Nick looked out at the narrow strip of grass below the window and waited and waited. Nick turned himself from wolf to boy and wolf again in a series of ripples that seemed to be the air moving.

'Can't you tell us stories?' Chinku finally demanded of Nostromo. 'We heard you are the best storyteller in the world.' So he sat them down and told them all the stories that he knew of the Chosen One, a girl who was destined to come out of the rising sun. She would be born from a sun fruit, an apricot that split into two halves and she would walk the earth with the sun glow on her.

'Definitely not,' Nick said, looking at Chinku. 'You're burnt as brown as a walnut, but that's all.'

'Stories don't always tell the truth as we know it,' Nostromo said. 'Very often they convey a deeper message.'

Chinku was too busy thinking of herself as a saviour to pay attention to what was being said. It did not seem very possible. At least if there was a saviour to be chosen she thought that Nick's mother would be a better choice, or one of the Old Ones. But then, the Old Ones had already lost their memories and none of them would have been able to hide in a rabbit's burrow. The knock on the door disturbed them. Nick quickly went out onto the balcony and prepare to change himself back into a wolf, while Nostromo went over to the door. Fowler was standing outside holding out a strip of golden parchment on a brocade cushion. Nostromo took it from him and ran his finger down the page. Chinku, who had been taught that it was not polite to read over someone's shoulder, stood shifting from one foot to another, impatiently waiting for him to finish reading.

'It is a poem,' Nostromo said. 'When beasts from the forests wide/Display their gentle selves inside/ And their true wild natures hide/ Stone walls and velvet hangings beside/The sages say/Go out and play...'

'Is it longer than that?' Chinku asked, totally missing the 'sages say' part. The jogging verse unsettled her and made her shake her head.

'The Lady has answered according to form,' Nostromo told her. 'But surely you understood the "Go out and play" part?'

He turned to Fowler, 'Was a time set for this? There is nothing in the poem.' Fowler shook his head, remembered himself and with a bow said, 'The Lady just handed me the poem. She said that she might be wandering in the gardens herself and if you chose to meet her there, she would be delighted.'

'The quicker we go down, the better. The wolf will get the fidgets out of his system and will hopefully practise with his owner and then we can decide whether it is at all worth it to inflict them on the Lady.' Nostromo sounded exactly like a bored and tired grown up.

Fowler recognized the tone and quickly withdrew. 'It is your wish, Nostromo. The guards will guide you to the gardens whenever you choose.'

'The guards?' Nostromo asked. 'In case the wolf gives you any trouble.' There was really no arguing against that. Nostromo shrugged, and said, 'Bring your wolf and let us get this over with as soon as possible. I hope the animal will behave himself.'

Chinku went out onto the balcony where Nick was draped over the railings looking down into the darkening gardens below. 'You heard that?' she asked. 'Come on. And be good.'

'Do you have the other thing?' Nostromo asked her as she led Nick through the room. She knew he meant the matrix stones.

'Yes, Wise One,' she answered. Fowler was standing at the door. He moved away hastily as she and Nick walked up, but the wolf's head did not even turn in Fowler's direction.

'Does he play?' Fowler asked timidly.

'Yes, he's exactly like a dog sometimes. But,' Chinku added, 'he doesn't like strangers petting him.' Fowler backed away, then clapped his hands and the two guards who had been escorting them appeared.

'They have to go to the gardens,' Fowler said. 'The Lady has allowed it.'

'Follow me,' Nostromo told the guards. 'If the wolf runs, I want you to let the boy run with him so that he does not escape.'

They looked sceptical but agreed. It was remarkable, Chinku thought, what a silly-sounding poem from the Lady could do.

20

Once they were out of the room, they half ran down the corridors, taking the turns dangerously fast with Nostromo running swift-footed, though not fast enough, after them.

'Wait!' he gasped. 'How will you know the way?'

'He can smell grass,' Chinku answered. 'That tells him which way to go.'

'Well, you cannot outrun the guards,' Nostromo told her, 'so please rein him in a little. I know you are excited, but the palace has rules.'

They went slower after that, but still fast enough to leave Nostromo and the guards behind. Nick pulled her round corridors and down stairs. Then he finally dragged her through a large hall, which had pillars of crystal down the centre and doors on both sides. He stopped beside one of the doors. She could see a darkening patch of green outside and glimpse the spray from a fountain. The guards and Nostromo dashed in and saw them standing there.

'Your wolf led you a little astray,' Nostromo told Chinku kindly. 'This is indeed one of the ways to the garden, but there is a proper door. I don't think these windows have been opened in years.'

At Nostromo's command the guards ushered them out of the hall into a little antechamber which had a door. Nostromo put his hand on the knob and it swung open. Both Chinku and Nick were too excited to wait. He leapt forward in a wolfish spring and she sprang after him so that they landed in an angle of legs and paws on the grass.

'I'll have to slip the leash,' Chinku told Nostromo, 'so perhaps you should have the door shut.'

The guards looked doubtfully at each other, but Nostromo went and shut the door.

'As long as he comes back when you call and does not interfere with anything in the garden, it should be safe,' he told her. 'And of course, as long as he does not attack the guards.' That made the guards fidget uncomfortably.

'You heard that,' Chinku told the wolf. 'Now bow your head to show that you understand. Bow!' Nick slowly inclined his head.

'That in itself is a tale for the Lady,' Nostromo said. When Chinku slipped the leash, the guards visibly cringed. Nick, however, ignored them and went bounding in the direction of the fountain. That too was a dragon, its head arched back to let an arc of fine rainbow spray out into the last rays of the sun. Chinku, still sitting on the grass quietly took the matrix stones from her pocket and cast them. Her palms were sweating out of sheer nervousness. Perhaps it was too early for it to seem natural – too early for her to start being bored enough to play with her marbles. However, there was no time to waste. She hoped that the dragon fountain would not interrupt the stones but when she took them out, they did not look like dead marbles. And they flashed their crosses as they rolled onto the grass.

One of the guards showed signs of interest. 'What is that?' he asked and began to walk over. At that moment Nick chose to bound back. The guard hastily stayed where he was. The wolf stood in front of Chinku and cocked his head at the flashing stones; Nostromo came over to see.

'You do not have long, child,' he said. 'You must leash your wolf now.' The beams of light from the stones crossed each other.

'Wake the dragons,' said a small growl, a very low growl from Nick who dared not be heard. His muzzle was tickling Chinku's ear. 'Wake the dragons.'

Chinku quickly put the stones in her pocket and leashed Nick. Her head was spinning because this seemed even worse than before.

How were they to wake the dragons, unless she was to run all over the palace throwing scraps of meat to the statues? And once the dragons were awoken, then what?

The guards led them back to Nostromo's room, visibly relieved that the wolf had not escaped. When Chinku told Nostromo what the stones had said, he was no happier.

'There must be something in the old stories,' he said, after a long silence. 'But the only person who has actually seen dragons is that old sculptor.'

'If we gave him back his memory?' Chinku asked, 'Wouldn't that help?' She was suddenly bubbling over with the thought.

Nostromo looked at her. 'I begin to understand why you were being trained as a Memory Keeper. I am sure you have some idea of how this could be done?'

Nick in his human shape said, 'That's easy. All you have to do is say that she needs a dose of memory to prepare her for the storytelling session.'

He and Chinku looked at each other and grinned. Sometimes, they thought, grown-ups underestimated children, especially when it came to rule-breaking ideas.

Nostromo thought that it would be best to try the attempt the following afternoon. 'You will have another practice session with me in the morning. The other children will be there and you must be certain to perform badly,' Nostromo said. 'In fact, the more people who see you do it, the better. Then at least we have a chance.'

Chinku said, 'The dragons wake when you feed them though. I wish we had some meat in the garden for the fountain dragon ...'

When they finally did go to sleep, they all slept very badly. In the morning they were all silent and listless. Nick changed back to a wolf again as soon as the knocks on the door began. It was not hard for Chinku to put on a bad performance. Excitement and lack of sleep made her fumble in front of all the other children. Nostromo corrected her twice, three times. At the fourth stumble he warned her to be careful. 'The Lady is not as patient a listener as we are.' And to add to the tension, Fowler came running with a message from the Lady, in verse again, demanding to know whether the ramble in the garden had been useful for the wolf.

Nostromo read out two sentences and said, 'Even if the wolf is prepared, it is quite obvious that you are worse than before. I think a trip to the Story Vat may improve your memory.' There was a mutter from the other children and a few sympathetic glances thrown at Chinku.

Nostromo said, 'Tell the Lady that we should be ready to present tomorrow evening. No, I will go to her myself and give her the news. Request an audience from her for me this evening. As to the wolf, tie him to a window and do not go near him.'

He held out his hand to Chinku. When Chinku took it, she found that it was sweating slightly. Well it was more dangerous because now they would have to steal a few drops of potion from the room.

Almost in a dream she wound her way through the corridors and up the stairs again through the curves of the mirage tunnel till they were standing outside the door of the room. Nostromo looked down at her once before opening the door. They stepped into that place of shadow and light and the man in the white coat materialized again. 'That child yet again?' he asked. 'Surely he must be a glutton for punishment.'

'A bad performance,' Nostromo said. 'The Queen allowed them out of the palace last night and the result is that this boy is wandering in the head.'

'Sometimes the smell is enough to restore the memory,' the white-coated man suggested.

'A drop of the fluid,' Nostromo said. 'Surely that would be enough?'

The man looked hard at Chinku. 'Are you sure a few hours' stirring would not be a better treatment? The fluid can be volatile and its effects on children have not yet been established. The younger they are, the sharper their memories.'

'Not all children have a natural talent for storytelling,' Nostromo said. 'But yes, you may be right. Let me take Chinku upstairs and set him to stirring the vat.'

Obediently, she went up the stairs after him and that smell grew stronger and stronger around them. 'If you stir hard enough,' he muttered, 'I might be able to bottle a few splashes without anyone being wiser. But stir clumsily as if you were not used to it.' He took her right to the edge where the colours swam, shifting and melting into each other and pulled down one of the great rods. He put the rod into the vat. Immediately, the lights seemed to flow up it. Chinku clung to it and found it hard to move. The rainbows seemed to resist her efforts while the smell filled her eyes and nose. Blindly, she pushed as hard as she could. The rod moved a little. Then a little more. With her eyes shut tight, she pushed as hard as she could. Something stung her hand like a cold lash and she flinched and almost lost her grip.

'Harder,' Nostromo said. 'You are not putting any effort into it. Lazy child – and you think you will tell stories in front of the Lady!'

His hand was on her back pushing her forward. She tried to open her eyes once but found them stinging so that she shut them again involuntarily. The rod moved so slowly that she was afraid Nostromo would not be able to catch any drips at all. She pushed and pushed. The rod seemed stuck.

'Please,' she whispered, unaware that she was whispering aloud. 'Please ...' And then suddenly it moved so fast that she found herself thrown hard against the rim of the vat.

'How did you do that?' Nostromo asked, amazed. 'The rod has never moved so fast before.'

'I said *please*,' she whispered, finding her feet again. 'Was that magic?' Magic or not, the rod moved, stirring like a spoon through sludgy porridge, but moving easier than before. She still could not see whether Nostromo had managed to capture a drop. She groped and pushed and groped and pushed.

'I'm going,' Nostromo said quietly. 'He'll find it odd if I stand here with you. The children perform their punishments by themselves.' And then there was space next to her, a stirring of the air. So he had managed to do it, she thought, gripping the slippery rod and grimly pushing it forward. Colours lapped the edge as she had seen them before.

The colours were nameless, some of them – the tint of a sunlit wall on a summer afternoon, or that of a young spring moon or a round pebble glimpsed through mossy water. Those were the peaceful shades that rode the swell and swirled away as her rod swirled. But then there was the pale no-colour of a drowned man's lips as she had seen them once on the lake shore before her father had quickly hustled her away, scolding till she was safely delivered into her mother's arms.

She wondered whether the nail in her collar was taking them all in for Nick. Shrieking pink with jaws reared up at her and splashed down again before she could drop the rod in sheer fright. What bad memory was that, she wondered, though could not associate it with any nightmare at all except limp hair ribbons on a rainy day. Still she was glad that the pink had not snapped at her knuckles as it seemed it was going to do. Tangerine lights took over, blinking in mesmerizing dots above the silver rim, contracting to pinpoints and then opening to the size of sunflowers. She tried to look away from them as well because she saw egg yolks dancing in front of her eyes.

After a while she lost count of time in her whirling thoughts, moving mechanically with the rod round and round the platform. Ages passed and even more ages. Then she heard scuffing sounds and the metallic ring of the spiral staircase treads.

It was Nostromo. He said, 'It is over. Now come downstairs and tell us your story.'

Chinku blinked and saw him standing there through a haze of rainbow fog. Letting go of the rod she followed him down the stairs. Getting her balance was hard with the smell and the reeling thoughts in her head. As soon as they reached the bottom, the white-coated man came and stood before them.

'Is it sufficient?' he asked.

'Tell us your story,' Nostromo said. And pushing at her thoughts, the way she had pushed at the memories in the vat, she began.

They did not talk till they were through the shell of the corridor again.

'Did you take the potion to the sculptor?' Chinku asked in a low voice. She noticed Nick was still not there and half her mind was worried about him.

'Yes,' Nostromo said. 'I am taking you back there now.' He walked through another corridor and round a corner to a door that stood open. An old man was in the room.

'Draconis,' said Nostromo. The man turned and Chinku bit her lip to stop herself crying out. He was silver from head to foot, the rainbow colours running down him as he caught the light from the window, scaled almost like a dragon round his throat. When he looked at them, she saw that his eyes had long slit pupils.

He said, 'How long has it been?'

'Years,' Nostromo told him. 'Don't you remember?'

'I remember finishing the designs for Princess Draga, carving the last flick of the tails. They said I was tired and brought me to a room, a dark room where a man stroked my head with something …' The slit eyes were frighteningly snake-like, but looked calmly into them. This was the first person she had seen who had drunk the potion, and it seemed to be working. 'Who is this child?' he asked, stopping in his story.

'Someone who needs your help,' Nostromo said calmly.

'My help? To do what?'

'To wake the dragons.'

Draconis's slit pupils grew even longer. 'I carved them in stone,' he said, 'not out of dragon flesh and scale.'

'But they are alive,' Chinku said. 'They eat meat.'

The slit eyes searched her up and down. 'This is not a boy,' Draconis said to Nostromo, the scales around his throat rippling. 'This is a girl.' The eyes were cold and his voice was almost a hiss. 'What treachery is this?'

Nostromo seemed unmoved. 'If you know that,' he said, 'and you are the only one who does, then you surely know the old story.'

'The Chosen One? That story?'

'Yes.'

The two of them looked at each other. Draconis turned his gaze on Chinku again.

'And if I awoke the dragons for you, what would you do with them?'

'Restore everyone's memories,' she said simply. How the dragons were to do that, of course, she could not tell. Perhaps they would fly away with the palace on their wings. Perhaps ...

'Then perhaps that can be done, though that would mean the end of the Empire of Kalabash and my master's daughter.'

He could read minds she thought, almost like Nick, and then she looked into the slit eyes and tried to force some other thought into her head.

'Would that be a bad thing?' Nostromo asked. The two looked at each other, then the two men were suddenly shaking hands.

'It will be good to end an Empire,' Draconis was saying. 'And perhaps restore the stories to all our people.'

'But how will you do it?' Chinku asked. The slit eyes swivelled to her, 'On the night of the Dragon's Moon,' he answered, 'I will say the magic word.' It sounded terribly impressive as he announced it with the light glimmering on his scales. She was already not thinking of him as human at all. But then, Nick was not human either, was he? A boy who changed from wolf to boy at will could not really be called human. She was about to ask when the Dragon's Moon was when Nostromo quickly hustled her out of the room.

'Nick is still tied in the hall,' he said. 'He has never been left out on his own for so long before. At least not chained.' They were half running as they reached the hall, but when they got there, Chinku saw that there was nothing to worry about, Nick was still leashed and sitting patiently where they had left him. 'We tried to pat him,' one or two of the children told Chinku reproachfully, 'but he snarled at us.'

'He's not a tame wolf,' Chinku said, 'but he's my friend. He'll let you touch him if I tell him to.' She quickly untied him, wondering whether Nick's mother had seen it all in the silver bowl and kept watch over her son. Then she said to the other children, 'You can pat him now.' Nick gave her a disapproving glance out of his amber eyes but stood there suffering the hands that touched and patted him, and one or two that tweaked his ears. Finally, they were allowed to return to Nostromo's rooms. Nick's hair was standing on end when he changed back into his normal self. 'Don't you ever do that again,' he told Chinku fiercely.

'But why did you growl at them?' she asked.

'Because they were talking about taking me for a walk through the palace,' he said.

Nostromo intervened, 'He did wisely. If the children had taken him elsewhere who knows what would have happened?'

Nick interrupted, rudely for him, but everyone understood it was because he was so excited. 'Did you find the sculptor? Did it work?'

Nostromo told him the story in brief.

'And did he say *when*?' Nick asked eagerly.

'The Dragon's Moon,' Chinku told him. 'He said he would do it on the Dragon's Moon. When is that?'

Nick suddenly fell into silence and Chinku understood why.

'The Dragon's Moon,' said Nostromo, 'is a term from the old Hunter's Almanac. It is a moon like the glimmer of a Dragon's slit eye. There will be one very soon.'

'Is it a full moon?' Chinku asked, looking anxiously at Nick.

'The Farmer's Almanac names only the Full Moons. The Dragon's Moon is also known as the Full Red Moon because of its colour when you see it rise through the haze,' Nostromo said. 'Don't your villagers name the moons?'

'Yes,' Chinku said, and put up her hand and began to count them through her fingers, 'There is the Crow Moon, the Strawberry Moon, the Sturgeon Moon when the fish rise in the lake and spawn…' Even as she spoke she kept her eyes fixed on Nick's face. 'And there is the Wolf's Moon in January when …'

'When amid the cold and deep snows of midwinter, the wolf packs howl hungrily outside the gates of the villages …' Nick was quoting from the same almanac. Was it that late, was it time for another Full Moon again?

'What is the matter?' Nostromo asked, looking from one child to the other. Nick's eyes gleamed suddenly amber and he turned away and went out onto the balcony.

'Wolves,' Chinku said, 'and the moon.'

She did not want to say any more. The memory of that night was something she knew Nick would not want to share. Nostromo looked at her with the beginnings of understanding in his eyes, but he did not ask further. Instead, he went out onto the balcony and stood in the early evening light beside Nick, the two of them bathed in tranquil pale pink and black light. Peaceful colours, Chinku thought, unlike the turbulence she had seen in the Story Vat.

After a while they came back in again. 'Until the Dragon's Moon and Draconis's plan,' Nostromo told Chinku, 'you two will have to continue as if there were nothing wrong. Which means you will have to prepare for your story session with the Lady. So tomorrow it will be back to practice again.'

Chinku stood there looking at Nick and thinking that a great deal of the excitement had gone. Whatever happened on the night of the Dragon's Moon, Nick could not be a part of it.

22

The days that followed seemed remarkably dull to Chinku. They were allowed the run of the palace as long as Nostromo was with them and all he wanted to talk about was Demetra, now that the matter of the Story Vat and wakening the dragons seemed to be settled. Chinku wondered how her parents were and thought of mornings by the lake with the other girls and boys of her village. Even her clothes which were left far behind. As her mind wandered over dresses and fabric turning and twisting as it was washed, she suddenly thought of the strips into which she had plaited the story of that moonlit night. 'My clothes,' she said to Nostromo, 'my red and black clothes. I left something in the pockets.'

Nostromo asked, 'Another magical nail?'

She shook her head, trying to remember whether she had hidden them with the other tunics under the shadow cloaks. 'No, it is important only to me. I'm forgetting my memory lessons.'

'If Draconis works his magic, the Old Ones will be able to teach you again,' Nick said, with a dull edge to his voice. When Nostromo was not there, she tried to talk to him about it, but he would hang his head and Chinku did not know what to say or do.

Nostromo considered the plan about going back to the turret room very carefully.

'Though if I say that you left something behind there, they may be suspicious. Perhaps if you told me what it was, I could go on my own and bring it to you.'

Chinku told him about the plaits she had knotted.

'But what did you knot into the plaits?' he asked.

'That's a secret,' she said, glancing quickly at Nick.

'All right,' he said, 'I will try. This at least will be less dangerous than stealing drops from the Story Vat.'

Feeling sorry for not being able to tell him what she had knotted, Chinku said, 'And if you take a piece of meat with you, you can watch the dragons come alive.'

When Nostromo was gone, Chinku turned to Nick, 'What will you do when the Dragon's Moon rises?'

Nick did not answer her. 'What did you send him to get? What have you left in the room?'

'My notes,' she said, 'stories about you that I put down as the Old Ones taught me.' Nick shuffled around the room, not really listening to what she was saying. He looked towards the sliver of sky that could be seen from the balcony. 'I could escape,' he said, 'jump down from the balcony.'

'Only a cat could do that,' Chinku told him. 'I don't think a wolf could.'

'Supposing Nostromo reads whatever it is that you put down in your notes?'

Chinku pointed out that not everyone understood the language of knots, especially not an outsider. 'You might because your mother is one of us. But no one seems to know where Nostromo comes from.'

'For a storyteller,' said Nick, 'he's very silent. If he's talked to my grandfather, he would know what happens to wolf people at the time of the full moon.'

It was a very bad kind of gift, Chinku thought. It had been given to them to ensure that they would not starve and yet on one night every month, they had no control over what they did. Impulsively, she put out her hand and caught Nick's.

'Don't,' he said, 'I'm trying to see how I can escape.'

'By changing shape? Will you be able to jump down and miss those spikes?' They both went out to the balcony and peered over the rails. Certainly the space between the walls and the spear topped railings looked incredibly narrow. Fur was bristling through Nick's skin – Chinku still had her grip on his hand in case he jumped without telling her. 'I want you to be there,' she said, 'when the dragons finally come to life. I want you to see the Story Vat for yourself.'

The door in the room behind clicked and Chinku found herself holding a wolf's paw.

'You were lucky. No one bothered to search the room,' Nostromo was holding up the strips of hide in his fist. 'What are these? I have seen something like them in the accounting system that the Mountain People use. Quipus they call them, where each knot stands for a hundred or a ten.'

Chinku took the strips from him. 'Here each double knot means an article,' she explained. 'This is one of the ways in which the Old Ones teach us to keep secrets, especially secret records of history.'

'Secrets – what secrets would someone so young have?' Nostromo asked. He was smiling as he said it and Chinku realized that the question was not serious, though at the same time she resented his assumption that children could not have any secrets worth keeping.

'It is a record,' she said, 'of the day when the Dream Stealers came and stole our memories.'

Nostromo's smile ebbed from his lips. 'I had forgotten that. However,' he added, 'they are aware that a suit of clothes is missing. In all this confusion Fowler has not been able to come to ask you where they are, but he remembers and so do the guards at the foot of the stairs. They asked me about them. I could truthfully answer that I did not know.'

'If Nick stays a wolf,' Chinku answered, 'they will never be able to find them.'

'But the royal laundries are very careful about details like these. They will need an answer. Be prepared for Fowler.' Chinku pocketed her plaits and said nothing further. They could return the clothes of course and perhaps Nick could wear some of Nostromo's, but that would mean going up and moving the cloaks. She looked worriedly at Nick but he was not looking at her. And she was not sure whether she wanted to talk about the cloaks at all, even though they were Demetra's.

The children in the hall were wary of Nick now and watched Chinku dance with him in wide-eyed amazement. Fowler came once briefly and stood at the entrance watching, but said nothing about the missing clothes. The other pages tiptoed by several times.

Nostromo finally thought that it was time to present Chinku's formal story to some of the lords and ladies of the court and sent a poem request around.

When the winds caress the air

Out into the garden fair ...

He had thought it best to stage it in the garden by the dragon statue. Chinku would have to have new clothes for the occasion and Nick would have to be brushed and trimmed, perhaps even bathed if the Master of Revels thought it appropriate.

The Master of Revels was formally dressed in a blue and purple robe with a silver wreath around his head. He looked Chinku up and down and tilted her chin. 'The child's hair needs trimming,' he observed. 'When do you plan to present his performance to the Lady?'

'That will depend on the response the Court gives him tonight,' Nostromo answered. 'Perhaps it would be better to reserve the hair trimming at this stage and wait till the Lady summons the boy.'

'But the Lady has seen me,' Chinku pointed out.

'With shorter hair,' Nostromo retorted. 'For a boy your hair is remarkably long.' When the Master of Revels had left he said, 'If you hair grows any longer, people will soon start to think that you look more like a girl than a boy.'

Nick growled, 'The Dragon's Moon is not too far away. Supposing the Lady chooses to have us perform on that night?'

'Draconis says that the Dragon's Moon is known only to a few. Lady Draga has done her best to forget all dragon customs except the more pleasant ones.'

The royal tailor came and measured Chinku for new clothes and the old blue ones were taken away once she had carefully emptied the pockets and given the nail into Nostromo's safekeeping. She was brought a new tunic which seemed to be no colour at all first, but when it caught the light, greens and blues and purples swirled. It was almost as wonderful as the Story Vat – or at any rate, wonderful for a piece of fabric.

Nostromo said, 'If you were a music student it would be red and gold and orange. Do your formal best in the evening and let us hope that everything goes well.'

Chinku was a little full of herself – after all, she had already danced once with Nick in front of the Lady without any preparation at all. And then there had been the story she had told in Demetra's inn. She danced the fabric up and down the room until she was tired of its feel. Then she realized that Nick was standing there quietly with his eyes glued to the end of the Spy Nail. 'What are you looking at?' she asked.

'The Story Vat, since I am never likely to set eyes on it.'

'If Draconis awakens the dragons we can be certain that the whole world will set eyes on it,' Nostromo tried to console him. 'Now change back into a wolf and let Chinku brush you. They will probably bring a new collar to put around your neck.'

He was right. The new collar seemed to be made of hammered metal, brass and silver, though it was light and bent easily.

'This cannot be removed until the person who put it on wills it so,' the Master of Revels told Chinku. 'It also ensures that if the wolf escapes, it will signal his whereabouts to anyone looking for him.'

'And how does it do that?' Chinku asked.

'There is a voice detector in it. The voice screams out loud. This is only being given to you this evening, since it would be unwise ...'

'To let a wild animal loose in the palace gardens,' Chinku completed, a little insolently. However, she thought she could get away with the insolence for once.

The Master of Revels looked at Nostromo, 'This one is asking for another session by the Story Vat.'

'After the performance this evening,' Nostromo answered. 'But you are right. Apologize at once, Chinku. How dare you say any such thing when your wolf has already escaped once and frightened the children?'

Reluctantly, Chinku apologized. And even more reluctantly she fitted the collar around Nick's neck. He pranced uncomfortably when it clicked shut, but settled down again. Then she took up the silken brush they had brought her and stroked his coat with it. He stood perfectly still under the brush as Nostromo and the Master of Revels observed her. 'Perhaps a touch of silver rain would make him shine more,' the Master of Revels said thoughtfully.

Nostromo seemed to know what it was. 'Has it been used on animals before?'

'Once or twice,' the Master of Revels answered. 'It would be a good evening to test it before the final performance.' He bustled away and returned with a tube that looked very like the Memory Stealers'. Nostromo had already explained to the children that all it contained was the essence of silver that made things glisten. The Lady used it to put shine into fountains, to coat a dancer's skin, to give flowers the look of precious metal – she used it in fact on anything she pleased. Chinku, politely, asked the Master of Revels to let her spray it on Nick.

'Lightly then,' the Master of Revels cautioned. 'Just one pass with the spray.'

He handed her the tube and she gingerly pointed it at Nick. A cloud of silver filled the air briefly, so briefly that she almost thought she had imagined it. But then she saw Nick shimmering, as if something had lit him up. 'How long will it last, Jaxartes?' Nostromo asked.

'Long enough,' the Master of Revels replied, studying Nick. 'Just make sure that they do not go rushing around. Rushing air disturbs the silver.'

When he was gone, Nostromo told Nick that he had better sit quietly on the balcony in wolf form. There was no knowing what would happen if he changed his shape. Nick quietly obeyed him, looking even more depressed.

23

Eventually, story time came. Chinku slipped into her new tunic and twirled around in front of the long mirror that stood in one corner of Nostromo's rooms. It was odd she thought how the people of Kalabash excelled at things that were unreal and artificial, but could not do a simple thing like tell a story straight. The Master of Revels came into the room and walked around her to see that nothing was crushed. 'Now bring that animal,' he told her. Chinku went to the balcony, clipped the leash onto Nick's new collar and brought him in. Then they walked through the corridors to the gardens; the mirrors they passed reflected a rainbow figure with a silver ghost by its side.

They came out into the same patch of garden as before, by the dragon fountain.

'Be careful,' the Master of Revels warned, 'Don't get wet.' Seats had been arranged in a fan shape and those were gradually filling with ladies and gentlemen who glimmered quite as much as Nick did, though in their case with little star points of precious stones.

The Master of Revels stepped up when they were all seated, 'Gentles,' he said, 'tonight we crave your indulgence. By the light of the young moon, under the firefly glimmer of the stars, a young talent performs in front of you. A gift that creeps soft-footed on the paws of a silver wolf.' Chinku was trying so hard to take in the speech that she almost missed her cue when he twitched his fingers.

They stepped forward in a rush and she thought that it was a bad beginning. However, the soft-footed starlight, or whatever it was, at least made them shimmer as they moved through the steps of the formal routine. And as Chinku spoke her words, there were soft notes of music from behind that fell like the drops of water from the dragon's mouth.

The performance was not a long one. Nostromo had told them that the Lady was easily distracted, so it was wise to keep any entertainment short. Nick's fur, stiffened by the Silver Rain pricked Chinku's fingers and the grass tickled her feet, but those were minor things. Her tunic changed colour with the changing sky and was soon sprinkled with dots of starlight so that she was glimmering like the audience. It was not difficult, she thought, it was not difficult at all.

When it was over a few of the nobles came to congratulate Nostromo. 'Very fresh,' they said. 'And the voice hasn't broken yet so that it sounds half girl half boy, almost not quite human.'

'Birdlike,' said the ladies. 'You will be presenting them soon?' One or two of them pinched Chinku's cheek and murmured how soft it was, though they skirted cautiously around Nick. When the audience had left, Jaxartes told Nostromo that it was time to send a formal message to the Lady. 'I think she will be happy with this standard of performance. And the King may be interested too.' Nostromo was not paying attention – he was speaking to the orchestra, 'Yes, Darya, that was a good note but you came in one beat too soon. You must be careful not to do that when we finally perform. Rigel, you went off key in the …' Listening to him Chinku wondered how he knew. She had forgotten all about the music behind her, as she tried to remember her words and movements. The Master of Revels continued to speak, 'We will have to fix a suitable date. If there is a full moon next week, that may be a good evening on which to hold it.'

Chinku said, 'You will hold it out in the garden?'

Nostromo heard the words 'full moon' and 'garden'. He turned from the orchestra, 'It would be fresh certainly, to hold it in the garden, but aren't there certain ceremonies that take place during the full moon?'

'Not on all full moons,' Jaxartes said. 'I will soon discover whether this is one of those.'

'You were good,' said Nostromo to Chinku and Nick. 'But next time, pay attention to Jaxartes when he introduces you.'

Back in Nostromo's rooms Chinku said, 'Is the next full moon the Dragon's Moon?'

'It may be. We need to talk to Draconis.'

Nick, desperately trying to keep the sadness out of his voice said, 'Would someone brush this silver paint off me? And remove this collar?'

Chinku hugged him, 'I'm so sorry, I'm so sorry.' And her fingers quickly undid the collar and then she busied herself with a brush, separating the silver from Nick's fur. That was not easy because if you touched the silver rain, it vanished under your fingertips to shine somewhere else, so she found herself chasing glimmers of light here and there.

'Let Nick meet Draconis,' she said, a note of pleading creeping into her voice. 'He hasn't met him; he hasn't seen the Story Vat. And if the next full moon …'

'Is the Dragon's Moon,' Nick said hoarsely, in one of those more-wolf-than-boy voices of his.

'You know that for sure?' Nostromo asked sharply. 'Haven't you finished girl?' There was a tense snap in his voice.

'Yes, I've finished,' Chinku said, disentangling the last of the silver beads from the fur.

'Then let us take Nick to Draconis. We must talk to him before we make any other plans.' Nostromo was in so much of a hurry that Chinku did not even have time to change out of her colour of light tunic, though Nick was able to become a boy. There were still a few glints of silver on him, especially in his hair, but in the blue tunic no one would look at him twice. Nostromo hurried them down the corridors. 'It is late,' he said. 'Soon the guards will begin their nightly rounds. And someone will come to my room looking for us.'

There was a guard outside Draconis's room, a sleepy disgruntled man. The guard saw them and got reluctantly to his feet. 'This is late, Nostromo, what is the purpose of your visit?'

'To show the sculptor to my students.'

It was a very strange way of putting it, but the guard was too sleepy to ask why anyone should want to show a strange sculptor to his students at half an hour to dinner. He pointed in the direction of the door and Nostromo tapped on one of the brass knobs that studded its surface. Then he turned the knob and opened it. A sliver of yellow light sliced into the passageway. A light that was almost the colour of fire.

'He's at his strange practices again,' the guard grumbled. 'All these days he was so peaceful and then, suddenly, he's been doing these heathen things.'

'Have you reported it to anyone?' Nostromo asked casually, still holding the door a fraction open.

The guard shrugged, 'What's to report? After all, he is from the Lady's homeland.'

Nostromo opened the door carefully, almost as if he were afraid something would run out. He gestured to the children and they stepped in quickly. Nostromo shut the door as soon as he too was inside. It was like walking into a globe of fire, except that though the flames flickered around them, there was no heat. Chinku looked around to see where the fire was coming from and saw that it came from the sculptor's strange slit eyes. Draconis was seated on a chair and a kind of globe hung in the air in front of him. 'Draconis,' Nostromo said, 'supposing someone else had seen you?'

The slit pupils seemed to fold within themselves. The fire faded. Draconis blinked. 'This is a very late visit, Nostromo. And I see you bring a wolf with you.' The yellow eyes turned to Nick, and Chinku saw an answering flame leap for a second in his eyes before dying down again.

'Yes,' Nostromo said, 'he comes from that village. We wanted to talk to you urgently about the next Dragon's Moon.'

Draconis was still looking at Nick, 'And you come with a wolfboy to ask me about the Dragon's Moon? Wolves and Dragons share one moon in the year. Didn't the boy tell you that?'

'Yes, I did, but we wanted to ask you about the Dragon's Moon. We have no Hunter's Almanac and there is more than one Wolf Moon in a year.' Nick was stiff and very polite as he spoke to Draconis, but Chinku could feel him bristling.

Draconis said, 'Look out of the window.' In the sky they could see glimmering a watery moon, with cloud trails floating across it. In that light, distorted by the moving clouds, it looked like a crouching figure with a tail.

'The next full moon,' Nick said dully. 'I forgot to look at the sky.'

'Very strange, wolfboy, considering the effect the moon has on your people.' Draconis rose from the chair, Chinku would have liked to say he slithered because he seemed to move with the boneless ease of a great lizard. Half-dragon, half-human, he seemed closer to Nick in some way.

'Are there any rituals the Lady would perform on the night of the Dragon's Moon?' Nostromo asked.

'Draga, I hear, does her best to forget that dragon blood ever ran through her family's veins,' Draconis said, 'but she would probably sprinkle the wild fire in honour of her father. If she can still conjure it up, that is.'

'Which means the storytelling should be the evening before?'

'Or earlier?' Chinku asked.

'Ideally, yes. Because I intend to use the wildfire to bring the dragons to life and that would require my presence at her ceremony.'

'Where does she perform this ceremony? In the garden by the dragon fountain?' Nostromo asked.

'If she did that the whole palace would know. No, it takes place in the most secret room in the palace. Beside the Story Vat.'

'Fire beside the vat?' Nostromo frowned. 'That endangers the whole ...'

Draconis lowered his head. 'That was what she used to do when I was still sculpting the dragons. I see no reason why she should have changed her custom. I will know before that night if she intends to perform the rituals. There are certain preparations that have to be made.'

'Or,' said Nostromo, 'we could send her a request for an audience on the night of the full moon and see whether she accepts it or not. That would give us time to make our plans.'

'Not too many days are left,' Draconis said, pointing to the window again. 'The moon is growing. And it is getting late, you had better leave my room now before the guards come to find out what it is you are doing here. It was nice meeting you, wolfboy.'

Nostromo and the children wished Draconis good night and left the room. When they approached their own room, Nostromo made them slow down. 'No one must see Nick enter.'

Chinku said, 'Nick can tell us whether anyone is around. Nick?' He cautiously sniffed the air every few paces and shook his head. Nostromo opened the door and they dashed inside.

'What is wildfire?' Chinku asked Nick.

'Fire drawn from the moon, that does not burn human skin, but trees and plants can catch it. And only the dragons can conjure it.'

'He said sprinkle. How will she sprinkle wildfire next to the Story Vat? The Memory Fluid reacts to any kind of light or fire in its presence. It draws it into its heart and the fluid starts to bubble up. Apparently someone lit a torch in the room once and the fluid almost flooded the palace. That's why the room is so dark,' Nostromo told them.

'Wildfire is cold fire,' Nick said. 'It would probably not disturb the Memory Fluid.'

The children went to bed after that. Nostromo was planning to compose a sonnet inviting the Lady to a performance in the garden on the Night of the Dragon's Moon. In the sonnet he would give it another name, like Plover's Moon or Hunter's Moon. If she did not accept the invitation, it would prove something.

'I have to be out of the palace before that,' Nick whispered sleepily to Chinku.

'But aren't you glad you saw Draconis?' Chinku asked. 'Have you ever seen a half-man half-dragon before?'

'No,' Nick answered slowly. But his amber eyes gleamed in the darkness for quite a while after Chinku fell asleep.

Next day, the sonnet was sent to the Lady on the gold cushion. Nick stayed locked up in Nostromo's room, which was just as well, because Nostromo's classes kept being interrupted by courtiers who wanted to shake his hand or stroke Chinku's hair. There were even requests to meet the wolf. Chinku privately thought that Nick would have been tempted to snap at a few of them, but she smiled demurely and said thank you like a well brought-up child.

A flurry of pages came with the information that the King had heard of last night's performance and had expressed a wish to be present when Chinku and the wolf entertained the Lady.

'Am I to treat this as official?' Nostromo asked. 'Because I have just sent an invitation to the Lady. I will then have to write another one for His Majesty.'

The pages looked at one another in dismay and finally confessed that they heard someone telling someone about it.

Nostromo said, 'Then we shall have to wait on his Majesty's intentions. If he wishes to attend the performance I am sure we will be sent word by the right sources.' The pages looked crestfallen and scuttled away. Nostromo turned to the children, who were listening eagerly to all these exchanges and clapped his hands.

'Enough of this, now back to your rehearsal. And where is the Music Mistress? She should be here this morning.'

Chinku had learnt that most of the children had their individual classes on the floor below. However, for a story session they practised with Nostromo. Quite a few of them had in fact played for the Lady and were telling Chinku about it.

'I have seen the Lady,' Chinku had told them. 'And Nick and I have already danced for her without music. Have any of you seen her by daylight? Does she still glitter like metal then?'

'Yes,' said one of them, 'but she has this thing like golden armour around her throat.'

Nostromo called them back into order and told the guards not to allow any more visitors into the hall unless they were messengers from the Lady or the King. Then he took them through a new piece, which he said would help them to play as a team. Chinku had to tell a story about a little girl who went to visit her grandmother through the deep woods and who met a wolf on the way in the formal storytelling pattern.

'I want to see whether that helps you anticipate her story with your music,' he told the musicians. 'After all you all know this tale.' Chinku did her best to tell it, embroidering the woods with tapestries of flowers as she went along. She expected that the Lady would respond by the end of the class but even when Nostromo was finally satisfied with their efforts, no gold strip of paper or even Fowler came along. As she was following Nostromo back to their room she said, 'Couldn't we go out into the garden again?'

'You were out there just last night,' Nostromo answered. 'I have no reason to ask for permission again. Now be patient.'

Nick was in a bad temper when they finally returned. He was standing on the balcony just as they had left him and he did not bother to turn when they entered. 'She hasn't replied,' Chinku called out. When he didn't answer, she went out to him and caught his sleeve. He whirled round so fast that she was startled. Surely the moon could not be that close? Or perhaps it was. He said, 'I don't trust that dragon man.'

Nostromo said, 'But you have no reason to distrust him either. What is it that the philosopher said, "The enemy of my enemy is my friend"? In any case, have you forgotten the message of the matrix stones? We shall hear from the Lady very shortly. Until then, find something to amuse yourself with.'

Nick told Chinku, 'The Dragon's Moon is in three days' time. I must be out of the palace by tomorrow.' He said it very low, glancing over his shoulder to see whether Nostromo could hear them.

Chinku said, 'You could hide in one of the rooms, like our turret room. I could lock you in the garde robe, you would be safe there .... If you vanish there will be a hue and cry.'

There was a knock on the door and Nostromo said, 'Nick,' warningly. Reluctantly, Nick turned into a wolf.

It was just another courtier bubbling over with congratulations and sweets for Chinku. 'My wife sent them for the child. She said it was such a fresh performance .... Everyone is talking about it, even the Lady has heard. My wife is one of her ladies-in-waiting, as you know. When is the final performance, Nostromo? Will it be private or shall we all be bidden?'

'It might not be fresh for those who have already seen it,' Nostromo pointed out.

'But there is so little to amuse us at Court these days. It is a long time since we have had something as new as this.'

'We are waiting for word from the Lady. And perhaps from the King.'

'His Majesty is busy,' said the courtier. 'The Shadow Riders were sent to the borders this morning.'

He and Nostromo looked meaningfully at each other for a moment and then the courtier took his leave.

'Are they stealing more memories?' Chinku asked.

'The Shadow Riders are the King's army. They are dispatched to put down signs of rebellion the moment they occur. Kalabash was after all a very small kingdom. It grew only after the memory stealing rays were invented,' explained Nostromo.

'Another stolen sculptor?' Nick sneered.

Chinku said hastily to Nostromo, 'He doesn't mean to be rude, it is just that he is worried.'

'We are all worried,' Nostromo said. There was another knock on the door and he whirled around in irritation. It was a page this time with the velvet cushion that they had been waiting for. Nostromo took the message and read it.

'The Lady has asked us to reschedule the performance till later in the week, after the Moon Day. She has heard only good things and would be sorry to miss the results of my training.'

'She wrote that all in verse?' Chinku asked.

Nostromo waved the parchment at her, 'Read it if you want.' Chinku saw the elaborate lines marching down the sheet and quickly shook her head. He dismissed the page.

'We shall have to go to Draconis again. He obviously has a plan. No, perhaps I had better go by myself this time. It would look strange if I kept taking the two of you along.'

'But it was my plan,' Chinku pointed out.

'That it was. Well come along, wolf and all.'

Draconis was hardly surprised to see them or hear their news. In the daylight, his room looked almost normal and his eyes were shadowed so Chinku could not shudder at their slit pupils.

'If she is by the Story Vat,' said Nostromo, 'how will we be able to do anything with it?'

'There is more than one way to deal with that,' Draconis replied, 'especially since you have told me to wake the dragons. Even Draga herself will be half-dragon by then and subject to whatever commands them.'

'But what are we to do?'

'Wait for me in the garden by the fountain.' He looked at Nick standing there in wolf shape. 'Yes, almost completely wolf. How will you explain him away to the guards, I wonder?' Chinku thought he was a savage old man with no kindness about him. If the dragons are like that, she thought, then perhaps they should stay stone. The slit eyes turned to her as if he had read her thoughts and she flinched, but then the eyes turned away again. 'It may or may not work – it's an old spell after all, but if you say that the stones have told you ....'

'What does the spell require?'

'Nothing much, but a vial of fluid from the Story Vat would be useful .... Take the children and get me some. The quicker you do it the better, because the room will have to be prepared for Draga and that takes a good many hours.'

When they came out of the sculptor's room, the guard outside commented, 'It's strange how you and the sculptor have got so thick these days. Since he lost his memory no one else in the palace seems to have any time for him.' He said it idly, of course, but it was enough to make Nostromo hurry Chinku and Nick away.

'He should have told us about the Story Vat,' Chinku grumbled as soon as they were safely in their room.

'I agree with you,' Nostromo said. 'I am going to that room so often these days that I wonder the Keeper is not suspicious.'

'Who will you take?' Nick asked. 'You can't take her again.' He said it in an oddly excited tone of voice and then in a rush added, 'Take me.'

'Take him,' Chinku agreed. 'The Keeper surely doesn't know all the children, does he?'

'It would make more sense if I took some of the musicians that played with you.' Nostromo looked at the two eager faces confronting him and laughed. 'All right, all right, don't look at me like that. I will smuggle Nick up to the Story Vat and he can stir the pot. I hope he thanks you for it. Well Chinku, you will have to stay in the room while I take Nick to the hall.'

That was something Chinku had not expected, but she agreed. Nostromo had Nick change back into his wolf form. 'We will go out like this and then when I find a quiet place you can go back to being yourself.'

'Where do all the children come from?' Chinku asked as Nick was transforming himself again.

'Some are sent by their parents. Others are brought by bounty hunters who kidnap them from their homes. A rare few are brought by the Dream Stealers who find them wandering in devastated villages. It is not always cruel. And some of the unfortunate ones gain an education.'

'What about their parents?' Chinku asked.

'Those who have their memories stolen do not remember their loss for long,' Nostromo replied. And he and Nick left Chinku on her own with that thought sinking into the pit of her stomach, as cold as ice.

The ice stayed in her stomach and refused to melt. Even though Nostromo had a special place in the palace, what would happen if he were caught stealing from the vat? He would have to steal the fluid and then go to Draconis again with the hidden phial. Angrily she walked from one length of the room to another and out onto the balcony. To distract herself she took the matrix stones out of her pocket, though as she had feared they had reverted to being marbles again.

A crow landed on the balcony railing and startled her with its harsh croaking. She flapped her hand at it, but the bird just cocked its head at her. It was a large glossy black bird with blue lights bouncing off its feathers in the sunlight. Chinku thought that what they needed was a crow to fly up into the Story Vat Chamber and steal a beakful of the fluid, then drop it on Draconis' head. The crow ducked its head again and cawed three times with a rusty sawing edge. After a while, the bird flew away. She watched it fly up into the satiny patch of sky, trying hard to see whether she could decipher something from the way it flew, but all it seemed to say was that it might rain in the evening.

Helplessly she took the strips of hay and hide out of her tunic pocket and began plaiting them, not really knowing what she was plaiting, but doing it because it occupied her fingers. Her mother used to walk through Qlwri with a string of knotted silk between her fingers on the days when she was especially worried, or had had an argument with Chinku's father. Her fingers would run up and down the knobbles of the knots one by one and the silk would grow longer and then grow short and then long again. Was her mother doing that now, she wondered, or had she forgotten the Worry String along with everything else? In three days, or was it two, she would know whether her journey to Kalabash had been successful or not.

A scratching, clicking kind of sound distracted her. It came from the door. She went towards it and listened. The scratches continued. Then she heard Nostromo say, 'He missed his master. That's why he's bounding at the door like that.' So they were back in one piece and none of them was arrested or thrown into the Story Vat! The door opened and Nick bounded in followed by Nostromo. As he shut the door, Nick began to transform himself. The grey shape blurred, stood upright, and gradually dissolved into fluid blue air. The air thickened till it became sea then solid colour and finally Nick. His eyes were brighter than Chinku had seen for quite a while.

'I saw it!' he exclaimed, 'I saw it.'

Nostromo shushed him with a quick glance at the door. 'Yes, and he did it all,' Nostromo said. 'The Keeper would not let me go up this time. He kept me talking and talking.'

'So while stirring the vat, I stole a phialful and put it into my pocket,' Nick said happily.

'But where did you get a phial from?' Chinku asked.

'That was the strangest thing. A bird flew down from the ceiling, where the pipe goes up towards the roof. And it had a phial in its beak.'

'What kind of bird was it?' Chinku asked, suddenly alert.

'A fat glossy crow,' Nick answered. 'Large enough to be a rook or a jackdaw.'

'That bird was here,' Chinku said. 'It perched on the balcony and cawed at me thrice .... I was standing there thinking about how we needed a crow to steal the Memory Fluid in its beak. Who could have sent it?'

'Whoever sent it,' Nostromo said, 'knows that there is a way to get down to the Story Vat from the roof. It might be useful.' Nick took the phial out of his pocket and proudly held it up. In the sunlight of the room, it flashed jewel colours across the walls, almost like a diamond, but brighter and stronger. And while he was holding it up, Chinku noticed the fur on the back of Nick's hand. Part of him had stayed wolf. She decided not to point it out while he was so excited. In any case he probably knew that it was happening to him.

'How do we get the Memory Fluid to the sculptor then?' Nick asked.

'Yes,' Nostromo said, 'that will have to be my task tomorrow. Not today. Let it rest for a while.'

Nick looked at the phial again and wanted to know how long it would stay like that out of the vat. Nostromo told him that no one had ever tested that. 'In any case, we had no choice. We had to take the fluid from the Story Vat as soon as possible. Thankfully, the Keeper of the room does not know one child from another.'

The next day Nostromo managed to arrange for the children to practise in the garden again – all of them with their instruments. Chinku noticed that Nick's transformation was quicker than before and that even before he transformed, the point of a tooth could be seen, glinting sharp in the sunlight. She decided that when she had a chance she would take the matrix stones out and get Nick to read them.

The other children were filtering in by twos and threes, so she sat in the shade of the dragon fountain and took the stones out of her pocket. One of the children spotted them flashing. 'What are those?' the child asked in a high voice that turned quite a few heads.

'My marbles,' Chinku said, quickly scooping them up. Nick snarled at the child and blocked the way. Chinku said, 'Stop that!' and added hastily to the children, 'There are times when my wolf is out of temper. Don't come too close, please.' She held him by his collar, the stones clutched protectively in her fist. They had flashed twice before the child had come up. She hoped that Nick had been able to read the message.

Nostromo swept up. 'Form your ranks,' he said to the other children. 'Chinku take that wolf up to the clearing.'

From where they were standing she could see parts of the palace, the ornate stone moulding at first-floor level with carved flowers and twining leaves. Above every window was an architrave guarded by a winged dragon. Both she and Nick were distracted and late on their cues, but the orchestra seemed to be equally slow.

'I should have had you practise in the hall!' Nostromo declared. 'Where were your teachers yesterday? Atika, did you practise this morning as I asked you to?' Atika was the girl who had asked Chinku about the stones. Even though she seemed much older than Chinku, she blushed guiltily when Nostromo spoke to her and looked down at the grass. The guards were sent running for the Music Teacher.

Chinku, hugging Nick whispered, 'What did the stones say?'

'Tomorrow the dragons will fly,' said the growl in her ear. 'At least not the tomorrow, but I assume that's what the stones meant.' Nick's breath was hot, so hot that it almost scorched her cheek and it smelt more wolfish than before.

'I need to lock you in the turret room tonight,' she told him, thinking that at least he seemed better than she had seen him on the road. He ducked his head in assent. After the snarl none of the other children came near them, so the conversation had largely gone unheard, except for a boy who said with a sneer, 'He looks like he talks to that wolf of his,' loud enough to attract Nostromo's attention and of a small round person in metallic plum satin who came bustling out of the palace.

'If you paid more attention to your octaves, Mihit,' said a sharp voice, 'we might have less problems with you. Now what's this I hear about lack of discipline?' The round woman halted in front of Nostromo, the sunlight painting her robe pink and purple and blue.

'Didn't your students tell you my opinion of their performance last night?' Nostromo asked.

'Nothing except that they were expected to play second fiddle to your storyteller,' the woman replied. 'And, as you know, that is such a waste of my teaching.' She had lively brown eyes and eyebrows that seemed to stray all over her forehead in tune with her expressions. Chinku thought she looked nice and she clearly knew Nostromo well. The two of them were arguing like old friends, with no real heat in the argument. 'Perhaps if they practised while I was here, things might be clearer,' the woman said. Her name seemed to be Harmonia. 'That is, if those two have finished their conversation. I don't think we ever had a child here who spoke wolfish before.'

'That is why they are so valuable,' Nostromo replied. 'That is why the Lady is so keen to see them perform.'

'Well. My children have a perfect right to be jealous,' Harmonia answered. 'But perhaps a song might enliven things. Let us start off with a song.' She clapped her hands sharply and said, 'Children, the song I made you practise this morning. Let Nostromo hear it.'

Chinku watched the children group themselves. They had their hands in front of them, one cupped in the other. Harmonia stood in front with a small silver wand in her hand. Chinku wondered whether she would see stars fly out of the end when Harmonia waved it, but nothing that exciting happened. Instead, the children began to sing and Nick threw his head back and howled.

It was the song of a timber wolf sung over the shimmer of snow when the moon first rises, but no one there knew that. Chinku shuddered because the howl seemed to trace its path down her spine with a cold finger. The other children gaped though they bravely tried to continue with their song. Chinku said, 'Ssh!' but the wolf ignored her. She was too worried to notice the wand waved to silence the children. 'Ssh!' she said, trying to catch his attention, but he ignored her. 'Hounds sing on the trail of their prey,' said a cold voice. 'Some people say that there is a kind of music about that. But this kind of music enlightens neither man nor beast.' The owner of the voice was Harmonia and she was definitely furious.

Chinku put up her hand to his collar and he suddenly snapped at her, his teeth missing her fingers by a whisper.

'Nick!' she cried, amazed.

What faced her was a dangerous animal with teeth bared. The singing behind her had ceased and the air was still. She faltered. The wolf seemed to be hesitating between attacking and retreating. He took a half leap towards her so close that the claws on the extended front paw scratched her hand, but then he seemed to pull up short.

'What's the matter?' Nostromo asked from behind.

'Nick!' She was terrified Nostromo would come towards them and the wolf would attack, but she did not know what to do.

The stones were heavy in her pocket she put her hand inside and found that they were hot to her touch. Carefully, she took them out. They caught the light immediately and flashed their beams into the wolf's eyes. He backed away, shaking his head. She advanced towards him and he backed again. Nostromo said again, 'What is the matter?'

She heard Harmonia's high-pitched voice muttering something about children playing with dangerous animals. 'It is obvious that the creature is not properly trained, Nostromo. How could you put the children's lives in danger like this? Have him sent to the menagerie and locked up!'

Chinku said, 'I need to take him upstairs. He can be locked into the turret room where we were first. He should be all right there.' The wolf was shaking his head as if something was in its eyes. They glinted at Chinku in a bewildering tangle of amber. With the stones clutched firmly in her hand she went up to him and though this took a great deal of courage, she caught him by the collar. The wolf stayed dazed, and even when Nostromo came up, did not seem to want to attack.

'Is this part of some plan you two have hatched up to ruin the rehearsals?' Nostromo demanded. He too looked as if he were baffled by what was happening. Chinku, clutching onto the collar with slippery sweating hands, tried desperately to explain, but found the words stuck in her throat. It was alarming the way the wolf had become a wolf in a flash just as she was telling herself that Nick was better and that the Dragon's Moon had not touched him in any way. Stones in one hand and collar in the other, she began leading him back into the palace. The guards, who had seen what had happened, melted out of her way.

'Where are you going?' Nostromo asked.

'The turret room,' she replied. That at least came from her throat loud and clear enough for the guards to hear.

'Follow the child,' Nostromo said. 'If the wolf turns vicious …' but then his voice died because it was quite obvious to Chinku that he did not know what to say.

'If the wolf turns vicious,' said Harmonia, 'kill him. There is no other option. And what is this turret room nonsense? Take him to the menagerie with the other beasts at once!'

Chinku started walking again, stones still clutched in her hands so hard that they bruised the palms. The wolf walked with her, his claws clicking on the paving stones.

Inside the palace, they walked, the claws clicking and scratching, a constant irritating sound. It was the only sound she heard as she half dragged the heavy beast through the passages. How had she never realized that Nick was so heavy? She seemed to know the right way too by magic, finding the stairs and the heavy door. There she waited. A guard sidled by keeping as far from the wolf as possible and opened the door. She dragged him inside and took him to the garde robe.

'When you're a good Nick again,' she told him, 'I'll let you out.' He hesitated at the threshold, but then went in. She shut the door after him. The moment the door was shut, there was a snarl and a scratching from the other side.

'Vicious, isn't he?' said the guard.

'No,' Chinku answered coolly, 'it's only the moon that does this to him.'

The guard gestured at the sunlight streaming through the window, 'Moonshine is it?'

'Tomorrow night's a full moon,' Chinku answered. 'Please don't lock this door. He will need to be fed …'

The guard went out muttering things about unnecessary problems. He would need to be fed, Chinku thought, but she would have to bring the meat with the stones clutched in one hand.

Harmonia was still rehearsing with the students in the garden when Chinku went downstairs. Nostromo was pacing up and down beside the bay windows.

'What on earth happened?' he demanded, the moment he saw her, gripping her arms with a grip so hard that it hurt.

'It's the moon,' she said. 'The full moon has that effect on him.'

Something like understanding dawned on Nostromo's face. 'Ah,' he said. 'I thought the old stories were myths.'

'The Old Ones say that no story is completely a myth,' Chinku parroted. 'There is always some element of truth to them.'

'And what if the Lady has asked us to perform for her today? What then? You should have warned me.' That had not occurred to Chinku at all and she hung her head.

'Well, I must take the phial to Draconis now, while everyone is listening to the music in the garden.' He turned in a whisk of his cloak and Chinku ran after him.

Everyone was not listening to the music in the garden. They passed flurries of ladies-in-waiting carrying pointed gilt bottles and bolts of fabric here there and everywhere. Some of them greeted Nostromo with cries of pleasure. 'Master you must tell us a story when you have the time …' And some of them took advantage of Nick's absence to squeeze Chinku's cheeks. 'Sooo soft … almost like a girl's, almost like a peach …' One or two of them asked where Nostromo was going and showed an inclination to linger. Nostromo politely explained that he had work with Draconis.

'That weird creature,' one of the ladies shuddered. 'I asked him to sculpt me and he looked at me with those snake's eyes of his as if he were going to devour me instead.'

'He might devour that child,' another giggled. 'Such a delicious boy …'

'Ladies,' Nostromo said, 'your conversation is charming, but my work is urgent. I must take my leave. And surely the Lady is waiting for you.'

'She is, she is,' the ladies chimed and bustled away, their skirts trailing after them.

'What, no wolfboy?' Draconis said when they entered his room. He was sitting by the window whittling at a piece of wood. Out of its rough shape, Chinku could see a springing wolf beginning to form. Nostromo held out the phial without a word.

'Ah yes,' Draconis said, 'the rooks told me you had succeeded in getting it.'

'The rooks?' Chinku asked.

'They are old friends of the dragon folk. They were keeping watch on you for me.' Draconis's fingers moved over the wood as he spoke. The wolf seemed to leap out of it, growing into a fierce springing shape every second, as if it were shaking off the splinters in its quest for freedom. 'It will not be easy. I will have to go to the Story Vat while Draga performs her rite.'

It will not be easy was casually said. The wolf aimed a frozen growl at them over the moving fingers.

'Here, give this to the wolfboy for me.' Draconis handed Chinku the carving. She took it carefully, trying not to touch those scaly fingers. Now that she looked at them up close, they seemed almost like talons, the nails long and curving.

Nostromo said, 'And what is our role tomorrow? Where should we be?' There was an edge of tension in his voice.

'I have no idea,' Draconis answered, still easy, sprawled back in his chair by the window. 'No one has ever woken the dragons before. We shall have to wait and see what happens at moonrise.'

Nostromo was uncomfortable, Chinku could tell by the way he walked, his shoulders hunched as they left Draconis's room. Adding to their discomfort came the shrill sound of a trumpet, followed very soon by the pages who had blown it.

'The Lady comes this way,' they announced. 'To your knees, all of you!' The pages were followed by the ladies whom they had met on their way to Draconis's room. All of them plumped down on the floor in pools of skirts and cloaks.

'What is the Lady's pleasure now?' Nostromo asked.

'She is bringing a robe of honour for the old sculptor,' one of the ladies whispered. Chinku, looking down saw gold slippers enter her field of vision. Then hard fingers found her chin and forced it up.

She found herself looking into a golden idol's face with circles and dots in gold radiating around the eyes. She recognized it, of course – she had seen the face before. And it wore what looked like a scaly necklace around its neck – having seen Draconis now, she knew that they were living scales and no goldsmith's work. Draga's eyes too were slit, she had not noticed that before. The eyes narrowed like a contented cat's then widened slightly.

'The child who danced with the wolf! You were to dance for me again, weren't you?'

'Yes,' she answered, as before not waiting to be told to speak by the pages or the ladies around. As before, she heard a slight gasp at her boldness.

'Very bold, very bold. My sons enjoyed your storytelling session. And the company of your wolf. Where is he?'

'He's been a bad wolf,' Chinku answered because it was the only answer she could give. And even when she said it she thought it sounded childish. 'He's been locked up.' She was still looking up, because the Lady had her chin firmly between her hard fingers.

'Stand,' the Lady said to everyone. 'I do not like looking at these bowed heads.' She released Chinku's chin and Chinku scrambled to her feet. She could hear a rustle behind her as everyone else did the same. 'I thought you said it was a tame wolf?'

Chinku answered, her heart thudding in her mouth, 'You saw me dance with him. So did the nobles the other night.'

There was a polite cough from behind her. 'If I may speak Your Majesty.' Chinku recognized Nostromo's voice.

'Speak then, Nostromo.'

'Animals we all know, even the tamest of them, are subject to strange fits and starts. That is why the more dangerous ones are confined to the menagerie. In this particular case, the child was insistent on keeping her wolf with her. And the wolf has behaved well so far. Today, it may be related to the weather, the moon, a gleam of sweat, who knows.'

'The moon?' the Lady raised her head swiftly at that. 'He responds to the moon?'

'It is well known that wolves are particularly active on full moon nights, Milady,' Nostromo said. Chinku thought that for someone who did not know what was wrong with Nick, he was lying very well. 'You may have heard them singing at night in the country.'

The Dragon Lady bowed her head thoughtfully. 'And if I had been foolish enough to ask for a performance today, what then? Perhaps it would have been a good opportunity to test His Majesty's experiments on animal memory. Would it not?' She raised her voice suddenly and Chinku realized she was speaking to someone at the back of the gathering.

'Your Majesty, that particular fluid is still volatile. No one knows what it can or cannot do.' Chinku wanted to glance around to see who it was she was talking to, but she could not – after all Nostromo's lessons on hierarchy and discipline.

The Lady sighed, 'A pity. Then it will have to be the evening after. We shall hope that your wolf has regained his temper then.' She turned abruptly on Chinku and the ladies began to bustle forward in their waves of colour, going around Chinku, shuffling and teetering and leaving her behind. And then, all at once, she and Nostromo were left alone. His shoulders slumped again.

'That was close,' he said. 'Thank god there are to be no more visits to the sculptor. Now child, do you have any notion of what might happen at moonrise?'

Chinku said, 'You forget, I can't read the stones. Only Nick can.' The next time, if there were a next time, she would take that parchment from the huts of Baghen and learn it by heart. She thought again of Nick's mother and the silver bowl and wished there was some way she could communicate with her.

Tomorrow, Chinku thought, all her questions would probably be answered. At least they should be, in one way or another.

Between today and tomorrow, however, was a long stretch of time that was difficult to fill. Both she and Nostromo were restless and despite the fact that the palace was filled with stories, there were none when she needed them. Chinku should have been happy – all the questions would be finally answered, her parents and her village would regain their memory, well, she hoped they would.

Interrupting her thoughts, Nostromo said, 'Life can occasionally be full of uncertainty. It's a pity the stones are not clearer about what they have to say.'

'They brought me to Kalabash,' Chinku said, 'and if they say the dragons will fly, then the dragons will definitely fly.'

The rooks were flying overhead – she caught sight of a thin line of them making the messages that birds always make when they fly. She studied their flight and tried to make sense of what the wings said, but perhaps it was just nothing at all, the usual stories of flight and a nest back home.

'No,' said a voice, Draconis's voice they realized two beats later. 'Not quite as usual.' Both of them looked around. 'Up here,' the voice said, from somewhere above them. They looked up, first at the sky with its bird patterns and then, since they could not see him there, backed against the balustrade of the balcony and craned their necks up what they could see of the building, the first row of stone dragons looking down on them and then a golden scaly head and slit eyes. He seemed to be poised like a lizard upside down on the stones. Looking at him like that sent the blood whirling through Chinku's head in a dizzy rush. 'I thought,' said Draconis, speaking quite effortlessly for someone upside down, 'that it might be easier if I came to see you. The birds have seen me and are telling you that, Saviour girl.'

'You mean you came down like that from your chamber?' Nostromo asked in wonderment.

'It's surprising what dragons can do. Half-dragons too have skills that most people don't know. Except for Draga, perhaps. But till you returned my memory to me, I had forgotten all this.'

'What did you want to tell us?' Nostromo asked.

'Wait, let me come down.' In a rush he seemed to trickle down towards them getting heavier and heavier like a water drop coming closer and they quickly scattered. Then he was standing there breathing lightly surrounded by the folds of his cloak. He glanced around the room and Chinku was certain he was looking for Nick.

'He's not here,' she said. She had put the carved wolf on a shelf where, when the old Nick was back, he would be certain to see it, but following Draconis' gaze she suddenly realized that they might not ever return to that room again, once it was tomorrow.

Nostromo said, 'Time is getting short. Will the guards not look into your room?'

Draconis replied carelessly, 'They shove the food into my room and leave me alone as much as possible. Now to work. Tomorrow, Draga will be in the Story Vat room from the afternoon till the rising of the moon. I will enter the room in the morning before her. There is a task for the girl to do. She must sprinkle some fluid from this phial onto the head of the dragon fountain. We shall have to divide this.' He took the phial from his pocket and held it up. 'Half should do. Is there a glass tube in this room?'

Nostromo produced one from a chest and Draconis deftly transferred some of the Memory Fluid, rainbows splintering from the walls as he did it. 'Climbing up will be easier,' he said, handing the bottle to Chinku. 'I was afraid the phial would slip from my pocket.' Folding his cloak around him, he leapt up and then was slithering over the balcony.

'Nothing for me,' Nostromo said. 'But then, I was never the saviour.'

Even as he spoke they heard a thumping on the door, 'Nostromo! Nostromo!'

'The guards,' Nostromo said. The thumps became pounding. Nostromo went to the door and opened it. 'What is this disturbance?' he asked. 'Has the wolf escaped?' Chinku gasped when she heard him say it, but that was not the problem.

'The mad sculptor,' said the guard. 'We cannot find him.'

Nostromo's hand came down hard on Chinku's shoulder. 'That is impossible. Have you searched every corner of the room?' Chinku thought of the lizard slithering up the wall. She quickly whisked away from under the hand and darted back onto the balcony. As she half expected, there was nothing on the wall.

'What's the matter with that child?' the guard asked. She caught Nostromo's glance and shook her head. 'I think we should go upstairs again,' Nostromo said to the guard, 'and look for Draconis.' Which was what they did with Chinku scampering after them. She was almost certain he would be back in his room again by the time they got there and he was, sitting by the window with another splinter of wood in his hands. This time he was fashioning it into a lizard.

'You weren't here when I looked in before,' the guard told him.

Draconis smiled, 'Did you look for me? But here I am.'

'The sculptor never leaves his room,' Nostromo said, 'I told you that.'

'But it should be reported,' the guard said. 'Because I am sure he wasn't here before.' He was shifting from foot to foot and looking anxious.

'I was inside,' Draconis said. 'I heard you looking for me.'

'But you didn't say anything.'

'I was busy trying to find the right piece of wood for this lizard. You must have heard me scrabbling in the woodpile.' He looked hard at the guard and the guard began to look confused. In a few deft strokes of his knife, Draconis finished carving the lizard, just as he had carved the wolf before. 'Here,' he said to the guard. 'I seem to have caused you some trouble. Take this as a gift from me'

The lizard raised its frilled ruff and seemed almost alive as he held it out on the flat of his hand. To Chinku it looked more like a lizardragon than anything else. The guard took it hesitantly, his fingers shying away from contact with Draconis.

The sculptor slithered, there was no other way to describe it, to his feet. 'Now, if I can have my room back again? I have things to do. I must try on this robe that the Lady has so graciously given me for tomorrow's ceremony.' There was a bundle of material flung across the table; it looked like liquid metal. Draconis's slit eyes indicated it as it lay there taking in the changing light. The guard backed away involuntarily though Draconis did not come towards him.

'We have orders to check on all inhabitants of the palace frequently,' the guard said. 'So if you hear me open the door, please make your presence felt.'

'Are you checking on my wolf too?' Chinku asked, suddenly alarmed.

'That vicious thing?' the guard looked disgusted. 'He's not worth bothering about as long as we know he's locked up safe and sound.' Out of the corner of her eye she saw Draconis fling the metal cloth over his shoulder. It flowed like bronze water covering him in ripples, so that scales around his throat seemed to extend all over his body.

'Come,' Nostromo said. 'I think Draconis needs his privacy.'

Outside, the guard shoved the lizard into Chinku's hand. 'Here,' he said, 'keep it. Children play with these things.'

Chinku could see that Nostromo was angry; in fact when they were back inside the room, he exploded in wrath, 'Of all the careless … he could have endangered this whole plan.'

'It is his plan,' Chinku pointed out, though she agreed with Nostromo. Of course, if the stones had said that the dragons would fly, then they certainly would, in one way or the other, with or without Draconis's help. Perhaps the dragon man knew that too. She put the lizard carving on the shelf with the wolf.

Nostromo left the room abruptly without saying anything to her. At a loss, she stood on the balcony looking out at the sky. She could see the moonlight growing in the early evening and wondered about Nick locked up in the turret room. The door opened and shut behind her – she could feel a rush of air on her cheek and turned to find that Nostromo had returned. He did not give her any explanations for where he had been. Instead, he said, 'If you have to be up at first light, you should go to bed. I will wake you when the moon is still in the sky.'

'Will the guards let us wander through the palace in the dark?' she wondered.

'Go to bed,' he said quietly. 'I have taken care of some of that.'

27

Chinku thought she would not be able to sleep, but a heavy hand shook her out of her dreams. She opened her eyes and blinked at the yellow light shining into them.

It was Nostromo. 'Just put on your tunic and come with me. Once you have done your task, then you can go back to bed again. There should be time.' What he did not add was, 'if nothing goes wrong ...' Bleary-eyed, she climbed out of bed and splashed some water on her face. Then she pulled her blue tunic on over her sleeping clothes. The matrix stones swung heavy in the pocket and she instinctively put her hand inside to touch them. They were quite warm to her touch and would probably grow warmer during the day.

Nostromo said, 'Put the phial into your pocket. Its glow will give us away in the darkness.

He opened the door and looked around. Chinku could see that it was absolutely dark outside except for stealthy gleams of what looked like moonlight.

Nostromo said in a low voice, 'If anyone asks, we are going out into the garden to watch a rare conjunction of stars, the dragon stars, Draco and Dromos will cross each other and as they do so, the night birds will break into song. This is a phenomenon that is said to occur once in a lifetime.'

'But is it real?' Chinku asked, finding her feet through the patches of silver light. They seemed to lead in shining tracks down the corridors.

'Certainly the morning stars will be out,' Nostromo answered, 'though at this hour they are low in the sky. What is useful for us is the fact that they can only be seen from the garden and the roof. Now, while the roof is strictly forbidden, there are no such rules surrounding the garden. As to which star is which, no guard ever knew one from the other.' He sighed a little as he said that. 'The stars create their own maps in the sky and tell their own stories. Stories that can never be stolen by mortals. Only those who study the stars know them by their true names.' He continued speaking loudly as they walked through the passages, as if it were all part of a lesson. 'There are hunting dogs in the sky and goldfish and dancers.'

'And dragons,' Chinku said.

'Yes, and dragons. Draco or Draconis, the star of the firedrake. It rises red in the east and rides the sky some nights in a trail of fire before falling to earth. You may see it now if we arrive in the garden at the right time.' One of the shadows moved as they approached and then stood back, almost as if it had heard Nostromo's words.

The problem with the moonlight or whatever kind of light it was, was that though it showed you your way, it made it very hard to see anything else, turning rooms and their contents into patches of lighter and darker shadows. A hundred guards might have been hidden in the stillness and they would not notice them, while the guards might spot two swiftly moving shadows with ease.

They came into the hall that led to the garden and Chinku noticed that the moonlit glimmers vanished. Nostromo walked towards the two pale squares and as he did so the doors silently seemed to swing open. Fresh air came in and ruffled her hair. Outside, Nostromo led her towards the fountain and pointed up into the sky. She could see a pale red light hanging low just over the dragon statue's head. At a distance was another glowing yellow star. 'Are those the dragon stars?' she asked. Her hand was clutched on the glass phial but, strangely, she was in no hurry to finish her task.

Nostromo said, 'Do what you have to quickly – we may be watched.' His hands pushed her almost to the brink of the fountain bowl. Dark shapes moved in the water. Something rippled towards her – was it a fish, or a dragon? Quickly, she took the stopper out of the phial and flung the contents clumsily towards the dragon statue and hurriedly put the phial back in her pocket. An arch of rainbow colour flared briefly in the night and was gone. She waited, hanging on to the fountain rim in expectation, but the night was still.

Nostromo pointed up to the stars, 'See how clear they are,' he said loudly. 'This is the hour just before dawn when the lords of the night arrange their strategies for the year.'

She looked up at the red and yellow specks but they seemed no larger than before. 'What did the firedrake do when it came to earth?' she asked.

'It took on the form of a human prince, a prince of fire with hair that streamed liquid gold. The young hero strode out of the flames and everyone who saw him gasped at his beauty. He seemed to have drawn into himself all the light of the last sun, all the power of a fire on a winter night. The first of the dragons married the daughter of the kings of the western lands and from that union came the race to which the Lady Draga belongs.'

Looking at the stars she thought that they seemed to move no closer to each other. It was like waiting for something to happen that irritated her by not happening. She dipped her fingers in the waters of the fountain quite forgetting the moving shadows. A streak of light lanced up her arm and she cried out, jerking her hand up and out of the water. The few drops that fell were rainbow drops, though the water looked as silver and dark as before. 'The Memory Fluid,' Nostromo murmured. 'It is in the water. Now let us go in. As I told you, we are being watched.' There was a shadow standing at the palace door and there was no telling how long it had been there. Perhaps it had been listening to Nostromo's story.

'Wait till the light fades,' Nostromo said. 'He will not have seen it.' Not seen light in that darkness? When you could see a fire for miles and miles away from a high hill! 'Look around you,' Nostromo murmured. 'We are under someone's protection.' She looked, following the shape of his hand and saw rainbow specks that seemed to float through the air. 'Dragonmoths,' he said. 'The dragon flowers breed them.'

'We call them fireflies at home,' she told him. The tingling in her arm had ceased and the light was gone.

The dragonmoths seemed to be all around, in rainbow flickers close by and in scatters of twin red sparks in the distance close to the palace. Chinku thought of catching one in the palm of her hand and having it light the way back to her room.

'Come,' Nostromo said. 'Enough of stars. It is time to go in. Are you feeling cold? I should have brought my cloak with us.'

In all this talk of cloaks what Chinku had forgotten were the Shadow Cloaks, which were still, as far as she knew, lying in the turret room. With the cloaks she could have vanished like a shadow through the moonlight patches without worrying about being seen by the guards. And Nostromo could have used one to slip in and out of Draconis's room at will. It came to her as that ray of light lanced up her hand from the fountain. However, she chose to wait till they had returned to the room without attracting undue attention from the watchers in the dark.

'There's something I forgot to tell you about,' she murmured to Nostromo, so wide awake that she was certain she would not go to sleep even if she crawled back into bed.

'What?' he asked. He sounded tired in that pre-dawn darkness.

'Demetra gave us two cloaks,' she said. 'They reflect whatever is around them so that the wearer seems to be invisible.'

'My cloaks!' he cried. 'She gave you my cloaks and you never told me! They were woven for me by the Water Nymphs of Atlantis. They are the only ones who know the art of creating that kind of fabric …' He blew on one of the darkened lamps in the room and the light sprang up throwing the shadows of his face into prominence. 'If we had those cloaks we could go unseen from one end of the palace to another, even into the room of the Story Vat. We need to get them.'

'I can go now,' she offered guiltily.

'The Shadow Hounds will be on guard,' he replied. 'Did you not see the red glints in the darkness?'

'I thought they were more dragonmoths.'

'The Shadow Hounds are the stolen shadows of living beasts. They can only hunt at night. During the day they stalk the heels of real animals.' She shivered at the thought – thank goodness she and

Nick had never thought of wandering through the palace in the darkness, wolf though he was, he might have found it hard to tackle a ghost hound. Holding her arm Nostromo led her into the palace. When they reached the door the shadow beside it had melted away into the others.

'Do Shadow Hounds attack?' she asked, glancing around fearfully.

'Yes, if they are told to. No one wanders round the palace at night.' After that Nostromo said nothing further, lapsing into silence as they made their way back to the shelter of the room. 'Wait till daybreak,' he told her. 'Then we shall see what you can do.'

'I will have to go to feed Nick in any case,' she said. And her heart sank again as she thought of what awaited her in the room upstairs.

'It is strange that I did not hear the waves,' Nostromo muttered. 'The cloaks have their own unique call, like the echoes of a shell in the chambers of the sea. Go to sleep,' he told her. 'There will be enough to talk about after the sun rises.'

Though she went back to bed under the huddle of covers and shut her eyes, all she could think about was the forgotten cloaks locked in the turret room with Nick. And there was a noise when everything was still and dark, a kind of crack like a great tree being uprooted and a whistle that stirred her coverlets briefly. She stiffened under her coverlets, but the sound was not repeated.

28

When the light behind her eyelids began to glow, Chinku realized it was day. The final day, the day on which she would accomplish what she had been sent to the palace for. At least she hoped she would because there was a song in her name and the stones said so. Her eye was caught by the shelf on which she had put the carvings Draconis had given her. The wolf was still snarling at the room, but he snarled on his own – the lizard was gone.

She looked at the floor in case it had fallen there but could see no signs of it.

After washing her face and hands she found Nostromo on the balcony gazing down at the garden. He heard her footsteps and turned. 'Nostromo,' she cried, 'the lizard's gone!'

'Lizard? What lizard?' he asked. He had been about to say something when she had interrupted with the lizard outcry.

'The one that Draconis had carved. It isn't there.'

He clicked his tongue impatiently. 'This is hardly time,' he said, 'to worry about toys.'

'But …' she was about to say that it wasn't a toy, but saw that he was in no mood to hear her out. 'What shall we do for the rest of the day?' she asked.

'I will take classes with the children as usual,' he said. 'Everyone will expect it. And you?'

'I will get the cloaks as soon as they bring me the meat for Nick.' She said it simply, wishing that she would not think of awful things like a vicious wolf tangled up in a shadow cloak who would spring out at her when she could not see him. No, she told herself, it was no point thinking things like that. Or even wishing that the stones would wake from their pebble selves and shield her with their light. A knock at the door startled them. They opened it and found an excited Fowler outside.

'Such chaos!' he said. 'The dragon from the fountain in the garden has vanished!'

'Vanished? What do you mean?' Nostromo asked. 'It was there before dawn. We saw it.'

The guard beside Fowler said, 'Yes, that's what the Night Watch told us. But the dragon vanished just at the moment the watch was changing.'

Chinku said, 'I heard a noise, a crack and a whistle as I was falling asleep.' That must have been a dragon thrashing its wings and rising up into the air. She wished she had been out on the balcony to see it. What had the Shadow Hounds done when that terrible shadow rose up in the darkness between the flecks of floating light? And that whistle, what was that?

Nostromo had obviously not heard the noise. He said, 'Is there anything that needs to be done?'

The guard shook his head, 'No, sir. The Shadow Riders have been summoned. Everyone in the palace has been ordered to go about their daily business.' From Fowler's excitement it was obvious that he was having a hard time doing that. He had forgotten to bring their breakfast and when Chinku said, 'Food for my wolf?' Fowler paused in his excitement and made a face, 'I forgot that creature.'

Nostromo told him, 'You had better hurry and complete your chores if you don't want us to be late for class. The child will deal with the rest of it.'

When they were gone Chinku said, 'Did the dragon come to life?' She tiptoed to the balcony and tried to look over the edge but all she could see was the patch of grass as usual.

'If it has gone, Draconis will know where it is,' Nostromo told her. 'If he chooses to tell us, that is. He must have known that this would happen.'

'I think that's where the lizard carving has gone too,' she told him. 'I think that came to life too.'

The major domo arrived, bustling up with Fowler and the food. He wanted to know whether they had seen anything suspicious in the darkness before dawn. 'Just the dragonmoths,' Nostromo replied, quite truthfully.

'The fountain has been totally uprooted,' the major domo told them. 'If the Lady hears of this today, I don't know what she may do. On the day when she celebrates her father's memory, was there ever something so unfortunate ...'

Another guard came running in, 'That wolf of yours needs to be silenced. His howls are making the upper storey unbearable. The Story Vat Keeper is afraid that the Story Fluid will curdle!'

'He's hungry,' Chinku said.

'In the middle of all this chaos, a ravenous wolf!' the major domo grumbled. 'As if I did not have enough to do. A new fountain must be installed by tonight!' He flung up his hands and turned to Fowler, 'At least get the meat and silence that wolf. I must find the sculptor.'

'Will he be able to sculpt a statue by tonight?' Nostromo asked.

'If we cannot find that dragon, he must do so. Something will need to be in place in the garden. Perhaps the tisane will make his hands move faster. It has been known to kill in large doses of course, but this is an emergency.' When he said that, Chinku wished Nick were nearby to sink his teeth into him instead of howling uselessly in a turret. The major domo walked up and down the floor wringing his hands and totally at a loss.

'The Shadow Riders will hunt for whoever it was who did this deed. It cannot have been anyone in the palace ....' Before he completed the sentence, he swung on his heel and left the room.

Chinku said, 'I will get the cloaks ....'

'What is the matter with Nick?' Nostromo asked. 'Is he trying to draw your attention to something?'

'It is the moon,' Chinku answered simply. 'It does this to him.' Both of them secretly hoped that Draconis would appear to explain everything to them, but there was no sign of him.

Fowler took his time about returning. Nostromo was about to leave the room for his class when the page reappeared with the breakfast and Nick's meat precariously poised on the prong of a pitchfork. 'I'll take it up,' Chinku said. She was afraid he would want to accompany her, but he handed the meat over gladly. 'I have work in the garden,' he said. 'They have us brushing the grass and straightening the basin.'

'Is the fountain still there?' she asked.

'The basin, yes. It's the dragon that has disappeared. The guards found the basin on the other side of the palace wall. Something had dragged it over the wall! They had such a time bringing it back to this side – the Shadow Horses were totally useless!' His eyes were wide and literally dancing at what he had seen in the morning.

Chinku thought she knew what had dragged it over the wall, but there was nothing she could say except, 'Could I come to the garden after I've fed my wolf?' she asked.

'I can't tell you,' he answered. 'And the palace is crawling with ladies-in-waiting because of the Lady's rituals tonight.' He scampered out leaving the door open.

Fowler was right about the ladies-in-waiting – the corridors were filled with trails of them carrying cushions, flowers and chattering like so many caged birds. She had to hold the meat carefully, so that the drips from it did not spoil their rich robes. Luckily no one gave her more than a glance. She made her way through the corridors, on the alert for more guards and pages or for anything unusual – she half wondered whether she was looking for the flutter of a dragon's wings. One of the guards tried to field her and send her to the kitchen.

'Where are you going with that meat? Go back downstairs. This is no time to be running around the corridors ...' but even before he could pursue that line of argument another guard came and took him away. She heard a murmur of, 'Should the Lady postpone. Tonight ....' Draconis had obviously known what would happen once the Story Fluid was sprinkled over the dragon.

Quickly she ran towards the tower. Even as she reached the foot of the steps she could hear the howling, so unearthly that it was like an icy finger running down her spine. She halted involuntarily wondering whether she should go up at all. Her foot touched one step and retreated from it, then touched and retreated again. 'Saviour,' she said firmly to herself and biting her lip began the climb up towards that howling. Being a saviour without stones to defend her did not seem to make her feel any better.

The guard at the top was still there. 'Come to feed that beast of yours, have you?' he asked. 'Just open that door and throw it in.'

'No,' she answered, 'he will be inside the garde robe …'

'Well, I'm not leaving that door open without a weapon,' he answered. 'I'll have to shut it behind you. But don't say I didn't warn you.' The door yawned in front of her like a mouth and as it opened, the howls were suddenly cut off.

'Perhaps he smells you,' said the guard. As she walked in towards the garde robe to open the door, her heart falling into her stomach, the floor seemed to lurch under her feet. Her field of vision swam. She stopped. There was a howl from inside, an awful rising up a scale kind of howl.

'What's the matter?' the guard asked.

'Did you feel the floor move?' she asked.

'Fright that's what it is, pure fright,' he answered. 'I didn't feel a thing.'

'Nick,' she said cautiously as she went in, holding the meat at arm's length. Two things happened. She heard the door shut behind her and at the same time, a snarling rush. A grey streak of wolf shot towards her from the garde robe, all teeth, foam and bloodshot eyes.

'Nick!' She thrust the meat at him as if it were a kind of shield. The teeth took it and as the pitchfork shot up relieved of its weight she held that in front of her.

The wolf took the meat in one great lunge and retired to a corner of the room to eat it. Chinku could see that the garde robe door was open and, waiting for a moment, when she thought his attention was focussed on the meat, moved towards it, the pitchfork firmly clutched in one hand. She was careful not to move fast – at home that was the first thing she had been taught, do not attract a wild animal's attention, blend in with the place. She was almost within reach of the garde robe door when the wolf leapt up and came at her in a great snarling rush. Instinctively, she threw up the pitchfork's prongs and thrust it at the wolf, though she did not want to jab him with it. His breath smelt of blood and meat and she almost choked on it. The red eyes, no longer Nick's golden ones, were narrow slits blazing at a prospective enemy. She sidestepped quickly and fended him off with the teeth of the pitchfork, yelling, 'Nick!' again and hoping the guard would open the door so she could dodge out. The wolf's teeth snapped at the pitchfork, then lunged for the handle.

An ordinary wolf might have continued attacking the pitchfork brandished in front of it, but this was Nick. The grey head lunged low under the pitchfork towards her. She hit him on the head with the tines wondering desperately what to do next. She could feel his hot breath on her feet. Her blue tunic caught and sent her stumbling and she fought for her feet while keeping the pitchfork in front of her. The floor lurched again hard like the back of a wild horse and sent her flying – she had not imagined it and it was so unfair that this should happen now. 'Nick!' she cried, her voice pleading now.

'The phial,' said a voice in her ear. 'The phial!' She did not pause to wonder where the voice had come from but scrabbled for the phial, jabbing the pitchfork up and up to keep the wolf away from her. In her fall the phial had broken so that a sharp edge stuck out. She thrust it forward just in time to catch the fleshy part of the wolf's extended paw. It sank in. Useless, she thought, there was nothing left in the phial and began to cring, waiting to feel the teeth in her flesh. They were there, almost there, an inch from her arm, when light streaked, the rainbow colours flaring out over the fur.

The wolf reared up and checked in mid spring, shaking its paw with a surprised kind of air.

'Chinku …' the voice was not a growl but clear. Nick's voice. And then Nick was standing there.

'What happened?' he asked.

'The Story Fluid,' she said. 'There must have been some left in the phial …' She was about to tell him what had happened in a rush of gratitude, but the floor bucked again.

'Earthquake!' he said. 'We have to get out of here!'

'No, it's the dragon from the fountain.' Even as she spoke she rushed inside the garde robe.

'What are you looking for?' Nick asked.

'The cloaks. Demetra's cloaks.' They had taken the clothes to wash, she remembered Fowler asking for them. She looked at the empty shelves with a sinking heart.

'They're there,' he said. 'I can see them,' and he walked past her. As he did, she flinched; she could not help it. The memory of the wolf attack was still too near.

'What's the matter?' he asked, turning. His hand scrabbled on the shelf for a moment, briefly seeming to disappear into the stone. Then when he raised them he was holding the two cloaks.

'You attacked me,' she said wonderingly. 'And the Dragon's Moon is tonight.' He did not look tired or ill, in fact he looked like her everyday Nick. He cocked his head and thought about it.

'I remember something,' he said, 'an enemy with ... with that,' and he pointed at the pitchfork. The hunted, embarrassed look was on his face.

She hugged him, 'Never mind. You're yourself again.'

'Tonight – what about tonight?'

'I don't know, but oh, the dragon from the fountain has gone!' And she told him all that had happened since he had been locked up in the room. 'We'd better get out of here,' he said, 'if there is an earthquake on .... But I don't feel like changing back into a wolf again.' He put one of the cloaks around his shoulders and held the other out to Chinku.

'Wait,' Chinku said. And she pitchforked up the piece of meat lying on the floor and took it to the turret window. Even as she did that the floor started shifting again.

'Don't be silly,' Nick said, 'we have to get out of here.' Fighting to keep her feet she held the meat out of the window peering out. As a drop of juice fell, she could see the stone dragon below look up and its tongue shot out like a lizard's flypaper tongue capturing the blood drop. Then it saw her and froze almost into stone again.

Nick said, 'You had better leave that to Draconis. They obviously won't listen to you. Now come on! Lock the door in case someone comes to find out why the wolf isn't howling any more!' And he grabbed her by the arm and pulled her towards the door. Before they went out he threw the cloak over his head and abruptly merged in with the background. Not knowing what to do with hers, Chinku stuffed it under her tunic and pulled the belt tight around her waist, hoping that it would not slither out onto the ground.

The passage outside was empty but voices were echoing up from the floor below. 'We should tell the King ....'

'No, evacuate the palace. Take everyone outside ....'

'It's a plot, that's what it is ....'

'What happens if there really is an earthquake?' Chinku wondered. 'You can get earthquakes to forget what they are doing ....'

'Shut up,' Nick hissed. 'You can't be heard talking to nothing!'

'It would be better off if I was heard talking to a wolf,' she retorted, but at heart she was relieved. Whatever the voice had told her had miraculously brought Nick back to himself. They quickly went down the stairs, she was aware of Nick's footsteps like a kind of echo under hers, but they were soon lost in the scuffling of frantic guards and pages. 'Have you done something about that wolf?' one of them asked as he ran past her. 'There's an emergency on, there is!'

'Yes,' she answered, 'he'll be quiet now.' They passed the ladies-in-waiting teetering on high-heeled sandals wondering whether to carry cushions or excuse themselves from ceremonies. Every so often the floor lurched. In a quiet space Nick wondered whether they should creep up to the Story Vat corridor to see what was happening there before they went back to Nostromo. 'It was actually a good idea,' Chinku said. And it wouldn't really take them too long. So they went scuttling in that direction but found the way barred by a phalanx of Dream Stealers, memory tubes in their hands.

'No one can pass,' one of them said. 'Any punishments today will be on hold.' Behind them they heard more excited voices spiralling down the corridor. 'The King would never allow it! Not when the vat is shaking like this ...'

The ladies in the corridor were not standing straight, Chinku saw, but were hunching down involuntarily. She realized that the illusion of the corridor was affecting them. The Dream Stealers blocked the way. 'We have no orders to let anyone pass,' the one who seemed to be their leader said. The ladies were indignant, 'We have the Lady's permission to leave,' they said. Chinku could see a rainbow aura around one of them and thought that they must have been splashed by fluid from the vat. Would it, she wondered, inspire the Lady to tell stories of hairdressers, or list the jewellery she had worn, numbering their stones one by one? The Memory Tubes, which had shifted during the floor shaking, swung up again. 'Child, you must leave this place now!'

There were footsteps again in the corridor and the ladies-in-waiting gathered themselves into groups, leaving the way clear. Chinku saw the golden idol approach. She seemed to be wearing a mask that covered her head and came down to her chest, so that from the neck up she was all dragon.

'Send for the King,' she said. The guards swung around on hearing her voice. 'He must be brought here as soon as possible. The palace is being attacked by some kind of creature.'

The Dream Stealers' heads turned to each other briefly. 'It is an earthquake, Your Majesty,' the leader said respectfully.

'Earthquake? This can be no earthquake. There is a beast in the centre of the earth trying to push the palace over.'

The Keeper of the Story Vat had come out after her; Chinku saw his white coat glimmering in the shell-like depths of the corridor.

'The Lady is possibly right. Earthquakes shake and then die away. Whatever this is, it keeps on moving.' Nick's hand closed on Chinku's arm and he pulled her away. She followed the pull and no one noticed her go.

'Whatever is doing this to the palace,' Nick whispered, 'we need to get to Nostromo.'

By the time they reached the hall, the palace floor had lurched and shifted several more times, so that they stumbled and swung as they walked. Once it bucked when they were going down the stairs and Chinku found herself almost thrown down the flight. Nick, invisible as he was, seemed to be no better at managing because his hand occasionally touched hers under the cover of his cloak. Nostromo was in the hall by himself.

'There you are!' he cried when he saw Chinku. 'I wondered what had happened to you. I sent the other children out into the garden ...' even as he spoke, he turned his head. And then, in two quick steps had whisked the cloak off Nick's shoulders.

'This time I heard it!' he said triumphantly. 'My wife's cloak!' And despite everything strange that was going on around them, he ran his fingers up and down the folds of material, almost Chinku thought, as if it were his wife's cheek. 'Now, children, out into the garden!'

'What about the sculptor?' Chinku asked. She wanted to pull the cloak from out under her tunic, but she could not do that in the hall. She also wanted to give the wolf that Draconis had carved for Nick.

'Draconis will deal with his problems himself. If you remember, all he asked you to do was ...' Nostromo glanced over his shoulder. 'Give me the cloak,' he said. 'And then go out into the garden.' He draped the cloak over his shoulders and vanished into the surroundings. Nick's nostrils flared slightly and his head turned. Chinku realized he was watching Nostromo leave the place.

'If we go into the garden,' she said, 'we could consult the stones ...'

'He's going to the sculptor, 'Nick said. 'I think whatever was going to happen has already begun.' The floor slipped and slid. 'The Lady was right about one thing, this is definitely not an earthquake. It feels as if the palace is shaking loose from the ground.'

'Loose?' Chinku's eyes sparkled. 'You mean the palace may ...' but whatever she was saying could not be completed because the floor bucked so hard that they were both thrown onto the ground, flat on their faces.

'Ha!' said Nick. 'I'd like to see what those Dream Stealers do with their memory tubes now.' They lay on the floor and waited to see if the movement continued, but the floor seemed to be still, so they cautiously found their feet again. They could hear the corridors echoing with screams and cries. 'The Lady must call off her function. We must evacuate the palace!'

Chinku slipped her cloak over her shoulders and said, 'Wait for me.'

'Where are you going?' Nick asked.

'To get something from our room. Stay there.' And she had whisked away before he could stop her. It was not an easy journey because every so often the floor heaved, but she scrabbled at walls and tapestries as she went and finally found her way to their room. The wolf was still there, lying on the shelf though luckily it had not fallen on the ground. Quickly she picked it up, stuffed it into her pocket and went running back to Nick as fast she could.

'Here,' she said, holding out the carved wolf to him.

'What's this?' he asked.

'Draconis carved this for you.'

He balanced it in the palm of his hand and looked at it in wonder. The wolf snarled up at him, one paw in the air poised to leap. Nick was about to say something when the floor shook again and they heard more shouts and people running past the alcove.

Nick said, 'If they are evacuating the palace, perhaps we need to stay in here?'

'Why?'

'It's just a feeling I have. I think we should hide here till after dark and wait and see what happens.' Taking Chinku's hand, he took her into one of the alcoves off the main hall.

'What about Nostromo?' Chinku asked.

'He'll come looking for us here. I'll smell him when he comes,' Nick assured her. The alcove was more like a marble cupboard than a room. It had a small sofa in it and tapestries cascading down the walls, but that was all. Nick looked behind the tapestries to see how much space there was between them and the wall.

Chinku said, 'Then the other children should also stay in the palace!' and went running out again.

29

It was a silly thing to have done with the floor bucking and heaving like that, but she thought it was the only thing she could do. If they had to stay there and it was safe for them, then perhaps it was safe for the other children too. She ran down and out into the garden and heard the patter of Nick's feet behind her. The children were there, standing under the trees or playing marbles. There were no teachers with them. What caught her eye was the patch of raw brown ground behind them where the fountain had been. When they saw Chinku they said, 'What are you doing here? Where's your wolf?'

'You've got to come inside!' she said. 'It's an adventure!'

'It's an earthquake.'

'No it isn't.' Nick had caught up with Chinku by then and he added his voice to hers.

'Who are you?'

It could have been an awkward moment, but a voice said, 'Chinku, what do you want the children to do?' At some point Nostromo had come out into the garden unnoticed except by Nick.

'To go back into the palace,' she said simply.

Nostromo looked at Chinku curiously then said, 'Yes, that is what Draconis wants us to do too.'

'You met him?' Chinku asked.

'Yes …,' he glanced at the children and raised his voice. 'There is no need to worry. It isn't an earthquake. Something strange and wonderful is about to happen. But for that I need you to go inside and wait in the hall. Yes, the floor will lurch and you will be frightened. But I want you to forget your fear and sing.'

They began to get up and form themselves into the lines as they had been taught. While they were doing that, Chinku quietly got up and going over to Nick, took the matrix stones from her pocket. Nick followed the movement of her hand and watched her fling the stones onto the grass. 'It's the same thing,' he said. 'The dragons will fly. Don't say much, these stones, do they?'

'Well one dragon has already flown,' Chinku said. 'And no one knows where it's gone.' She and Nick fell in behind the last rows of children.

Inside the palace there was utter chaos. People carrying bundles and bags were scurrying all over the place. One of the guards halted Nostromo and said, 'Master, it would be better if the children were outdoors. This is not safe.'

Nostromo gave him a smooth answer, something about the children being hungry. Chinku did not remember what it was that he said, but it was obvious that the guard was so eager to get out of the palace himself that he did not question Nostromo further. In fact no one seemed to be interested in the children at all, they were trying to escape from that cage where the floor bucked so alarmingly.

'Hold onto each other,' Nostromo told them. 'That way you might keep your balance when the floor lurches.' And it worked. They rolled with the swaying floor hand in hand. The major domo was running. He stopped when he saw them.

'A message has been sent to the King. I am certain His Majesty will want the palace evacuated.' He looked old and tired, the wrinkles on his face making him look as if no one had ironed him for a very long time.

'Where is the Lady?' Nostromo asked.

'In the Story Vat chamber. She is adamant that she must finish her ritual by moonrise. God knows what will happen when the moon rises. In all my days I have never seen such a thing!' He shook his head and Chinku felt quite sorry for him.

'Has she begun the ritual?'

'Her ladies were frightened and wanted to leave the place. However, they have been persuaded to stay on.'

Chinku did not like the sound of that word 'persuaded'. Perhaps the Dream Stealers had stolen their memories so that they did not know what it was they were so frightened of. There was another wave of movement. This time the floor tilted up, so that they all found themselves sliding to one side. Holding hands helped, though not as much as they had hoped. Then it sank down again with an almost audible thump and several of the vases were shivered from their stands and crashed onto the floor. Normally pages would have come running from all directions to pick up the shattered pieces. This time nothing happened and the children found that absence of normal activity the most frightening thing of all. The major domo shivered and went in search of someone.

'Hush,' said Nostromo to the children. 'Nothing will harm you. Sit down on the floor. That will be safer. Let us practise scales. Find a place where there are no shards of glass of course.'

After a wobbly beginning, the children started singing. In between with the thumps in the palace, their voices jumped. Chinku sat there listening, the stones clutched in her hand, wondering about the voice that had told her to throw the phial at Nick. She had not found time to think about that.

'It was my mother,' Nick said. He had been listening to her thoughts the way he sometimes did; his pale yellow eyes fixed on her face. 'It must have been,' he added. And rose and fell in front of her eyes on another wave.

No pages came to clear the room that long afternoon, though at one point Chinku thought she heard the call of trumpets in the air.

'The King must be coming,' she said aloud, so loudly that everyone stopped to look at her. But though they listened for a long time after that, they could hear no more sounds of any kind. The movements had stopped too, as if whatever it was that had been trying to lift the palace had given up. But the major domo had not returned, nor had any of the guards. Then, when everyone was beginning to look a little accusingly at Chinku, they heard the trumpet again. 'Certainly His Majesty must have arrived,' Nostromo said. He rose to his feet. 'Wait here.' And he left the hall.

What difference could the King's coming make, Chinku wondered, would he have any power to stop whatever it was that was happening? 'The princes have gone to the country,' one of the children piped up. 'They were sent there the moment the palace started shaking, at first light. His Majesty must have come for the Lady.'

'But the Lady never does what he tells her,' another child said, with an air of knowing it all.

'Why is that?' Nick asked.

'Because she comes from the land of the dragons and is as fierce as a dragon. The Lady Draga never allows the Story Vat to be used except for her own entertainment these days.' They looked at each other's faces as they said this and Chinku and Nick realized that they were talking about forbidden things. 'Some people even say that she changes into a dragon at night ...' followed by a giggle. 'Imagine a dragon in a frilly nightdress!'

The tramping of feet silenced them. The curtains swished open and the King stood there flanked by his guards.

'What are you children doing here?' the King demanded. 'This building is not safe!'

He had Dream Stealers on either side of him, memory tubes in their hands, their cloaks long and black and grim, and their red eyes glinting even in all that light. The children involuntarily crept towards each other and there was a long silence.

'Where are the major domo and the pages? Why is this room like this?' The King's gaze wandered over the broken glass and the fallen paintings.

No one had any answer for him. Chinku wondered where Nostromo was and thought she should at least say something. 'Nostromo felt that we should stay together here...'

'With that beast on the roof?' the King looked hard and long at her. 'Aren't you the child with the wolf? Where is your pet?'

'In the turret,' Chinku answered. 'He was howling.'

'It may be a good opportunity to test the ray,' the King turned to one of the Dream Stealers. 'Do you have the new ray?'

One of the dark men held up a tube that looked exactly like the other tubes, as far as Chinku could see.

'All right child, take us up to the turret,' the King said.

Nick pushed forward, 'The wolf attacked her in the garden. It may not be wise ...'

'Sire,' one of the Dream Stealers said, 'with all respect, whether it works or not, we have no time to experiment on the wolf.' Chinku could have hugged that Dream Stealer, repulsive as she found them.

The King turned reluctantly and agreed that he might be right. All of them turned and left and the curtains swished behind them. The moment the sounds of their jackboots died away, Nick was on his feet and running to the curtain.

'Come on!' he said to Chinku. 'Let's see what's on the roof!' She could guess of course that it was the dragon from the fountain and she thought it was silly of Nick not to realise it too, but he grabbed her hand and took her in a rush after him before she had time to say anything. He was so fast that very soon they could hear the echoes from the boots again, that crunching tramp, tramp, tramp.

'Wait, they'll hear us!' she panted. He halted and let the echoes grow fainter, then took the stairs in a rush, up and up, till they came to a pair of great gilded doors folded wide open like wings.

There was a beast all right; a golden dragon that looked like the wings of the huge door could have belonged to it. And behind it Chinku could see the sun lowering in a burning fringe on the horizon. The Dream Stealers were silhouetted against it exactly like shadows. One of them had run in ahead of Chinku and Nick. He was carrying a larger bulkier tube that needed both hands to manage its heft. It was just as well; otherwise he might have noticed the children. The men gathered around him while the King stood a little to one side. 'How does it work?' the King asked.

'Probably like the rest,' one of the others muttered. When they talked like that they almost seemed human. The slit eyes turned towards the cluster of men and Chinku saw the mouth open. White fanged teeth shone in icicle points in the dark cave of its mouth.

'Quick, His Majesty!'

'Beware, he's raising his head!'

Nick grabbed her by the arm and pushed her behind a wall. 'Fire?' he murmured. But there were no flames, at least not then. They peeked around the corner and saw the men raise and point the tube quicker than the children had thought possible. The dragon raised its wings and the palace lurched again. The men lost their balance and as they did so, like arrows out of the sky came a flock of ravens, the birds that had been making sunset patterns against the sky on their way home. They flew at the men, stabbing at them with their sharp beaks, clutching their hair with their claws. One of them flew straight at the King. Chinku saw him duck convulsively. In the confusion the men dropped the tube. Two of the ravens snatched it up and flying in perfect formation together carried it away into the evening. The dragon had settled peacefully on the roof again. As the light grew darker, the golden eyes flamed.

'Good dragon,' Nick observed. 'Another one would have been spitting fire!'

The Dream Stealers were regrouping on the roof pointing the tubes that they did have with them, but another wave of ravens swept over, upsetting their formation again, darting and snatching the tubes.

'Good ravens!' Chinku said. 'Draconis has trained them very well.'

'Or knows how to speak their language,' Nick answered.

Quietly, they backed away from the roof and made their way down the stairs. At the foot they found Draconis wearing the ceremonial cloak that Chinku had seen. On his shoulder perched a small lizardragon, exactly like the one he had carved. The little creature raised its head and briefly spat a puff of smoke at them. Draconis appeared to be unaware that it was there at all.

'So wolfboy,' he greeted Nick. 'How do you like my cousin on the roof?'

'Are you going to the Story Vat?' Chinku asked. 'Can we come with you?'

'I have already made my preparations there this morning. Yes, you may come if you stay quiet and in the shadows,' Draconis answered. He swept past them. And vanished round a turn in the corridor leaving a fold of golden material to follow him like a tail. Then that too was whisked away. The floor resumed its lurching dance, but now they knew what was causing it.

'Let's go and see whether the guards are still there.' Nick said. 'They may all be on the terrace with the King.'

And he twisted and turned this way and that till they found the shell corridor again. It was empty, as he had said. 'I smelt that it was empty,' Nick admitted. 'You didn't notice. Only the ladies and the Dragon Man have been this way.' The 'Dragon Man' was to get back at Draconis for calling him wolfboy.

As they walked on, that unforgettable pungent smell filled their nostrils, flowing like a river's currents and confusing Chinku who had still not got used to the corridor's mirage tricks.

When they reached the door, their eyes and noses were streaming. And the door was flung open. Draconis had whisked through it just before because they saw a whisk of the golden lizard's tail. It was not empty because there were ladies all around, holding wisps of lace up to their faces in an attempt to mask the smell. 'The ladies rarely go up to the Story Vat,' Chinku remembered someone, the major domo perhaps, telling her that since none of them was a storyteller or had any kind of talent, they were never allowed up.

'Today, Draga,' they heard Draconis's voice say, 'you will perform the proper rituals. Not the ones that you have been performing in the past.'

'How dare you suggest ...' That was the Lady's voice hissing in anger.

'All this stealing of children, all these stories. We are dragons, Draga. Our task is different.'

'Blame that on my husband's ancestors, not on me!'

'But your husband's ancestors encouraged storytellers and musicians. It was only after you came to this kingdom that the Story Vat began.' Chinku looked at Nick and Nick looked at Chinku.

'You thought I would forget this, but I have not. I remember why you stole my memory from me after I carved the dragons for you.'

The Lady replied, 'My father would have been proud of me. The Kingdom of Kalabash is stronger than Dragonara ever was. Who has wise men or storytellers like the ones in our court? Who has a palace like this?'

'And who has the countryside so filled with terror as Kalabash? The Shadow Riders and their tubes, Draga. Those were your doing.'

'But the experiments that gave rise to them were my husband's.' Nick nudged Chinku and pointed down. Trails of rainbow vapour were curling around their feet, rising slowly in snaky trails. Dead man's lips, afternoon amber, whispers of stars, all the colours that she had seen in the vat and, amongst them, Chinku thought she could see a dragon's head in the mist, shining like the head of that beast on the roof. Flecks of rainbows danced in the air. She caught at one and it shimmered between her fingers like the dragonmoths she had seen in the darkness of the garden.

The Lady said, 'You cannot stop me Draconis. The rituals must be completed.'

'No, I cannot stop you, but I will make sure that you complete them as you are meant to.' The children crept even further into the room, blinking away the tears in an effort to see what was happening. The darkness below the vat was lit up with vapour. And there, surrounded by the rainbow dragon trails, stood the Lady and Draconis. The Lady had a small eight-metal bowl on a tripod in front of her. In one hand she held a trident. Around her neck was a garland of dragon flowers. Chinku could see that the flowers were alive and moving as she had seen them that night in the barn. Every now and then one of them flared puffs of yellow into the air, though she could not tell whether it was pollen or smoke. The Lady raised the trident.

'Wait,' Draconis said.

There was a strange smile on the Lady's face. 'And how will you stop me?' she asked.

Chinku whispered, 'Where are the Keepers?'

'Perhaps they ate them,' Nick suggested.

'No, wolfboy,' Draconis said. He had obviously heard them. 'Dragons do not eat people like you wolves do. The Keepers have been sent away because the rites are secret.'

The Lady half turned her head, distracted by the voices. Aware that there was no point hiding, the children walked up. Draconis held up his hand, 'No closer.'

'What are these children doing here?' the Lady asked. 'Is this part of your treachery? And what do you mean by 'WolfBoy'?'

'The boy is the wolf who you laughed at,' Draconis answered. 'And the girl is the Saviour.'

The Lady obviously knew what 'Saviour' meant because under the gold paint and scales her face froze till she really looked like a statue. She was obviously distracted by Nick and the wolf story, but she began to raise the trident again. 'Saviour or no Saviour, I will continue as I have begun.' The tip of the trident plunged down, not into the bowl as the children had thought, but into the Lady's forearm which was stretched out over the bowl. The three prongs rose up, and blood followed after, welling up out of the Lady's arm. At least the children thought it was blood, but it looked golden, taking on the colour of the skin. 'This you will admit is part of the ritual,' the Lady said to Draconis. Draconis inclined his head. The Lady held her arm over the eight-metal bowl and the drops of her blood fell into it. As they did flames burst from the bowl, streaming upwards towards the ceiling. Surprisingly, the children could feel no heat from the flames. It was cold fire as Draconis had said. The room was now filled with so many kinds of smoke that it was hard to tell where one ended and the other began; though the fire cut through the rainbows like a strong white torch beam.

'What would you have me do next?' the Lady asked Draconis. There was an edge of sarcasm in her voice. 'Shall I sacrifice the boy you say is a wolf?'

'Show her,' Draconis said to Nick. Reluctantly, Nick began to change shape until he was standing there in wolf form.

Ignoring Nick, with her free hand, the Lady took the garland from her neck and dropped it into the eight-metal bowl.

'Was that right, cousin? Was that how the ritual should continue?' Not more vapours, Chinku thought, wondering how they would ever be able to breathe with all those smells in their nostrils.

'You're a child, Draga. Anything for distraction.' He put his hand to his shoulder and the lizardragon raised its ruff and walked on to his hand. Draconis raised his arm and threw the creature into the air. It rose like a hawk on transparent whirring wings and as it rose it began to grow with a fierce golden light that seemed to draw all the vapours to it.

'Yes,' Draconis said, 'You have the right thought. I will ask you for them shortly.' The lizard had vanished somewhere above and, in vanishing, had cleared the air.

Instead of vapour, a low humming began to ring in their ears. The bowl was singing. Chinku had heard of singing bowls, though never seen one before.

'Child,' said Draconis. 'Give me your stones.' Chinku's hand dropped to her pocket and she took out the stones.

'What stones?' the Lady demanded sharply. Chinku saw that she seemed to be melting, her golden robes streaming down like water and forming some kind of animal shape, the train elongating into a zigzagged tail.

Draconis held out his hand, 'Throw them to me!' Chinku had had practice skimming stones across the lake; thank goodness she didn't throw like a girl. The stones spun into the air hard as plum stones with not a glint to them.

'Marbles,' laughed the Lady. 'Children's toys!'

'But there is something you don't know about these toys,' he answered. And he flung them into the eight-metal bowl. Nothing happened for a minute. The Lady began to laugh. But then, suddenly the singing rose to a high shriek, so high that Chinku thought her eardrums would burst and Nick shook his wolf's head back and forth trying to escape the sound. And then there was a flash of something and two dragons stood there, wings beating in the narrow space, one red and one golden. The red dragon rose up in a leap and the golden dragon followed. The children backed away. The ladies, whom they all had forgotten, screamed behind them. And then light and air rushed into the room.

'The roof's gone!' Nick said, grabbing Chinku's hand. When had he changed back into a boy, she wondered and then stopped wondering in all the lurching and moving.

'What's the use of that?' Chinku muttered once she had recovered. 'How will the people get their memories back?' She could see the moon's red disc through the vanished roof over the rim of the Story Vat once she glanced up. 'The dragons have flown. And they're not going to …' Then she saw the taloned feet cross the moon's surface and the palace lurched and began to shoot upwards so fast that they were sent sprawling.

The moon vanished from their field of vision. Occasionally a star loomed up and flashed past. Nick and Chinku sat holding hands and looking up. 'Where is it taking us?' Chinku asked. 'And where are the King and his men?'

'Probably too scared to move,' Nick said. 'I wouldn't if I was in a flying palace.'

Behind them they could hear the ladies sobbing. 'But this answers your question. The Story Vat must be smoking into the air as it flies.'

30

He was right, but they did not know that till the next morning when light flooded through the vanished roof. The palace suddenly came to rest with a jarring thump that set the Story Vat rattling. For a moment everyone in the room held their breath in case it started again. But this time the stillness seemed to be permanent. Gradually the ladies filed out of the room and the children followed them through the empty corridor. Downstairs they found Nostromo with the children in the hall. And then they ran out where the glass doors had been.

The palace had been set down in a great clearing. There were trees around in which the surprised birds had been startled out of their early morning chores. Nick sniffed the air. 'We're near my village,' he said.

Nostromo said, 'Here comes the King.' They had forgotten that he had been in the palace all the time. And he had his Dream Stealers with him. They came out of the palace in a rush their tubes at the ready.

'What magic is this?' the King demanded. 'Where is my wife? And where are we?'

'I don't know where we are, sire,' Nostromo answered. 'The dragons brought us here.'

'Someone's coming!' said Nick. One of the Dream Stealers threw up his memory stealing tube and pulled back the bolt.

'No!' Chinku cried. But the Dream Stealer's face was surprised. 'It's empty ....' And the others were throwing up their tubes and discovering the very same thing.

A file of men in red and black came out of the trees with grim intent in their faces.

'Father!' Nick cried and went running. And Chinku realized that her home was not far away after all ....

Nick took her back. That was after the red and black men had surrounded the palace and Nick's father had scolded him in front of everyone with a mingling of pride and anger. She had stopped listening after that because home was the only thing on her mind.

'Take the child to her village,' Nostromo said. 'We can wait.' He wanted to go to his own home of course, to Demetra and the inn which he hadn't seen in more years than Chinku could imagine possible.

Nick's mother had come too and greeted her son first with a slap and then a hug.

'We saw you in the nails,' she said. 'And then I followed you in the bowl. Didn't you recognize my voice?' She put that question to Chinku who looked up at her in wonder.

'You mean that was you in the turret room when ...' She would have blurted it all out, but Nick's mother put a finger to her lips. 'It was very brave of you and very foolhardy at the same time,' she said, 'Still I am glad that this son of mine had the wits to go with you.'

'I could never have done it without him,' Chinku admitted. 'I would have been too scared.'

'Do you want me to look in the bowl, child?' Nick's mother asked. 'You can see your parents before you return.'

She was not sure what to do, shifting from one foot to another all of ten years old again and certainly no saviour. Nick's mother put her arm around her shoulders. 'Come and see,' she said coaxingly.

'No,' Chinku said. 'I want to go home.'

Nick's mother said, 'You can always come and live with us if things are not right in your village.' For all its kindness that made Chinku want to get home all the faster.

'Let her see what things are like at home,' Nostromo suggested, 'and then bring her back again. Her part in this adventure is not yet over.'

There was the matter of the Story Vat to be looked into to see whether it was really empty. And there were all the children to be sent home. Nick's father had the King by the arm, with his eyes glinting silver fire. Unlike Nick, he really was a silver wolf, Chinku thought. Cold, pale and dangerous. The Dream Stealers stood around, their tubes hanging uselessly from their hands. The light had drained whatever power the tubes had, or perhaps the dragons had sucked it out during their flight. No one was really sure – in the bright meadow with the shady trees whispering in the wind all harm seemed far away.

'Are you all right though?' Nick's mother asked him. Chinku realized that she was worried about what had happened to him during the full moon.

'I'm all right,' he assured her. 'Something wonderful happened last night. I'll tell you all about it as soon as I come back.' He held out his hand to Chinku, 'Come on then. Let's go home.'

And as soon as they had reached the sheltering trees, he was in his wolf's form again, waiting for her to climb on. Nick fell into his smooth swift stride that was half a run, and before she could have thought it possible they were flashing past the lake. She could see the girls at their morning chores and the arched white gates in the distance behind them. Before anyone was close enough to see them, Nick skidded to a halt.

'Get off,' he said. 'We walk from here.' Then he was boy again and holding her hand, though they were still running, Chinku so fast that she kept stumbling.

Someone by the lake got up and pointed and she could hear some noise. Then she saw that it wasn't just an ordinary morning. Behind the girls were two of the Old Ones who were deep in conversation. Her heart jumped straight up into her mouth. The Old Ones were looking at them – and then she saw her father and, dropping Nick's hand, ran to him and threw her arms around his neck without even waiting to see whether he recognized her.

'Where have you been?' he asked angrily. 'We've been out of our minds with worry! I went straight to the rabbit hole this morning in case you were there ...'

'You remember!' she sobbed, 'You remember!' and tears of happiness rolled down her cheeks.

One of the Old Ones came forward, 'This morning we woke out of a long dream. The birds told us that something wonderful was happening. And then your father came to tell us that he remembered where you might be.'

Word had spread and Chinku's mother came from her cooking pots to hug her daughter and laugh and scold all at the same time. Nick stood back a little shyly, not wanting to interrupt, but after hugs had been exchanged all around, Chinku turned back to him, took him by the hand and said, 'Mama, Papa, this is my friend Nick. He's the one who saved me.'

'A wolf,' said one of the Old Ones.

'And yet one of us,' said the other. They looked at each other and smiled. Chinku thought they were as slow and wise as ever, and as irritating. 'He went with me to Kalabash!' she said in a rush, interrupting their ruminations.

'You went to Kalabash!' cried her mother. 'You naughty girl! Do you know what danger you were in!'

A lammergeier fluttered by in a slow wheel when she said that and the morning sparrows hushed their chattering.

The Old Ones said, 'She has done a thing so great that even the bird lords of the mountains are acknowledging it. Chinku has freed us from the power of the Lady of Kalabash.'

Nick said, 'The King of Kalabash and his palace are sitting in the middle of Qlwri Forest. Chinku was so anxious to come home that I brought her here first. But there are things to be done.' He said it politely but a little firmly, flashing an amber eye at Chinku because he thought she was forgetting what was really important.

'The great Palace of Kalabash?' everyone in the village set up a shout at that. And then, reunions forgotten, they began bringing out mules, horses and carts, any form of transport that could get them to the forest.

The Dream Stealers and the King were sitting on the grass surrounded by Nick's village men. The children were running around or rolling over the meadows, while the ladies were trailing their wonderful gowns over the grass and chirping and complaining. They all stopped what they were doing when they saw the Qlwri villagers with Chinku. Nick's father came over to the Old Ones and greeted them. 'This is a matter that touches us all,' he said. 'Together we need to decide what to do with this King.'

The first thing they did was go through the rooms of the palace with Nostromo leading them. The corridor that led to the Story Vat looked more like a shell than ever with the light making the walls translucent.

The room was flooded with sunlight and smelt of clean air. All of them crowded up the spiral staircase to gaze into the vat. It was empty, though Chinku thought that perhaps she could see some rainbow droplets glinting right at the bottom. The silver tripod was standing where the children had seen it the night before, filled with that blood-like liquid. A dragon flower was floating on the surface. They found the Keeper of the room looking dazed in all that light, sheltering in one shadowed corner of the room, and they hustled him happily out and down.

The pillars in the great hall were clear crystal and rainbow lights seemed to flicker through them. On the dais was the throne, empty now, shaped like a great silver lotus flower tipped with gold.

'Those lights,' said Nostromo, 'were supposed to remind everyone who came into the room of the true power of the throne of Kalabash.'

Everyone thought that it would be safer if the King of Kalabash stayed where they could keep an eye on him. Nick's father looked at the Chief of the Old Ones and said, 'This is in your hands.' They conferred together for a moment before sending the village children running to collect leaves. The King demanded, 'What do you plan to do with us?'

Nick's father answered the King, 'That is for the Old Ones to decide. By stealing their memories you deprived them of centuries of wisdom. And for what? So that your Queen could laugh.'

'No,' the King answered steadily. 'So that my sons could sleep more soundly.' He held his head high and looked Nick's father straight in his silver eyes and that, Chinku admitted to herself, took courage. The children came back with their hands full of leaves. The Old Ones walked amongst them, choosing, taking one here and another there. Then the four of them separated, each one walking to a different point of the compass, chanting. Chinku was glad she understood some of the chants, incantations asking for the winds to bring them word of the fugitive, for the sun's great golden eye to shine on the wrongdoer with full angry force. Then the King and his Dream Stealers were formed into a great circle in the lower hall of the palace. The Old Ones ordered down the tripod and bowl from the Story Vat room. It was carried down by two of the pages who had been found hiding behind a curtain, one of whom was Fowler. The Old Ones converged on it and took the wilted dragon flower out of the silver bowl.

The dragon flower draped its petals like cloth over the hand of the Chief of the Old Ones. A rain of blood streamed over the hand and dripped onto the tiles. The three others dipped their chosen leaves into the bowl and spattered the Dream Stealers and the King with them. Then they walked in ever-quickening circles around them, faster and faster until they were almost whirling and the hall seemed caught up in the core of a mass of spinning energy. Their leader drew a ring around the King and his men and, putting out his hand, marked the King's forehead with a streak of red without crossing the red ring. 'It is done,' he said to Nick's father and the men of Baghen. 'If they try to leave the palace in secret, thunder will rumble from a blue sky and the winds will surround them with twists of dust and anger.'

'We are your prisoners,' said the King stiffly.

'Not quite. Any one of you who asks permission in a free and fair manner from any of our Chiefs will be allowed to walk out of the palace walls into the wood. But if he tries to cross the borders of the great wood onto the highway that leads towards Kalabash, he will find the creepers entwining him like living snakes.'

The Chief Old One turned to the others and said, 'And for as long as this palace sits on the meadow grass, it will be a meeting place for all the villages in this region. We ourselves shall hold classes for the children here in one of the halls, so that the palace can be used as the old king designed it to be. A place where children learn and grow and where people come together in harmony.'

The roof would not be put back – it would stay as it was to remind people of the Night of the Dragon's Moon.

It was like a picnic, Chinku thought. Especially when the women of Baghen brought out baskets of fruit and loaves of bread and cheese and honey cakes.

When finally the stories – for the meeting was more about stories than anything else – were over, a whole pack of wolves was sent scurrying over the countryside to find out where the lost children of Kalabash had come from and to summon their parents and families to fetch them home. They looked like streaks of silver shooting through the trees and no one had ever seen so many wolves by daylight before.

Nick's mother, who had been deep in conversation with Chinku's mother came and kissed Chinku. 'I know what you have done for my son,' she whispered. 'Thank you.'

Chinku's mother said, 'If I had known that you had married in Baghen ...'

Nick's mother laughed, 'If you had, you would never have spoken to me again.' Seeing Chinku look astonished she said, 'Your mother and I were playmates when we were your age. But one day like you, I went wandering in the forest and met a wolfboy and then my whole life changed.'

Nostromo was finally allowed to leave – though the Old Ones told him that he would have to return to continue his classes in the palace. 'Gladly,' he said, 'anytime you call me.' He was given a cart and took some of the lost children with him – before he left he handed the shadow cloaks to Chinku and Nick.

'I have a feeling,' he said, 'you two will need them more than Demetra and I ever will.' And then he was gone with a flick of the whip and without even a backward glance, his wife's face filling his eyes.

Sooner than they would have thought possible the wolves began to return with news from the other villages. There were children from Astandia, Baphomet, Deimos. As each wolf reached the meadow it became a man with a message. There was a rush of carts being ordered out and children divided and sent away with a lady or two in charge. The meadow gradually emptied of its laughing crowds.

It really was time to go back home. Reluctantly, Chinku got to her feet and began to follow her parents and the other people of Qlwri. She thought how strange it would be to wake up and go down to the Lake of the Moon with the rest of the girls, and then to start her classes and she said that aloud.

'No,' said an Old One beside her. 'Life for you is just beginning.'

Nick had been loping along with them all this while. 'And for this wolfboy too,' added the Old One. 'For these two together constitute a force that all the Shadows of Kalabash could not destroy.'

Chinku suddenly realized that the rest were all far ahead of her and only she and Nick were walking together.

'I'll be over tomorrow with the parchment,' he said cheerfully. 'And we'll be meeting when they start classes in the palace. Father says I am to stop sneaking into the classes at Qlwri.'

'But how dull life's going to be after this,' Chinku said wistfully.

He shook his head. 'It will never be dull again. Now the dragons are loose, there will be all sorts of things happening.'

As they walked towards home and bed, the rising moon, no longer a dragon, shone down on them lighting their way, free from darkness and fear.

About the author

Advertising consultant by profession, Anjana Basu also writes short stories and poems. In America she has been published in *Gowanus*, *The Blue Moon Review* and *Recursive Angel*, to name a few. In Canada a story appeared in *The Antigonish Review*.

Author of *Curses in Ivory*, her critically acclaimed first novel, in 2004 she was awarded a Hawthornden Fellowship in Scotland where she worked on her second novel, *Black Tongue* published by Roli Books in 2007. She has worked on the dialogues for the Amitabh Bachchan starrer *The Last Lear* directed by Rituparno Ghosh.